"You do want to come ~~**don't you, Jacob?"**~~ **whispered into the phone.**

"Yes. No. I don't know," he replied.

The flutters in her chest turned to stone and dropped to her stomach. He had to have heard her gasp.

"Wait. Don't hang up," he said quickly. "I'm not the same, Sally."

"Well, hells bells, neither am I. But forget about you and me. What about your kids? Don't you want to see them?"

"Of course I do, but . . ." He paused. "I don't want them to see me like this."

All of this was so unlike the Jake she knew and had loved at one time.

"I'm no hero," he said.

The tears she'd been holding back all day fi-na...

By Sandra Hill

A HERO comes HOME

A Bell Sound Novel

SANDRA HILL

AVONBOOKS

An Imprint of HarperCollinsPublishers

A HERO COMES HOME. Copyright © 2020 by Sandra Hill. All rights reserved. Printed in the United States of America. No part of this book may be used or reproduced in any manner whatsoever without written permission except in the case of brief quotations embodied in critical articles and reviews. For information, address HarperCollins Publishers, 195 Broadway, New York, NY 10007.

First Avon Books mass market printing: February 2020

Print Edition ISBN: 978-0-06-285419-3
Digital Edition ISBN: 978-0-06-285411-7

Cover design by Nadine Badalaty
Cover illustration by Shane Rebenschied
Cover photographs © Shutterstock

Avon, Avon & logo, and Avon Books & logo are registered trademarks of HarperCollins Publishers in the United States of America and other countries.

HarperCollins is a registered trademark of HarperCollins Publishers in the United States of America and other countries.

FIRST EDITION

20 21 22 23 24   QGM   10 9 8 7 6 5 4 3 2 1

This book is dedicated to all the hometown heroes out there, and their spouses, who hold down the fort. Yes, I mean the military, which I respect wholeheartedly, but also those local police and firefighters, and others who go the extra step in dangerous places to provide for our physical safety. There are heroes all around us, and I love them all.

A HERO comes HOME

Chapter 1

She was all shook up, for sure! . . .

Sally Dawson stood, momentarily transfixed, staring at the scene before her. She felt a little like Alice in Wonderland falling down the rabbit hole, except, in this case, it must be the Graceland hole.

A native New Yorker, she had seen just about everything on the streets of the Big Apple. And, really, she'd been living in Bell Cove for almost nine years now, ever since her late husband, Captain Jacob Dawson, had brought her to his hometown as a bride. So, she shouldn't be surprised by what the well-meaning wackos in this small town came up with. But this beat them all, even last Christmas's Grinch contest, where everyone was running around like a chicken with its head cut off, trying not to get "Grinched."

No, this was a new high for Bell Cove. Or was it a new low? In terms of corniness, that was.

"Jailhouse Rock" was blaring from the loudspeakers, the Sexy Senior Swingers (aka the Old Codgers Dance Club) were performing some amazing jitterbug moves on the newly laid asphalt parking lot, and a twenty-foot neon Elvis, with his trademark crooked grin, oversaw the entire event. Actually, it wasn't a jitterbug, but that Carolina favorite, the Shag. No Outer Banks event could be held without that homage to boardwalks, hot sun, and beach music.

The line waiting to get into the diner was twenty deep and, with all the new arrivals, hadn't gotten any shorter since the doors opened three hours ago, at noon. And, yes, with perfect timing, the town bells, each with their own distinctive sounds, began to chime the hour. First, Our Lady by the Sea Catholic Church. *Bong, bong, bong!* Then, St. Andrew's Presbyterian Church. *Ding-dong, ding-dong, ding-dong!* And finally the clock in the town hall tower. *Clang, clang, clang!*

No one even paused in their conversations at the ringing. It was, after all, a town that had been founded over a hundred years ago by the Conti brothers, Italian immigrants who built Bell Forge. The small factory became known for finely crafted bells, the kind that hung in cathedrals and big city towers and on college campuses, but they also made bells as musical instruments. Every business in Bell Cove—every residence, in fact—had a bell attached to its door, thanks to the Conti influence. The one over the door of Sally's bakery, Sweet Thangs, was a soft jangle that she'd come to love.

Still bemused, Sally noticed that everyone in line, not just the dancers, had made an effort to suit their appearance to the occasion. Women and girls, no matter the ages, wore sweater sets or pastel-colored blouses with Peter Pan collars tucked under tight cinch belts into circle skirts over bouffant petticoats, leading down to bobby socks and saddle shoes. Still others wore figure-hugging pedal pushers or dungarees rolled up to midcalf, with flat ballet slippers. Ponytails and poodle cuts abounded. The guys, men and boys, went either preppy with crew cuts, button-down shirts, and back-belted khaki pants with white buck shoes, or else they went full greaser with black leather jackets over white T-shirts and ducktail haircuts.

No, it wasn't a reenactment of that movie *Grease*. It was the grand reopening of the Rock Around the Clock Diner and the Heartbreak Motel, and it looked like everyone in the small town had shown up . . . and was commemorating the event as only Bell Cove-ites could in their own unique, wacky style.

Delilah Jones—rather Delilah Good since she'd recently married Merrill Good, treasure hunter and former Navy SEAL—was the owner of both businesses, but a little fact like that never fazed the good people of Bell Cove who tended to take over when there was any excuse for a celebration. No wonder then that they were using the reopening of the Elvis- and 1950s era–related businesses as a prelude to the town's new Lollypalooza Labor Day Weekend to be held in a few weeks. God only knew what they'd come up with for that!

George Saunders and Lance Bowes, whose Out of the Closet chain of North Carolina thrift shops, including the one on the town square, just down the street from Sally's bakery, must be doing a thriving business with all this vintage apparel. Sally had to admit, she was benefitting from increased traffic in her bakery today, too, a spillover from this event.

Enough dawdling! Sally readjusted the large bakery box filled with four dozen fresh-baked hamburger rolls in her arms and walked on. Here and there, people called out to her.

"Hey, Sally! Need any help with that?" Frank Baxter from Hard Knocks Hardware asked. Frank, who was renowned for his comb-over hairstyle to hide a bald spot, or rather a comb-forward hairstyle complete with bangs, wore an Elvis wig today. And a jumpsuit! At close to seventy years old, with a bit of a paunch, he was not a pretty sight.

But that was mean, Sally chastised herself. Frank was a nice man. In truth, everyone in this town was. A little bit crazy, but good-to-the-soul people.

Still, Sally blinked rapidly to avoid gawking. "Not now, Frank. But thanks for offering. Six blocks ago would have been nice, though," she chided in a teasing way.

"Ouch!" he said and grinned.

Standing next to Frank was his main squeeze, or the person Frank would like to squeeze. Everyone knew he had a thing for Mayor Doreen Ferguson, who owned the shop next door, Happy

Feet Emporium, which had to be doing a run today on blue suede and saddle shoes. Doreen, also close to seventy, wore purple capri pants with a white sleeveless blouse tied at the waist, à la Rizzo from *Grease*. Her brown hair had been teased into a bouffant hairstyle with the ends flipped up, thanks, no doubt, to her daughter Francine who owned Styles and Smiles hair salon. "Where's that outfit I sent you, girl?" Doreen inquired with an exaggerated glower. "You'd make an incredible Ann-Margret."

Hardly! I'm too skinny. Don't have enough on top. And my pixie hairstyle would never do for Viva Las Vegas. "Oops. I left it back at the shop. It's a little big, and I didn't have a chance to alter it," she lied.

"Excuses, excuses!" Doreen wagged a forefinger at her and said, "You better not think you're getting out of a costume for Pirate Day."

Wanna bet? "I wouldn't think of it." As part of Lolly Weekend, the town council had decided to set aside one day to celebrate the shipwreck treasure discovered several weeks ago by Merrill's salvaging company. What that had to do with pirates was anyone's guess. But then, Bell Cove folks put their own spin on everything that happened hereabouts. In a nice way, she reminded herself. And it *was* good for business.

With a little wave, Sally continued walking to the back of the diner. She was about to set the box down and knock on the door, but it opened suddenly and Delilah smiled warmly at her. "Thank you, thank you for answering my SOS call! We're almost out."

"Really?"

"Yep."

"Wow! You started with eight dozen."

"I know. Isn't it great?" She took the box from Sally and motioned for her to come in.

The narrow kitchen that fed the diner through a wide pass-through window was a beehive of activity: Orders yelled out, mixed with laughter, and an occasional muffled curse as grease spattered. A myriad of smells. Hamburgers sizzling, peanut butter and bananas melding in grilled sandwiches, and Delilah's trademark multiflavored cinnamon rolls. Overlaying it all was the voice of Elvis crooning through the sound system, "Don't Be Cruel."

Merrill, in a white apron and hokey chef's hat, waved to her as he helped Andy Briggs, the cook, at the stove. "You're an angel, Sal," he declared, referring to the rolls, she assumed, which Delilah set down on the counter near him.

One high school kid worked the fryers, while another was washing dishes, the two of them exchanging trash talk about some skateboard competition.

Delilah's grandmother, Salome Jones, whom some called the "Glam Gram," was plating dishes, even as she was dressed to the nines in a sheer, shiny silver tunic with a deep décolletage over tight black spandex yoga pants. Her dyed blonde hair was swept up into a beehive style. No surprise that the lady had been a Las Vegas showgirl at one time. From behind, she could have passed for her twenties, rather than her sixties. In fact, she could have played the role of Ann-Margret better than Sally any day, no matter what Doreen Ferguson said.

Delilah's five-year-old daughter, Maggie, was sitting on a high stool at the prep table mashing ripe bananas with a fork.

"How adorable!" Sally remarked to Delilah.

The little girl looked like a Mini-Me version of her mother, both of them wearing poodle skirts and bobby socks, their blonde hair pulled back into high ponytails, Delilah's silver blonde and Maggie's more of a gold tone.

"Thanks. You have no idea how many hours we spent picking out these ensembles. Maggie is *very* particular about not being too matchy-matchy."

"I'm surprised your grandmother isn't out there with the dancers," Sally remarked. "With her dancing background, I mean."

"Oh, she was. And she will be. But Stella, Andy's assistant, needed to take a break, and Gram offered to help out here."

"Lilah! Why didn't you ask me if you need help?"

"You have enough on your plate without helping me, too. Just keep baking those rolls for me. That's help enough."

"I am so impressed with what you've done here, Lilah. Really, how did you manage to pull this all together in less than a month?"

"Well, we're working on a shortened menu today,"

Delilah said, handing her a cardboard menu insert. "Just three appetizers, three entrées, and three desserts. Fried dill pickles, oysters Rockefeller, and catfish nuggets. Then, bacon-topped meat loaf with mashed potatoes, brown gravy, and Southern-fried corn; fat cheeseburgers with all the works and a side of French fries; and, of course, grilled peanut butter and banana sandwiches, with or without bacon. Then, for dessert, banana pudding, the Fool's Gold Cakes your bakery made for us, and my cinnamon rolls."

Sally had to laugh at Delilah being able to spout out her entire menu. Which wasn't surprising, really. Sally could do the same for her bakery offerings, even though they changed often. "Everything Elvis related, I notice."

"Right. Have to keep everything according to Uncle Clyde. Although I managed to squeeze my cinnamon rolls in, you'll notice."

"Your uncle must have been a character," Sally commented.

Everyone knew that Delilah had inherited the business—the diner, the motel, and the bayside land—from her great-uncle Clyde. Even as she'd been in prison! But that was another story.

"He was," Delilah replied. "The man loved Elvis, obviously, as evidenced by the Heartbreak Motel, and all the kitschy Elvis stuff everywhere—posters, jukebox music, food. But his business was a tribute to that whole rock 'n' roll era, as well, by naming this the Rock Around the Clock Diner."

"You could say he was lost in the fifties," Sally joked.

"For sure."

Sally glanced at the menu Delilah had handed her. "So, not a salad in sight."

"There will be eventually. We are a work in progress."

"Tell me about it! But, when I said I was impressed, I meant the diner renovation itself. I know you were doing all the grunt work yourself for a while but this"—she waved a hand to encompass her surroundings—"well, you made some major improvements in a miraculous amount of time."

"Money," Delilah said with a self-deprecating grimace, making a motion of her head toward Merrill. "My husband is a computer genius and he managed to find all these internet sources for equipment, even the specialized stuff like tabletop jukeboxes for the booths, and service sources, including, can you believe, there are actually people who repair neon signs? But he also used his computer skills to hire staff, set up staff schedules, and make menus. Bottom line, though, is money talks, and without the cash I made for my share of the shipwreck treasure, I'd still be sanding rust off the exterior of this diner."

"You're speaking to the choir here, girlfriend. I was sitting home with three kids just getting by on social security after Jake died. It was only when I got his death benefit check that I was able to open my business." Jacob Dawson, a captain in the

Army, Delta Force, had been declared MIA more than three years ago, leaving her with three kids, Matthew, Mark, and Luke, then aged five, four, and two. Six months later, the death notice came. "Sitting home" pretty much said it all where she'd been concerned in those early days. If it hadn't been for her young brood, she would have been comatose with grief and guilt. In the end, the bakery had been her salvation in more ways than one.

Delilah nodded, seeming to understand without the details, and said, "Where are the boys today, anyhow?"

"Kevin took them fishing."

"Woo-hoo!" Delilah said and grinned at her. "Do I sense a love connection here?"

Sally felt her face heat. Kevin Fortunato, or K-4, an ex-SEAL like Merrill, had been hitting on Sally since he'd arrived in town a month or so ago to join the treasure-hunting company. To no avail . . . until recently. Which was surprising for him, apparently, since he'd avoided the dating scene after his wife died of cancer several years ago. And surprising for Sally, too, since she hadn't been involved with any man at all since Jake's death, and given her vow never to be involved with a military man again, even an ex-soldier.

"Not a love connection." *Not yet anyhow.* "But an attraction." *Definitely, an attraction.* "I consider him a friend at this point."

"With benefits?"

Sally's face heated some more. "No." *But lots of almost benefits. Like kissing till my bones melt. Or touching that verges on sex.* Sally wasn't sure how much longer she could hold out. Not that he was pressuring her, but just being himself, sexy as sin, was pressure in itself.

"But you're tempted?"

"Oh, yeah!"

Just then, the cell phone in her pocket buzzed. She took it out and glanced at the screen. "Speak of the devil," she said, and read the text message.

Where R U?
Diner. U back already?
Already??!!##

Sally laughed. Eight hours with three energetic boys—on a boat, no less—would tire even the most patient adult. But one not used to kids . . . well, Kevin must be ready for a nap by now.

Before she had a chance to remark on that, Kevin wrote again.

U R needed at home asap.

Her heart skipped a beat. Emergency?

No. Visitors.
Who?
Just come.

On that ominous note, Sally said quick goodbyes to Lilah and the others, and hurried to her cottage, which was several blocks away in the row built more than a hundred years ago for the Bell Forge workers. Her home was across the street from the one where Jake had grown up with his mother and father. His father, Joseph Dawson, a commercial fisherman, still lived there by himself since his wife, Margaret, Jake's mother, died last year of a heart attack. Joe was a godsend of help when Sally had to work, as his wife had been before her death.

Sally was a half block away when she saw Kevin walking toward her. How nice, that he was coming to meet her! Away from the chaos of her house where her three boys would be vying for attention. They must be across the street with their PopPop. So, Kevin coming to meet her represented a rare, private moment.

Nice.

Kevin was wearing the same running shorts and raggedy Navy T-shirt he'd had on this morning with sockless athletic shoes. Tall, compared to her five-five, but no more than six feet, probably an inch or two less. And muscular, as all SEALs or ex-SEALs were. All Special Forces guys, for that matter, as she well knew, having lived in a house cluttered with the old-fashioned weights and barbells that Jake had favored. His black hair was short, but not as military short as when he'd first arrived in town. With dark Italian coloring enhanced by weeks of sun out on the ocean-salvaging expedition, he was one good-looking man.

Maybe it was time to move to the next level.

Maybe it was time to check out his bed at the Heartbreak Motel, where he lived, temporarily.

Maybe making love with Kevin would be the best birthday present she could give herself. She would turn twenty-eight next week, after all, and she hadn't engaged in sex in almost four years.

As they got closer to each other, she smiled at him. An enticing smile, accompanied by a quick flick of her tongue to wet her lips, which she hoped conveyed her invitation.

He didn't smile back. And there was no doubt he'd understood the message in her smile.

She faltered and came to a complete stop.

He came right up to her and put his hands on her shoulders. The expression on his face was stone-cold serious.

"Oh, my God! Did something happen to one of the boys?"

He shook his head.

"Joe?"

Another shake of the head.

He stepped to the side, deliberately. They were a short distance from her cottage by now, and she could see what his large body had been hiding from her view.

A black sedan with a white license plate and blue lettering, clearly marked "US Government," sat on the street. There were small American flags on either of the front fenders. Standing beside the vehicle was an older, gray-haired man in full military uniform, the four stars on his epaulets denoting him a general. Beside him stood a distinguished-looking, fortyish black man in a tan suit who she could swear was Senator Bolton Smith, North Carolina's newest bright star on the political horizon.

Sally's knees went weak and she might have fallen if not for Kevin's firm hold around her waist. This was shades of the death notification visit she'd gotten from the Army three years ago, but then it had been a lower-level Delta Force officer and a military chaplain.

What does it mean?

What is the worst thing these people could tell me?

Jake is dead. He can't be declared dead again.

Maybe it's some posthumous medal he's being given. Well, forget that. She'd had enough with the military long before Jake had left for his last deployment. But Jake had been gung-ho Uncle Sam and God Bless America to the end, bless his patriotic soul.

"Mrs. Dawson?" the general said when she got close enough to notice the grim expression on his face, which matched the one on Kevin's face, as well as that of the senator who had a cell phone in one hand, which he was tapping away at with an expert thumb. How rude! But then, maybe it was an important call he had to make. *Direct line to the president*, she joked to herself.

But then she heard him say, "Yes, Mr. President."

Holy frickin' hell!

"Yes. I'm Mrs. Dawson," she said to the general.

Kevin walked away, leaving her on her own.

It was all so strange. If she'd felt like Alice falling through the Graceland rabbit hole before, now it was more like Alice in Woo-Woo Land.

Only seconds had gone by, but her brain reacted like it was viewing a series of slides. Pictures on the walls of her brain that went *click, click, click.*

Kevin greeting her before she reached home, a warning of sorts in his caring eyes.

The black sedan with the government plates in front of her house. *Didn't they see the no parking sign?*

A high-ranking military man waiting. *For me!*

And a senator, for heaven's sake. In Bell Cove! *The townies will have him over at the Elvis diner doing the Shag, if they find out.*

The surprisingly absent sound of three boys laughing and shouting at the same time, each vying to get her attention, especially after a day fishing. *What does it all mean?*

The military man coughed to clear his throat and said, "I'm General George Parker from the Joint Chiefs. In Washington."

She tilted her head to the side and waited.

"I have some good news for you, Mrs. Dawson," he said, though the tone of his voice didn't sound like it.

"That's great. I could use some good news."

Was it ironical, or what, that the bells of Bell Cove began to ring then? A drumroll couldn't have done it better. *Bong, bong, bong, bong! Ding-dong, ding-dong, ding-dong, ding-dong! Clang, clang, clang, clang!*

When the reverberation of the bells stopped, into the silence General Parker announced, "Your husband is alive."

Chapter 2

He could "go home again,"
but he didn't want to . . .

Oompfh!" The muscles in Captain Jacob Dawson's scarred back screamed with agony as he lowered the bar on the weight machine. The compact multi-function gym station, which probably cost a cool fifty grand, worked every part of the body imaginable. Today, Jake was concentrating on lost upper body strength. An uphill battle to say the least . . . and painful!

"Jake, my man, you are sweating like a fisherman hauling in two-hundred-pound gill nets under a blistering Outer Banks' sun."

Surprised, Jake twisted around on his seat, too quickly, and about passed out at the lightning bolt of pain that struck the back of his skull. Even so, he reached, reflexively, for his trusty Ruger, which, of course, wasn't there. All this happened within a split second, and he was about to duck for cover when reality hit.

It was just his longtime friend, second lieutenant

Isaac Bernstein, who'd walked, unannounced, into his private room at the Landstuhl military hospital in Germany. "And, dude . . ." Izzie sniffed the air in an exaggerated fashion, ignoring Jake's reaction, "you stink like bad tuna, too."

"Bite me!" Jake said and stood, taking a moment to get his balance. He still wasn't used to the soft brace on his left leg. He limped over to the bench where he grabbed a gym towel and began to wipe the sweat off his brow and bare chest.

"How's the leg doing?" Izzie asked after watching his halting progress.

"Just super. After three surgeries and a titanium rod implant that weighs about five pounds, I still can't dance."

"Not even the Shag? Oh, man, you'll lose your Carolina creds."

Jake threw the towel at Izzie's teasing face.

Izzie caught it midair and tossed it back at him. "Remember the dance contest in Myrtle Beach? You and me and the Marconi twins from St. Bernadette's. I was the winner, as I recall. In more ways than one." Izzie waggled his eyebrows for emphasis.

"Dream on, brother. Even at sixteen, I could beat your ass in any contest, whether football, swimming, fishing, or . . . dancing."

"I don't know about that. I have fond memories of Angela Marconi. She was my partner that night, and . . ." He began to sing "Under the Boardwalk."

Grinning, Izzie stepped forward to give him a warm bro hug, despite his smelly body.

Jake barely restrained himself from shoving his friend away. He didn't like to be touched anymore, not even by his buddy since toddlerhood when they'd been dog-paddling side by side in the cool waters of Bell Sound, their mothers best friends since college, fellow teachers at Bell Cove Elementary School for many years. Of course, Jake's mother was gone now, but he and Izzie had many shared memories.

"Cool digs!" Izzie remarked a short time later, as he sipped at one of the beers he'd snuck in.

Jake was sipping at the other, the first he'd had in the three months he'd been residing there. Didn't matter that it wasn't even ten a.m. Beer was the breakfast of champions on occasion.

"A suite, no less!" Izzie continued as he gazed around the large room.

Yes, Jake had a suite, if you could call it that . . . a traditional patient room with an adjoining sitting area featuring institutional-style furniture, a barebones couch, coffee table, TV, and dining table, and an alcove for the gym equipment. It was located in a private—in other words, secret—wing of the hospital where Uncle Sam hid those high-profile soldiers it didn't want the public to know about. Down the hall, at the moment, were a congressman's pilot son who'd crashed a billion-dollar aircraft in some reckless *Top Gun* maneuver, and two unidentified soldiers rescued from a work camp in Russia, where they had no business being. Probably SEALs.

"Suite, my ass! They can call it that all they want, but, in the end, it's a jail. I'm just as much a prisoner here as I was for three years in an Afghan cave."

"You don't mean that."

"Yeah, I do. The surroundings might be more comfortable. The food a little better. And I don't get tortured every other day, except by Nurse Hatchitt and his happy needle."

"His, as in male nurse?"

Jake nodded. "Marine lieutenant Delbert Hatch, RN, as in registered nutcase. Solid gold butt-inator."

Izzie smiled at that reminder of the name the two of them, at the age of about ten, had given to anyone, mainly adults, they classified as assholes. "So, no pretty young things prancing around?"

"Be careful where you talk like that, man. Even I, isolated like I am, know what constitutes sexual harassment."

Izzie pretended to zip his lips.

"And, no, there are no pretty young things here, not that I've seen. Personally, I think it's just another form of legal torture Uncle Sam is inflicting on me. Visual deprivation."

Izzie popped the caps off two more bottles of beer and handed one to him. They moved to the low couch where they both leaned back and propped their shoes on the coffee table. A flat-screen TV on the opposite wall was showing yesterday's Yankees game against the Red Sox, with an announcer narrating, at a low volume, the play-by-play in German.

"Seriously, you know what would happen if I tried to walk out of this hospital with you, right?"

Izzie took a long draw on his brew, wiped his mouth with the back of his hand, and raised his brows in question.

"There would be so many sirens going off you'd think we were being attacked."

"They're just trying to protect you."

"Bullshit! I can't make a phone call, and my computer is locked so that I can read but not participate in any forum. Not even receive or send email."

"No interactive porn, huh?"

"Hah! They'd probably encourage that. Do you know what my shrink—Dr. Sheila—asked me last week?"

"I can't begin to guess." Izzie smirked.

Jake elbowed him, and Izzie elbowed him back. Immature, yeah. A sign of longtime companionship, more so. They grinned at each other.

"Dr. Sheila asked me if I'm suffering from wargasm."

Izzie's eyes went wide before he let out a hoot of laughter. "What the hell is wargasm?"

"Google it when you get home. You won't believe it." Jake took a small sip of his beer and set it aside. He really wasn't in the mood for alcohol. The combination with his meds was making him a bit nauseated.

"The private hospital wing, the mental and physical rehab, the isolation . . . all these things . . ." Izzie continued, "Well, I repeat, they're protecting you until you're well enough to return home."

"And I repeat, bullshit! They're protecting their own asses. I leave here and tell the press what happened to me in that Taliban shithole, it will jeopardize that ridiculous truce with the Balakistan rebels. If the brass had their way—and they've been trying to brainwash me with some asinine 'forgive and forget' philosophy, for the sake of peace, for three months now—I would go home and keep my mouth shut. It's all politics!"

"Everything in the military—hell, everything in life—is politics. You know that."

"Yeah, but I don't have to like it." Jake gazed at his friend, who was wearing Army fatigues, and smiled. "Is that another bar I see on your chest, soldier?"

Izzie puffed his chest out and grinned. "Yep. Finally made captain. Now I'm just like you."

"Hah! They want to make me a major and plant me in some defense department office, making 'Hail to the Chief' promo videos. Or some such crap."

"Be real, man, you're in no shape to return to active duty, if that's even what you'd want," Izzie said, not in an unkind way.

"Don't I know it!"

"A cushy job in DC sounds pretty good to me, short-term anyhow."

"Yeah, right. You'd be as miserable in a desk job as I would."

"Maybe." He studied Jake for a moment. "You do look a lot better than you did three months ago when they brought me in to identify your unconscious body."

That had to have been hard for Izzie, but then, Jake would have done the same for him in a heartbeat. "I saw pictures in my file this week. I looked like Frankenstein's younger, uglier brother. Now, I look like some Long John Silver Freakoid."

"You do not."

Jake put a hand to the patch over his one eye and then held out his hands to display his nailless fingers.

"The nails will grow back, and your other injuries will heal eventually. Maybe not totally, but . . ."

"Not my eye."

"The laser surgery didn't work?"

"No. They want to do another one in a month or so, but I am not sticking around this burg that long. Even if I have to rappel down the side of the building using bedsheets."

"And then what?"

"Hell if I know!"

"Still don't want to go home?"

"Still don't want to go home," Jake agreed.

A sudden idea seemed to occur to Izzie and he said, "Please don't tell me you had other injuries."

At first, Jake didn't understand until he noticed the blush on Izzie's face and his quick glance downward to Jake's crotch. "No, the package is still intact. Wanna see?"

"Hell, no!" Izzie relaxed visibly. But then he continued on the previous vein, "Don't you want to see Sally? And your kids?"

Jake shook his head.

"They miss you."

The kids might. He wasn't so sure about his wife. They'd exchanged words before his last deployment. Harsh words. As for the kids, three years was a long time in kid land. They probably didn't even remember him.

Jake had been sent recent pictures of his kids . . . and of Sally. The boys, Matthew, Mark, and Luke—yeah, he'd been on a Bible kick back then, and hoping for a John, eventually—were eight, seven, and five now. Luke had been only two the last time he'd seen him. He saw no resemblance to himself in the gremlins, except for their blue eyes . . . and maybe their mischievous grins.

The boys, even the littlest mite, had attached themselves to Jake like leeches—adorable leeches—whenever he'd been home on leave. And wailed like banshees every time he'd had to leave.

As for Sally, her long hair, a luxuriant light brown with golden sun highlights that he'd loved to wrap around his hands when—*Not going down that road!*—had been chopped off to an almost boyish style. The flighty girl's parents had been artsy-fartsy Broadway set designers and had raised their only child with only one aspiration, to sing on the Great White Way someday. Until she'd met him, that was. Sal did have a voice like an angel . . . a powerful alto for such a petite woman, like that singer Adele.

How had the girl who couldn't boil water or balance a checkbook managed to open and operate a successful bakery? And why hadn't she gone back to Manhattan and her parents and a possible singing career when he'd "died"?

In answer to Izzie's statement, though, about his family missing him, he replied simply, "They'll get over it."

"But why? I just don't understand why you'd want them to."

"I've changed."

"We all change. Hell, if you must know, you're probably better looking with that broken nose."

"I'm not talking physical changes. Inside"—he pounded his own chest—"inside I'm like an unpinned grenade. The least jarring and I might explode. And don't you dare tell that to my doctors or they won't ever release me."

"You do know you have a serious case of PTSD, don't you?"

"No shit!"

"PTSD isn't terminal, my friend."

"Really, Dr. Bernstein? Now you gonna give me the talk? Boot Camp 101. 'The Perils of Warfare.' Blah, blah, blah. I've heard that lecture before. Next you'll be telling me about STDs and the need for condoms, especially in foreign countries, complete with gory gonorrhea pictures. Did you bring pictures?"

Izzie sighed. "So, what . . . ? You gonna go off and live in the woods by yourself, or something?"

"Something like that. Maybe I'll be like one of those new frontier Alaska guys. Alone in the wild. Just me and the bears and wolves."

"You hate the cold. You're an Outer Banks boy to the bone. A sun lover."

"Well, maybe some warmer frontier," he conceded. "A jungle, maybe. Aren't there still frontiers in the Amazon?"

"Sorry, bud, but you gotta go back to Bell Cove. At least for a while. They won't release you if you don't agree to that." A slow smile twitched at Izzie's lips as he seemed to think of something. "Actually, you'll fit right in back home with that eye patch." Izzie went on to fill him in on the latest antics in their crazy-ass hometown, this time involving some shipwreck discovery which was being celebrated with a pirate theme during the Labor Day Lollypalooza, whatever the hell that was. They were even trying to get Johnny Depp to come, dressed in a Captain Jack Sparrow costume.

"Figures," Jake said. "I hope they don't expect me to play the part." Another reason for him not to go home.

Which brought them to the big elephant in the room.

"Don't you want to know about Sally?" Izzie asked.

Jake remained silent, working hard not to show any emotion. It wasn't as hard as you would think, being as dead inside as he was.

"My parents moved to Seattle to be near my sister Leah. So, not much reason to return to Bell Cove." Izzie sighed deeply and said, "I do talk to Sally occasionally on the phone, but that's kind of awkward, y'know what I mean."

"Because I was dead?"

"Well, yeah. Anyhow, I haven't seen her in three years, ever since they declared you dead and a memorial service was held, but . . ."

Izzie's nervousness raised some alarm bells in Jake's aching brain. He needed a Vicodin, or five, which he wouldn't take. The painkillers dulled his senses too much. "What?" he demanded.

"She just started dating."

Jake felt like he was kicked in the guts, even though three years was a long time for a wife to stay loyal to a husband she thought was dead. He shouldn't care. He didn't care. Still, he asked, "How do you know?"

"Uncle Abe told me. Did I tell you that Uncle Abe's deli was featured on that Food Network show, *Diners, Drive-Ins, and Dives*? They called his Reuben sandwich 'Reuben's Greatest Masterpiece.'"

"That's nice. So, who's the guy Sally is dating?" he asked nonchalantly.

"A Navy SEAL."

A SEAL? Fuck! "That's nice." *You hypocrite wife of mine! You berated me up one side and down the other for being in the military. You constantly demanded that I quit. Called me a selfish bastard. Now you take up with the most military of all the services? Shiiit!*

"Actually, he's an ex-SEAL. He's working on that treasure-hunting team in Bell Cove now."

An ex-SEAL? Who's now a hotshot Indiana-Fucking-Jones? Oh, that's better. Not! "I hope they'll be happy."

"If you must know, that's why I'm here."

"Ah, so you're not here out of friendship. You have ulterior motives."

"Don't be a dick. The brass figures it's time for you to go home."

"Let me guess. They sent you here to convince me that it's in my best interest to do what they want when they want?"

"C'mon, man! You don't want Sally to go getting married or something when she's already got a husband." He could tell that Izzie was trying to make a joke to ease the situation.

Jake wasn't laughing. In fact, he showed no emotion at all. It was a trick he'd learned during his long imprisonment. The best way to fight his torturers was to not reveal his feelings. After a while, it became second nature. "And you know what dating leads to." Izzie winked. Another lame attempt at humor.

Jake maintained his stone-cold expression.

"Apparently the guy likes kids."

Crap! "I hope they'll all be happy together."

His friend was nervously peeling the label off his beer bottle, which raised some warning flags for Jake. Something was rotten in the state of Denmark . . . or, rather, Germany, and one particular hospital room. Jake sensed that this wasn't just about his friend visiting him and casually asking about his plans to go home.

Jake could feel the red mist begin to form, a sure sign he was going to lose it any minute now. That's how the rages usually started. A mist in the distance, like a sunrise on the horizon. Sometimes, he was able to tamp it down at that stage. Other times, it swelled and got brighter. Still a haze, but hot. He could feel it. Then the haze would become thicker, more liquid, like water, coming at him in waves. Blood, that's what it became. He could not only see it, but smell it and, in the worst cases, taste it.

No! I can stop this. He gritted his teeth, clenched and unclenched his fists, and took several deep breaths before he calmed down. "All right, Izz, give it to me. The whole story. The brass sent you here to soften me up for . . . what? Spill! What is it you haven't told me?"

Izzie inhaled deeply, to brace himself.

Or was it to give Jake time to brace himself?

"They've informed Sally that you're still alive."

The waves were back. Crimson red. A slaughterhouse scent on the wind. A metallic taste on Jake's tongue. "Without getting my permission?"

"No choice. 'Gotcha!,' that WikiLeaks-style internet site, got wind of your rescue and deets on the two guys who didn't make it out. They're running with the story tomorrow, half of their facts twisted and unverified. It's a goat fuck about to happen if the Pentagon doesn't get a handle on the announcement themselves."

Jake licked his lips and swallowed hard, fighting the urge to hurl. "Sounds like a classic case of preventive damage control, fucked-up military style."

"Bingo!"

"When, exactly, did they tell Sally?"

Izzie glanced at his watch. "Taking into account the six-hour time difference, about an hour ago."

Waves crashed in his head. A tsunami. Slowly, he lowered his legs off the coffee table and stood. Inch by inch he turned to Izzie. "The pricks!"

"They've arranged for you to call Sally in a few hours," Izzie informed him. "Three a.m. at the latest, which would equate to nine p.m. back home. Not much time to prepare, but everything's happening at warp speed. Sally will be expecting your call. So, no reason to . . ." Izzie's words trailed off as he realized he was talking too much and too fast.

Jake gazed at Izzie as if he hadn't heard right. "Is that so? Have they arranged what I should say, or when we should meet, or whether we should have sex before or after saying hello? Did you bring cue cards with you?"

"Be reasonable, Jake."

"I have nothing left, man. I am nothing. What the Taliban didn't take from me, my own military is. They think they can control everything about me. When I eat. When I sleep. When I piss. What I can see or hear. They'd like to reach in and mold my mind to their specs. Well, fuck that!" Without thinking, he reached down, grabbed his half-empty bottle of beer, and threw it, smashing the television screen into a gray cobweb with the German baseball announcer still blathering on, before falling to the floor into a mess of booze and shattered glass.

"Oh, man! Oh, Jake! No!" Izzie said, as he stood, too.

Through the red haze of his vision, Jake barely registered Attila the Nurse come bursting through the door. Before he could react, the nurse had him in a head hold and was jabbing his arm with a needle. Almost immediately, he began drifting into the peacefulness of tranq-induced waves. Not the bloodred ones of his rage. These waves were crystal clear. Like a sweet summer day on Bell Sound.

It was a sign of how broken Jake still was that he could swear he heard the bells of his Outer Banks hometown ringing in his head. In fact, during his three years as a POW, he'd often heard those annoying bells. Back then, he'd thought they were calling him home.

The thing was, he no longer knew what, or where, home was.

Chapter 3

Facilitate that! . . .

Jake was lying flat on his back in bed when he awakened from his Ambien sleep.

He was calm now . . . and full of regrets. He hadn't had one of those "episodes" in weeks. Last time was after he'd gotten the results of yet another failed eye surgery.

Damn, damn, damn!

Was it a one-off, or was he regressing? It better be the former or they would have him on a tighter lockdown than they did already. But, no. He recalled what had prompted this wash of red mist. The fact that Sally was being informed of his existence, without his consent or input.

Damn, damn, damn.

His curse words were head whispers, more a gentle mantra of that mindfulness crap his psychiatrist was always hyping. "Just breathe, just breathe, just breathe."

Or his version, "Damn, damn, damn."

At first, he remained motionless, his good eye

shut. Then he realized what had awakened him . . . the sound of low voices coming from the other side of his room. It was a sign of his improvement here at Landstuhl that he didn't immediately jack-knife up and into a shooting position, sensing a threat.

Yeah, yeah, he'd lost control a short time ago—two hours ago, in fact, he realized by checking the wall clock—but he chalked that up to extreme provocation . . . as in, his cover was blown, or about to be blown. Not just with his wife, and family, and friends, and fellow soldiers, but the whole freakin' world. Who wouldn't overreact to that?

Slowly, he turned his head, without changing the position of his body. There was a group seated around his small dining table, talking softly. Extra folding chairs had been brought in. Four people. Izzie; Dr. Sheila, his shrink; Dr. Muller, his general physician here at the medical center; and some guy in full military dress uniform that he didn't recognize, probably a major if Jake's one eye didn't miss a stripe or see double.

Slowly, he eased himself up and over to a sitting position on the side of the bed. He hadn't showered since his workout this morning, but figured he'd have to wait until he faced the music from the "firing squad" over there.

That little bit of movement got their attention, and they all turned to look at him, with concern. Dr. Sheila Benoit, a fortyish woman from Louisiana whose Cajun husband was a pilot stationed at Ramstein Air Base, came over to him and said, "How do you feel? Is the red tide over?"

He regretted confiding in a counseling session once about his rages, which she constantly wanted to talk about. She was the one who'd given them the name "red tides." It would probably end up in one of her books on PTSD.

"I'm fine now. Just a blip."

She raised her brows at that dismissal but reached out a hand to help him up. "Come, join us. A cup of tea might help."

Yeah, right. He was going to guzzle down a gallon of her chamomile, which tasted like perfume to him, and lickety-split he would be cool, calm, and collected.

He'd rather have another beer.

Or a glass of iced water.

He got up on his own, without her aid, and walked over to the mini fridge. Taking out a bottled water, he chugged down half of it, then turned to the table, where everyone was gawking at him like he was some specimen under glass, or a bomb about to implode. "So, what's up?"

"Have a seat, Captain Dawson," Dr. Muller said, pulling out a chair for him. Muller was wearing a golf shirt and lime-green pants today, probably off to the links at Woodlawn or Barbarossa once he left here. Landstuhl had a mixture of military and civilian staff. Dr. Sheila and Dr. Muller were among the latter.

Jake sat and glanced pointedly at the military guy. "And you are . . . ?" Not the required protocol in addressing a superior officer, but at this point Jake wasn't in the mood for politeness or military etiquette.

"Major Raymond Durand, Pentagon, division of global communications. I'm here as part of a team to facilitate your Transition Plan, Phase One." He pointed to a folder on the table, which actually had those words on it. "Captain Jacob Dawson, Transition Plan, Phase One."

"Wow! The Pentagon has an interest in little old me? How many phases are there, exactly?" Jake asked, unable to hold back his sarcasm, which was probably a violation of another Army Code of Conduct rule.

Two checks against me. Big deal!

Man, I am in a fighting mood. Gotta get myself under control.

Undaunted, the major said, "Three. Phase One is 'Breaking the News.' Phase Two is 'Reentry.' Phase Three is 'Guided Media Opportunities.' There may be other phases, to be determined, as needed."

Jake turned to Izzie, who was seated on his right, and he gave him a stare that pretty much said, "Can you believe this butt-inator?"

Izzie just shrugged.

"So, are you one of my facilitators, too?"

Izzie shrugged again.

He hated Izzie's shrugs.

"We all are, Jake," Dr. Sheila said, patting him on the arm.

Jake hated being patted, like a kid.

Back to the clueless major, Jake asked, "Are any of these phases called 'Tail Wagging the Dog'?"

"This is serious business, Captain," the major warned, his voice clearly pulling rank on him. "You're already aware that the president is in volatile negotiations with the recently elected Qadir government in Balakistan."

It took Jake a moment, but then the major's words, *already aware*, clicked like a light bulb in his brain. Why would the major be so certain he was aware of current news regarding Balakistan? *Son of a bitch! They must be monitoring my TV watching habits. Probably my computer, as well. Too bad I didn't hit some porno sites.*

"Any adverse publicity about your treatment at the hands of the rebels would reflect badly on the new regime. Yes, you have reason to be upset about your long period in hiding, but for the greater good and national security, discretion is called for," the major continued. "Caution is the key in media relations from this point out."

"Long period? How about three years? And what's with the 'in hiding' nonsense? I was a prisoner, pure and simple, not roughing it in some cave, like a crazy-ass spelunker. As if I had a choice!"

"I'm familiar with the details, Captain. But here's the situation. As a Special Forces operative, you're well aware of the term *collateral damage*. Unfortunately, whether in battle or government, sometimes innocent parties are harmed. It's the price of freedom."

Me? Collateral damage? Oooh, I do not like the sound of that. He turned to Izzie with disbelief. "Are you okay with this propaganda?"

"Shhh. Calm down, Jake. He's only doing his job."

"I don't like your tone, *Captain*." The major bristled, pulling rank on him. "Keep in mind that I'm here to facilitate your return. That kind of attitude is getting you nowhere."

"You may be my 'facilitator' or 'handler' or whatever the hell you want to call it, but I'm still an American, and I have the right to speak my mind." He inhaled deeply to tamp down his temper. In a surprisingly composed voice, he said, "Number one, excuse my language, *Major*, but bullshit on the 'elected' government you mentioned. There is no such thing in Balakistan. Number two, bullshit on differentiating between the rebels and the new cabinet. They're one and the same. I had an up-close-and-personal acquaintance with the Qadir tribe and with Nazim bin Jamil, with or without the title of minister of defense, more like minister of torture. Number three, bullshit on sugarcoating my treatment at the hands of those Taliban assholes. Number four, bullshit on 'guided media opportunities.' The only opportunity the media will have with me is what I grant, and, frankly, I have no interest whatsoever in talking to the press."

"See, those are the kind of messages we can't have you portraying in the public sector."

"In other words, you want me to lie?"

"No, no, no! But there are ways to tell your story in a way that accomplishes our purpose without offending other parties. You have to think long game here, not what happens in the first or second quarters."

"Oh, now I get it. You're a spin doctor."

The major sat up straighter and flashed a glare at Dr. Sheila. "You said he was ready."

"I never said he was 'ready.' I said he was well enough emotionally to handle going home."

"And I never said he was 'ready' for the physical stress of some kind of promotion tour," Dr. Muller added. "This boy needs another eye surgery, and the rod in his leg will have to be removed at some point. Rest in a peaceful environment would be my recommendation, not some media circus."

"How about you, Izzie?" Jake asked. "Don't you have an opinion?"

"I'm more concerned about your phone call to Sally, which is going to take place roughly an hour or so from now. Do you have any idea what your wife has been told? Before you talk to her, you need to know what intel she's been given, or not, so you have your ducks in a row."

Jake had conveniently forgotten about that. He would need to call Sally, now that she'd been informed. "You're right, buddy. By the way, sorry for my outburst earlier. My only excuse is that I was caught off guard."

"No problem, my friend."

"So, what was Sally told?"

"Only the basics," Major Durand interrupted. "She knows that you were rescued and are recuperating here at Landstuhl. She knows that you have continuing eye and leg injuries to deal with. She knows that you'll be going home soon on a medical leave for continuing rehab and recovery."

"Is that all?"

"That's about it. Well, a few more things." The major took sheets out of his folder and passed them to Jake. "This is the news release that will be going out tomorrow, and that's pretty much what your wife has been told. The second page outlines the do's and don'ts of what you will tell your family, friends, anyone in the public. Not the media. Do not speak to the press until you get prior approval from the DOD. That would be me."

Jake took the sheets and scanned them. First, the news release, which was on heavy vellum with a Department of Defense letterhead.

"Army captain Jacob Dawson, who was declared dead three years ago after a failed mission to rescue two downed pilots in Afghanistan, is actually alive and will soon be on his way home to the United States.

Although Captain Dawson suffered serious

injuries to one eye and a leg following a HALO jump into the mountains of Balakistan on May 19, 2016, he managed to survive for three years by living in a remote cave in the middle of hostile territory, with the aid of some rebel friendlies. Survival skills mastered during his military training helped the soldier to endure the brutal conditions.

During recent high-level negotiations between the US and the newly elected Qadir government, the president first learned of Captain Dawson's amazing survival story and demanded his immediate return. The President thanks Balakistan Minister of Defense Nazim bin Jamil for his efforts in this operation.

Captain Dawson has been in Landstuhl Hospital in Germany, recovering from his injuries. Two other soldiers on Captain Dawson's team, Sergeant Frank Bailey and Corporal David Guttierez, died on the mission, according to Captain Dawson. The pilots who were to be rescued, Lieutenant Anton "Ace" Sampsell and Lieutenant Gerald Frank, were rescued in another section of Afghanistan soon after Captain Dawson went MIA.

For more information, contact US Department of Defense, Press Information, Major Raymond Durand, at the above address."

Jake's eyes got wider and wider as he scanned the page. "So much for not lying!"

"There's no lie in that document. A skirting of the truth, maybe, but no outright lies."

Jake arched his one visible brow skeptically.

"You were kept in a cave. There were rebels, maybe not friendlies . . . I can delete that word. Nazim did inform the POTUS of your existence. Two of your team members did die on the mission."

"Are you crazy? I wasn't even a POW in your version of events."

The major shrugged. "MIA, then."

Jake shook his head at the major's audacity in twisting the truth so boldly. "That news release isn't the real story. Not even close."

"It's all anyone needs to know, for now."

"Are you for real? Seriously, no one will ever believe this crap."

"I'd bet my precious DC parking permit that the press will buy it and beg for more."

Jake put his face in his hands, then looked up again. "This feels like some bizarre episode of that TV show *Homeland* where an Army sergeant was held prisoner by al-Qaeda for eight years."

"And nobody said that was unbelievable," the major pointed out.

"Oh, yeah! It was Delta Force that rescued the sergeant in that series. Ask any Delta Force guys what they thought of that scenario. We all had a good laugh over it."

The major didn't reply to Jake's specific criticism, but he did look at him with some sympathy. "I do understand your concerns, Captain Dawson, but

believe me, I've handled more complicated cases
than yours." He waved a hand toward the other
sheet. "Read your instructions."

CAPTAIN JACOB DAWSON: Do's and Do Not's

- Do not accept any requests for interviews,
  whether local or national, whether in person, via telephone or email, without prior
  approval of the DOD.
- Do not discuss the events of your time in
  Balakistan with family or close friends.
  Loose lips sink ships, and even those most-
  trusted individuals can inadvertently dis-
  close details that must remain secret.
- Do not, under any circumstances, mention
  the word *torture*.
- Do not voice an opinion about Nazim, in his
  present role or any past contact you may
  have had with him.
- Do not claim to have inside info on Balakistan, its history, culture, or tribes, such
  as the Qadir, battles, or political climate.
- Do be thankful to the president and secretary of defense for their actions in bringing
  you home. If you are so inclined, you can
  thank God, as well, though that might offend some sectors.
- Do express your continuing loyalty to the
  United States and its military.

- Do take advantage of medical opportunities to bring yourself back to pre-2016 physical condition, or as much as possible, including any eye and leg operations deemed necessary.
- Do meet ASAP with the psychiatrist hired to work with you at the VA hospital in Richmond, Lieutenant Colonel Martin Elliott, a specialist in military PTSD.
- Do maintain regular contact with your Army liaison during your medical leave.
- Do consider the Pentagon's generous offer of a promotion to major and a posting in the Department of Defense's Office of Communications.
- Do not hesitate to ask for help. Your country appreciates your service.

Jake blinked several times after finishing his quick scan of the document. "You've got to be kidding. I can't say anything about the three years I was a POW."

"Without getting prior approval from your contact at the DOD, that's correct. Army Code of Conduct, Section 108, part B. From this point on, the term we will be using is *MIA*, not *POW*."

"Actually, I don't mind keeping my mouth shut. Confidential intel has always remained private. But I draw the line at becoming your propaganda machine, being interviewed by the news media, parroting some political buzz words. And what's with your assumption that I would want to talk about Nazim. Hell, I even object to the assumption that I want to go home to the Outer Banks."

In the end, Jake and the major arrived at a compromise.

Neither of them was happy.

Honey, I'm home . . .

The phone rang at nine o'clock on the dot. Sally was sitting on her bed, the cordless phone in her hand, but she didn't answer right away. She couldn't.

She'd had more than five hours to prepare herself, but her body was still frozen with shock. A small part of her clung to the idea that someone was playing a morbid joke. Or that she was lost in a dream and couldn't wake up.

Her father-in-law, Jake's father, had done nothing but freeze up and go off on his boat to brood, ever since they'd gotten the news. Not unlike Sally, who'd probably scandalized both the general and the senator by not shedding a single tear. Why would she? She still didn't believe it. Finally, the bossy general had returned to DC. If the man, with his long list of "advice," had stayed longer, Sally might very well have knocked him over the head with one of her baking trays.

The boys were asleep due to overexcitement, starting with the fishing expedition this morning and then the news that they actually had a father—which they could hardly understand, but recognized as something huge in their lives. To them, it was like Christmas and birthdays combined, with surely the promise of presents on their greedy horizons.

The townsfolk didn't know yet that their lost hero was a live hero, thanks to orders from General Advise-a-Lot, but they suspected something was up. If the pretentious vehicle parked outside wasn't a clue, the presence of a general and a senator certainly were, not to mention two military security guards patrolling the perimeter of her property.

Which didn't stop some of the Bell Cove-ites. In fact, Laura Atler, editor of the local newspaper, *The Bell*, scooted around one of the soldiers and made a mad dash for the cottage, only to be picked up bodily by a grinning marine, then frog-marched back to her car.

Not to be deterred, the phone, which had been set on voice mail, hadn't stopped ringing. But the voice mail had been turned off now so that she could accept this all-important call.

On the fifth ring, Sally picked up. "Hello."

"Hey, babe!"

It's Jake. It really is! Oh, my God! And what's with this casual "Hey, babe!" as if he just returned from a normal three- or four-week deployment? But then she realized that he might be as nervous as she was. And so she replied in the way she would have in the old days . . . the days prior to his "death."

"Hey, dude!" she said, barely above a whisper, the usual response she made to his "Hey, babe."

They'd started that playful exchange back when she'd first met him at a Central Park concert eons ago. She had been a student at the Manhattan School of Music, waiting for her big break as a singer in a Broadway production, he a handsome soldier on leave in the big city. Her heart had literally skipped a beat on seeing the young man with blue, blue eyes in a spiffy dress uniform. More than nine years later, her heart still beat so fast she could scarcely breathe, but for different reasons now, of course.

Over the lump in her throat, she managed to get out, "Long time no hear, sweetie."

"The dead don't speak, *sweetie*." He laughed.

And, yes, she sensed nervousness from his end. "I'm sorry," she said right off.

"For what?"

"The things I said before you left. That's the one thing I regretted after we were told that you died, how I sent you out with bitter words."

"'You selfish bastard!' Are those the words you're referring to? Yep, those were definitely not the three words you usually said before I left."

"You didn't say them, either. The three usual words, I mean."

"You could say them now," he noted.

"So could you, Jacob." Although everyone called her husband Jake, Sally had gotten a kick the first time she was introduced to his mother to hear her refer to him as Jacob. In the beginning, she'd started calling him Jacob, too, in a teasing way, but then it became her pet name for him. By using it now, she might not be saying that she still loved him, but it introduced an intimacy to their conversation. He had to be thinking of those times when he'd relished hearing her breathy sighs of "Oh, Jacob!"

"Anyhow, I'm sorry, too," he said. "This was no way for you to get the news that I was alive."

"Three months, Jacob! You should have called. You should have come home. I can understand how you might not have been physically able to at first, but . . . three months!"

General Parker had explained that Jake had serious injuries when he was first rescued, that he was in fact unconscious for a while, but Sally knew her stubborn husband. If he'd wanted to come home, he would have, or at least found a way to contact her. With his Special Forces training, he had skills.

The fact that Jake remained silent at her condemnation was telling. "You do want to come home, don't you?"

"Yes. No. I don't know," he replied.

The flutters in her chest turned to stone and dropped to her stomach, making her nauseated. He had to have heard her gasp.

"Wait. Don't hang up," he said quickly.

Which was precisely what she'd been about to do.

"I'm not the same, Sally."

"Well, hell's bells, neither am I. But forget about you and me. What about your kids? Don't you want to see them?" She'd like to remind him that he hadn't seen much of his kids in the past, when he'd had the chance, with all the active duty crap he'd engaged in, some of it voluntary. He'd parked her in boring Small Town, USA, then gone off to his other life of excitement and adventure.

But now was not the time for that argument. They'd had it enough before.

"Of course I do, but . . ." He paused as if unsure what to say next, then revealed, "I don't want them to see me like this."

All of this was so unlike the Jake she knew and had loved at one time. He would be tossing out swear words like bullets. Arrogant on occasion. Always sure of himself. And, yes, selfish.

"Like what, Jacob? Do you think kids care about a limp, or an injured eye? They already have you built up into this larger-than-life Superman hero."

"See. That's what I mean. I'm no hero."

"Tell that to the town of Bell Cove. They'll have a marching band waiting for you at the ferry. Billboards, at the least. Yellow ribbons from every tree for miles around. A celebration to outdo their Grinch madness last Christmas, or the Independence Day wedding they put on last month, or Pirate Madness, or today's Elvis-Comes-Back-to-Bell Cove, or the upcoming Lollypalooza."

He groaned.

"Don't you dare say that you're not coming home," she continued. "You are not going to humiliate me, or disappoint your boys, or break your father's heart by staying away."

"Is that an order?" he asked.

"You better believe it, soldier. As I told that General Parker today, 'I'm a civilian, but you work for my government. Therefore, you work for me. You do not tell me how to handle my husband's homecoming.' What an ass he was!"

"You gave a general his marching orders?"

"You better believe it."

He chuckled.

"One more thing, Jacob," she added. The tears she'd been holding back all day finally let loose in a torrent. She was about to say, "I do still love you. Dammit!" But the words wouldn't come. They might not even be true anymore. Instead, she said, "Welcome home, soldier."

Chapter 4

Eye candy for the chocoholic . . .

(New York City, nine years and one month ago)

Well, that was a waste of time," Sally Fontaine said to her best friend, Melody Carter, as they left the Eugene O'Neill Theater.

"For sure! Even if we get the parts, the pay and the hours wouldn't be worth the effort."

The casting notice on Backstage.com had been misleading, to say the least. The two of them had skipped morning classes at the Manhattan School of Music to audition for supporting roles in a remake of *West Side Story*, which was expected to make its Broadway debut next March. It had been a cattle call for mostly chorus spots, resulting in hundreds of singers showing up, many of them with a smattering of experience, like themselves.

Ever since her parents had discovered that Sally had singing talent when she was about ten years old, they'd been encouraging her with voice lessons and auditions, all geared toward a Broadway career. Never the popular music scene, which they considered a meat market for drugs and exploitation. But the "legitimate" theater, yes, yes, yes.

Her parents wouldn't have minded her skipping classes, today or any other day, despite the expensive tuition they paid out each month. It was important to keep trying, whether through auditions or agent appointments, never knowing when the "lucky break" would come for her to hit the big time. As a result, this marked Sally's nineteenth tryout since she'd graduated from high school last year. Oh, she'd gotten numerous bit parts along the way, but none of them anywhere near the "big time," not even the three days of playing Annie when she was eleven and the lead actress was sick with the flu.

Mel fanned her face with a *Playbill* she'd picked up from the theater lobby. The temperature on the TV this morning had said eighty degrees, and they were both dressed appropriately for the weather in sundresses and flat ballet-style shoes, but eighty degrees in August in the Big Apple was comparable to about a hundred anywhere else.

Not that Sally knew much about "anywhere else," having grown up in the city with her parents, Max and Lola Fontaine, famous set designers who rarely left their beloved home territory near the Great White Way, except for occasional flights to LA where they worked on films, which was rare. Not for lack of opportunity. They just preferred live theater.

"Should we go back to school or hit the summer concert series in the park?" Sally asked.

"Definitely the concert," Mel replied. "It's 'Beach Music Without Sand' today. Eight bands, headlined by the Beach Boys."

"I thought they were dead."

"Some are, but the band is still cool. Well, their music is." Mel began to sing "Barbara Ann," which caused passersby on the busy street to turn and stare, then smile. She was really good. Unlike Sally, Mel and her doting family wouldn't mind a popular singing role. In fact, she was planning to try out for next season's *American Idol*.

Sally elbowed her friend to behave, and they headed across 50th Street, taking a shortcut through the park. Within ten minutes they were at the back of the crowd which stood about or sat on blankets listening to the band. The spectators were all ages. Some seniors who would have been teens in the heyday of beach music, but also some young couples with children, and lots of teens on the loose for summer vacation.

On stage at the moment appeared to be a Southern band called The Shakers, which was playing "Carolina Girls." Well, actually, there were two bands on the stage . . . The Shakers and the Beach Boys. They had a sort of duel of the bands going on, with The Shakers extolling the virtues of Carolina girls, while the Beach Boys did a counterpoint with their song about West Coast girls. Back and forth they went with contradictory lyrics from their once-popular songs, and surprisingly they worked well together.

Sally and Mel looked at each other and smiled.

"Should we try to get closer to the stage?" Mel asked.

"Nah. Let's sit on that picnic table over there. That family is leaving."

They rushed over and were about to hop up and onto the tabletop with their feet on the bench when Sally looked to the side, then did a double take. Standing nearby were a group of six physically fit men in short-sleeved khaki uniforms with green berets covering high-and-tight military haircuts. But it wasn't the group that caught Sally's attention. It was one man in particular.

He had dark hair and pale blue eyes. Broad shoulders. Small waist. Tall. Maybe six foot. But not too tall, compared to her five-five. In a pair of her favorite high heels, he would be just perfect.

What? Why make that comparison? Am I nuts? Suddenly attracted to hunks? My parents, true-blue pacifists, would have tandem heart attacks if I ever came home with a soldier. But, holy moly, he does look good in that uniform.

Sally was used to good-looking males in the entertainment business her parents worked in and the participants that they often brought home. Actors. Musicians. Singers. If they weren't born handsome, they used plastic surgeons, or aesthetic dentists, or hair stylists, or physical trainers to get to that perfection ideal. Eye candy for the sugar-deprived masses.

But this guy was different, somehow.

And, face it, I'm no beauty prize. Sally was realistic about her own shortcomings. Plain brown hair, except for some naturally blonde highlights. A slightly crooked incisor tooth, which her parents said made Sally stand out from the too–orthodontically perfect, too-white-toothed crowd. A petite figure that was far from voluptuous.

Men didn't stop in their tracks when she walked by.

Still, this guy, as he leaned against a tree, was staring, not at the stage, like his buddies, but at her. And he appeared to be equally poleaxed. Tilting his head to the side, his compelling eyes seemed to be asking a question, the same question causing her heart to leap in her chest.

Who are you?

But then he smiled, a slow, lazy twitch of impossibly sexy lips.

And Sally's world changed forever.

The Beach Boys launched into "Good Vibrations," countered by "Shagging, USA" by The Shakers.

Oh, yeah!

Forever is a long, long time . . .

Jake stared at the cell phone in his hand before laying it down on the bedside table. He'd just ended his awkward call to Sally and wondered, sadly, how they'd managed to land in this rocky place. Their marriage had been on shaky ground before he went MIA, too many tours, too many broken promises, and now . . . ?

Could it even be salvaged, especially with all the problems of his "resurrection" thrown in?

Would he really be welcome back in Bell Cove? By Sally, who'd made a new life for herself? By his kids who didn't even know him anymore? By townsfolk who revered a dead hero, not a live nonhero?

And how about the new boyfriend?

How had the love that had bloomed almost instantly between him and Sally nine years ago gone so far off course?

Lieutenant Jacob Dawson and five of his buddies had just come from a funeral for a fallen comrade when they sidetracked through Central Park on the way back to their hotel. The guys would have much preferred a bar with cold beers on tap in this heat and were griping about wanting to get out of their uniforms and into civvies.

Jake had heard that The Shakers, a North Carolina band, were playing in a beach music–themed concert. Being from the Outer Banks, where The Shakers were well-known and where Shag dance music was still popular, he'd convinced his friends to make the detour.

But then he saw her.

She was average height, about five-five, but small boned, making her look kind of petite. But maybe it was the sundress she wore, held up by thin spaghetti straps that gave a guy ideas. It was peach-colored, like her skin, with big splotchy ivory flowers. Her hair, brown with gold highlights, picked up by the sun, was long and luxuriously thick, but held off her face into a high ponytail. Freckles, which were oddly attractive, dotted her nose and cheeks and upper arms. The freckles, too, gave him ideas. *Can anyone say, connect the dots? Like with a marker? Or a tongue? And, hey, where else does she have freckles?*

This was crazy. He shook his head to clear it. There was nothing outstanding about this girl. He'd seen and dated ones much prettier. In fact, normally he would be more attracted to her friend, the taller blonde wearing a red figure-hugging sundress.

But, no, it was the one with the caramel eyes who drew him. He couldn't stop staring.

She noticed his staring. And stared back at him, her head tilted in question.

His heart skipped a beat, and then began pounding. *Ka-boom, ka-boom, ka-boom.*

She's the one, a voice in his head said.

The one what? he answered.

But he knew. The men in his family were reputed to fall hard and instantly for their "one true love." Yeah, hokey as that was, it was a tradition they all believed in, those who had fallen, that was. He'd always jeered at the notion. Until now.

This could not be happening to him. Not at this time. He was only twenty-three years old. A recent college grad, two years into his military duty, he'd recently joined the elite Delta Force unit.

Without thinking, he smiled at her.

She blinked several times, then smiled back at him.

And he fell, "hook, line, and sinker," as his dad, a commercial fisherman, was wont to say, into a deep, deep, forever love.

Or so he'd thought for many years, Jake mused now in his hospital room. Until the arguments with his wife kept him away from home more than necessary, until a sadistic Taliban operative taught him that maybe she'd been right, maybe he was not worthy of love.

Call me maybe . . . or not . . .

*F*or the next week, every evening Outer Banks time, Jake made phone calls home, which he loathed, but looked forward to with a passion that scared him. He didn't want to be that needy. Neediness made him weak, even weaker than he already was.

And, despite the option being open to him, he passed on FaceTiming calls. He wasn't ready to show his sorry self to anyone, not even his family. He didn't want to scare anyone, especially his young boys.

The first call to his father was the hardest. Their relationship had been broken for a while after he'd refused to go into the commercial fishing business with him after college, but they'd put that behind them in recent years, or so he'd hoped. After that, they'd been awkward with each other, always nervous of saying the wrong things. Like now.

"Jacob? Is it really you?"

"Yep. It's me, Pop. How's the fishing?" *That's certainly a safe question. Totally irrelevant but what the hell!*

"Up and down, as usual," his father said. Not to be diverted, he said, "I couldn't believe it when they told me you were alive. Three years in a cave? Really? You, who hated tight spaces! Could barely stand to sleep overnight in the cabin of *Lazy Days* when we went out on extended trips."

Jake had become adept at avoiding questions about his POW experience, per Major Butt-inator's Do's and Don'ts list. Mainly, he avoided any questions specific to his three lost years. Made a joke or sidetracked the conversation. Thus, he was prepared for his father's comment. "It was a big cave," he remarked. "But, hey, is that old rust bucket still staying afloat?"

"Bite your tongue, boy. *Lazy Days* will be riding the waves when you and I are both gone." He seemed to realize what he'd said then, referring to Jake's death, and muttered a curse under his breath.

Great! Now everyone is going to be overly sensitive over what they say around me. They'll be avoiding any words like pirates *(as in eye patch or peg leg), or* missing people *(whether soldiers or young girls off the streets), or* caves. *Well, fuck that!*

"And you, Dad . . . no thoughts of retiring?" Another sidetrack.

"Hell, no! I'm only sixty-two. Why would I retire?"

Maybe to relax once in a while. Maybe to spend time with your family. Maybe to stop beating up on a body that could take only so much abuse hauling nets and two-hundred-pound fish. But then, Jake realized that those same suggestions could be applied to himself. An unsettling thought!

"Is Old Mike still with you?" *Instead of answering a question, turn the tables and ask your own questions,* Major Durand had suggested in one of their annoying "facilitation" sessions.

Old Mike had been his father's first mate on the thirty-five-foot boat as long as Jake could remember. Even when he must not have been all that old, though he had to be close to seventy now. Jake had no idea where the crotchety character had gotten that nickname, or where he'd come from.

His father cleared his throat, then said, "You come home, son, y'hear? You and me have fences to mend."

Jake could swear he heard tears in his father's voice, which was impossible. His dad was not an emotional person, being a native New Englander who'd maintained his stoic, undemonstrative personality. In fact, he didn't think he'd ever heard him use the word *love*. Not that he doubted his father's love for him or for his mother, for whom he'd moved to her hometown in North Carolina after their marriage. It just wasn't ever spoken of. Especially not when Jake had about broken his heart in leaving the Outer Banks for a military career, instead of the damned family fishing business.

In truth, Jake couldn't ever recall telling his father that he loved him, either. Though he had loved him. Unconditionally. Despite his pigheaded, inflexible ways.

"Dad, there are no fences," he assured his father. "We're family. Always have been, always will be, even if you are a stubborn sonofabitch."

"Takes one to know one," his father choked out.

Definite tears. Especially when he said, "I wish your mother had lived to see this day. She prayed for you every day, even after we got the death notice."

He had to ask something that had been nagging at him. "Dad, did I cause Mom's death? I mean, she was only fifty-five when she passed. Was her worry over me what brought on the heart attack?"

"Forget that idea right now, son. Your mother had an undiagnosed heart condition. Runs in her side of the family. Good Lord! With all you've been through, don't go looking for trouble."

Jake didn't argue, but he wasn't convinced, either.

Then there were the calls to Sally, which were uncomfortable, to say the least. Mostly, they talked about all that had happened in Bell Cove the past three years, especially regarding the bakery she'd started with his death benefits. "A sweet reward!" he'd joked.

She hadn't laughed.

A morbid joke, yeah, but give me some points for trying to break the ice.

He liked hearing her talk about the bakery, how she'd started out there, working part-time for the former owner, Delia Kohler, after his last deployment, then buying Delia out when she retired.

"At first, I was such a klutz in the bakery, as you can well imagine," Sally told him. "Remember the time I made brownies and they were so underdone we had to eat them with a spoon?"

He remembered, all right, and he remembered where they'd eaten them, and where the splatters had landed, and how they'd cleaned them up. Smiling, he replied, "No, I don't remember that, but I recall you asking me one time what a whisk was."

"I've come a long way, baby. In fact, I· bet I have a dozen different whisks in my bakery at the moment."

"A girl can never have too many whisks, I suppose." *That was as lame a joke as anything I've ever heard. Jeesh! Stop trying so hard, man.* "So, what's the specialty in your bakery? Wasn't Delia big on pies?"

"Cookies."

"Huh?"

"That's my specialty. Yeah, I offer artisan breads and special-event cakes, and six flavors of homemade ice cream in fresh-baked waffle cones during the summer, but I wanted something people could buy and eat on the street when they're walking around the square. Something people could hold in their hands and not make a mess, like filled cupcakes. Donuts are good for that purpose, but practically every bakery on the Outer Banks does donuts, some very good ones. I had to have something unique."

"Cookies are unique?"

"Mine are. They are the size of saucers, and I call them Mookies . . . as in monster cookies."

He chuckled.

"Don't laugh. The most successful bakeries have something unusual, like the Apple Uglies at the Orange Blossom in Buxton."

"I love those! So, what kind of Mookies do you make?"

"It varies. Some of them are seasonal, like Cove Candy Cane Crunch at Christmas, and Strawberry Shores in midsummer. Jello Waves all through the tourist season because of the bright colors, which the kids love, and the usual ones, too, like Chocolate Chip Coasters. Surfin' with Ginger. Sandy Tarts. Butterscotch on the Beach. Tides of Peanut Butter. Walnut Wafer Waves. Salty Caramel Shells."

"Whoa, whoa, whoa! I get the picture. What I like most is how passionate you seem about all this. But I wonder, well . . ." Why hadn't she gone back to New York when he'd "died"? Why hadn't she resumed an aspiring career with singing? As far as he knew, the only singing she'd done since he'd brought her to Bell Cove was in the church choir, and he didn't know if she'd even continued with that. Surely, her parents would have welcomed her back to the city, even with three kids. But these were questions best saved for another occasion.

"What?" she prodded. "What do you wonder about?"

"I wonder why you haven't sent me any cookies this past week," he said.

"By the time they arrived there, you'd already be here," she pointed out.

Which was something he did not want to think about now. Not yet. Time was going by too quickly now that the decision had been made for him to go home.

So, in their nightly chats, he and Sally skirted around anything involving their personal relationship. Most guys in his situation would be engaged in tantalizing discussions of what they wanted to do with their wives when they got home, mostly related to beds and naked bodies. Once he'd teasingly said, "So, I guess we've been given another chance to get us a John," based on their naming their kids after the four Gospels, Matthew, Mark, and Luke, and John, which ended with that third son.

Jake's remark had been met with silence.

Guess there won't be any action in that regard, at least not right away. What had he expected when her last words to him when heading out for deployment three years and three or so months ago had been "You selfish bastard!" followed by a slammed door.

At first, Sally had asked questions about his captivity, but eventually gave up when she never got real answers.

Like "What did you eat, living in a cave?" As if his diet had been important during those brutal days!

"Bat wings," he'd replied. "They taste just like chicken wings without the sauce."

"Why do you always have to make fun of me like that? As if I don't have the brains to understand what you do. Or that I can't take the truth."

"I wasn't making fun of you. I was making fun of myself."

"Yeah, right."

Or, "How did your leg get injured? And your eye? Oh, Jacob! Your beautiful eyes!"

Sally had been attracted to his blue eyes from their first meeting, said they were among his best features. "I still have one left."

"That's not funny," she'd said. "How did it happen . . . the eye and the leg?"

"I always was clumsy," he'd answered.

"That doesn't even pass the giggle test."

Which was true. He'd never been clumsy. Just the opposite. Highly coordinated and able to spin on a dime and land on his feet.

Mostly, they talked about the boys.

"Matt considers himself the man of the family since you've been gone."

"That's quite a load for an eight-year-old."

"Yes, but he takes it seriously. You'll have to be careful not to step on his toes."

"Point taken," he said.

"Mark suffers from the typical middle child syndrome."

Sad to say, Jake had no idea what that was, and he'd said so.

"Middle children often act out because they feel their older siblings get all the privileges and can do things they can't just because of their age, while the younger children get more attention."

Jake groaned. "So, what do I do about that?"

"Just give him equal attention."

"How about Luke? What's his problem?"

"None at all. Happy-go-lucky and mischievous as all get-out. The most like you, I suppose. He's missing two of his front teeth at the moment, and he's very self-conscious about it. Whatever you do, don't mention his lisp."

Then there were the short conversations with the boys themselves.

Matt said, "I remember you."

"That's good. I certainly remember you." *And the day you were born. Six pounds, six ounces. Beautiful. And I was there to "catch" you when you came out, big guy. Sad to say, I was not there for Mark and Luke's births, being on active ops at the time.* "Guess you've been the man of the family since I've been gone. Hope you'll help me get the swing of things when I return."

"Yep. There's lots to learn," Matt said.

Jake could tell that Matt was pleased at his not taking over unilaterally. As if he would! Jake had been away too often even during normal times for that.

"Will you be back in time for the scout banquet?

I'll be getting my Bear badge. Mark and Luke are only Lions, but Mark will be moving up to Wolf, if he finishes his badge requirements in time." In a whisper, he confided, "Mark is terrible at tying knots, even with PopPop helpin' him."

Boy Scouts, Jake realized. Sally must have told Jake that they were in scouting, but it had slipped his mind. "When is the banquet?"

"Two weeks."

"I should be there," he promised and gulped at the prospect of appearing at such a semipublic event.

When Mark came on the line, the first thing he said was, "Just so you know, I can't tie knots worth diddly-squat."

"Diddly-squat, huh?"

"That's what PopPop sez. Not to me, but I heard him tell that to Old Mike. I'm just dumb."

"You're not dumb, Mark," he said to his clearly insecure son. "Can you keep a secret?"

"Uh-huh," Mark replied, tentatively. Probably no one had ever trusted him enough with a secret before.

"I had trouble with knots, too. In fact, PopPop told me directly, 'You're never gonna be a fisherman, son, if you can't tie a damn . . . darn knot.' I had the hardest trouble with slipknots. Almost didn't earn that badge."

"Really?"

"Really. I'll help you practice. I have a special trick for remembering the order of the ties."

"Yay! I can't wait till you get here," Mark said, then confided in a whisper, "Matt is too bossy."

By the time he got around to Luke, Jake was generally smiling.

"My birfday ith next month," Luke said with the cute lisp Sally had warned him about. "Thammy Thmith got a python for his birfday."

"Um. I don't think your mother would like a snake in the house."

"Thath what she said," Luke said dolefully. "Maybe a little one."

"Wouldn't a dog make more sense?"

"Whoop-ee! Daddy's gonna get me a dog for my birfday," he'd heard his son yell to whoever was in the room with him.

He hadn't exactly said that, had he?

And so it went, as the days went by way too fast before Jake got the go-ahead to leave Germany.

Chapter 5

*Turns out, you can go home again . . .
even if you don't want to . . .*

A week later, Jake was in the passenger seat of a small two-seater Viking Twin Otter, a float plane, being piloted by his old friend Ethan Rutledge. Both of them were wearing those heavy earphones that allowed them to speak to each other over the loud noise of the engine, while Ethan's connected to air control somewhere on the island, as well.

Both Sally and Jake's father had offered to pick him up . . . Sally at the airport in Richmond, or his dad on his fishing boat across the bay. But Jake knew from his nightly phone calls that reporters were bird-dogging them. Since the government would give the press no more information, especially not a timetable for his return to the USA, they figured his family would be their best bet for making contact with him. In fact, Landstuhl was glad to be rid of him after weeks of newshounds by the dozens trying to "storm the gates" of the hospital looking for him.

In any case, it was a short aerial trip over Bell Sound from the mainland to the Outer Banks, unlike the long but scenic drive along the beach road and several ferries to the barrier island, with the Atlantic Ocean on one side, and various bays and sounds on the other. Such a leisurely trip could take six hours or more from end to end in high season, which he would have, nonetheless, much preferred . . . in fact, which he'd dreamed about on numerous nights of his imprisonment, especially following days of torture.

Cruising along in his old pickup truck, windows down, a salty breeze coming in off the ocean. Fishing boats and sailboats in the distance. The occasional lighthouse. Surfers and beachcombers.

However, his leg could never have stood the pain of being in a driving position for that long. Besides, too many people would recognize him along the way . . . either from growing up on the Outer Banks, or from his picture being flashed on national TV, repeatedly, following the news conference last week in DC where his rescue had been announced by the president, along with the secretary of defense, a congressman, and other high mucky-mucks.

Jake had declined to attend, even when he'd gotten a personal invitation from the president himself via Skype. *Declined* was too soft a word for his "Hell, no!" refusal, delivered in as polite a manner as he could manage for the POTUS while still conveying his point. He never could have regurgitated all that "fake news" crap they'd concocted about his MIA (not POW) experience without . . . well, vomiting.

Back to the present. The aerial scene was beautiful, too, especially on this morning with the early-August sun sparkling off the whitecaps of the pristine blue waters. A squadron of brown pelicans with their distinctive oversized bills and throat pouches glided on a wind current that mimicked the waves. They were just waiting for the opportune moment to plunge-dive for a tasty breakfast of finger mullets or cigar minnows.

Home, Jake mused. *Beautiful, beautiful home.*

"Yeah, I know what you mean," Ethan said. "Every time I cross Bell Sound I get the same ache in my chest. The view never gets old."

Jake hadn't realized he'd spoken aloud and cringed. Even so, he admitted, "I never thought I'd see the place again." *And I certainly fought tooth and nail against returning . . . at this time, anyhow. But they forced my hand, as only Uncle Sam and his military brass can do.*

Ethan gave him a quick questioning glance, but when Jake didn't elaborate, he reached over to squeeze his forearm. "Things will get better, pal. You're home now. Your family and friends will help you forget."

No one can do that, and I shudder to think how they might try. Time to change the subject before he asks about my three years "hiding" in a cave. "This plane is new, isn't it? Last time I was here, you had that old Piper model. The Christmas-tree business must be doing well for you."

"Yeah, business is booming, even those stupid Rutledge trees," Ethan replied, then grinned. "Remember how embarrassed I used to be over those Charlie Brown–lookalike trees that my dad grew here on the island? Now they've become a holiday must-have, a conversation piece for the yuppie crowd all along the Outer Banks. I swear, I can sell thousands of traditional Douglas firs from my mainland tree farms, but the ones that get the most hype are those damn scrawny evergreen mutants, the only kind of Christmas trees that can withstand Outer Banks weather."

Jake recalled that Ethan had resisted ever going into the family business, just as he himself had baldly refused his father's offer of a partnership in *Lazy Days*, the Dawson commercial fishing boat, which followed the various fish through their seasons on the Outer Banks . . . sea trout, bass, flounder, red drum, bluefish, king mackerel, crabs, shrimp, and the prized tuna. Having been forced to help out from a young age, Jake used to hate fishing. Now, he wondered if, like Ethan, he might have grown into the career, if he hadn't opted for the military after college.

Well, that was the past. No sense dwelling on what-ifs.

He glanced sideways at Ethan, who was fiddling with one of the dials. "Your trees were even highlighted on a holiday segment of *Good Morning America*, according to Izzie."

"Izzie has a big mouth," Ethan commented.

Jake had to smile, having made the same observation more than once. "Yep, your trees and Izzie's uncle Abe with his Reuben sandwich being featured on the Food Network are Bell Cove's very own celebrities," he teased.

"Pfff! That was last week's news. These days, the big BMOC . . . Big Man on the Cove . . . is Merrill Good, the former Navy SEAL who started a salvaging/treasure-hunting company and hit pay dirt the first time out."

Jake winced inwardly, needing no reminders of ex-SEALs in Bell Cove.

"Then, there's Good's new wife, Delilah, who just reopened Clyde Jones's old diner and motel."

"You mean the Heartbreak Motel? Oh, man! Remember the time after senior prom when we . . . never mind."

The two of them grinned at each other.

"Of course, you won't be laughing long about me or anyone else being in Bell Cove's celebrity crosshairs. You have to accept that you are going to be the celeb du jour, my man."

Not if I can help it! "Holy shit! That is the last thing I want or need."

"Like that matters! Do you think my appearance on *Good Morning America* was my idea? No way! I blame Laura Atler at *The Bell*. You remember her, don't you? She took over the weekly when her grandfather went to the great tabloid in the sky."

Jake did know Laura from back in high school. She'd been dating Izzie at the time. More important, there had been several text messages on Jake's phone this week from Laura wanting an interview. *When tuna fly!* How she'd gotten his private number was beyond Jake. *Note to self: change cell number.* Neither Sally nor his father would have given it out. But then, the people in Bell Cove had their own network of sleuths. The FBI could learn a few things from them.

Jake remembered something else. "Hey, man, I was sorry to hear about Beth Anne dying." There had been a scandal right after high school when Ethan had been forced to marry a pregnant Beth Anne, despite being in love, for years, with someone else. "She must have passed right after I was last deployed more than three years ago," Jake remarked. "I told Sally to send flowers or a mass card. I assume she did."

Ethan acknowledged his expression of sympathy for his deceased wife with a nod.

"But then, you just got married again a few weeks ago. Good for you! Guess you and Wendy finally got your acts together, huh?"

"Between the Rutledge trees and my dumbass moves with Wendy all those years ago, I've given Bell Cove more than enough to gossip about." Ethan grinned. "Your turn now."

"Great!"

"My sympathies, too, on your mother passing. She was a good woman. A great teacher."

That was one of the many painful aspects of Jake's return to Bell Cove. His mother not being there to greet him. When she was alive, his favorite spicy crab and sweet corn chowder would be simmering on the stove, no matter the weather, with fresh-baked hot biscuits cooling on the counter. A chocolate layer cake sitting on the milk glass pedestal in the center of the kitchen table. Freezing-cold milk in a glass bottle in the fridge.

Sally had never been much of a cook, or she hadn't been before. But then, she'd always greeted him in other ways that had been equally sweet and hot. He doubted that would be the case today.

He had no chance to react to Ethan's remarks about his mother because they were descending now, not to one of the busier wharfs around town, but a deserted, rocky shore, at Jake's suggestion. Ethan brought the float plane down into the shallow water and dropped anchor. They would both get wet wading through the lapping surf, but no big deal. Better that than making his reentry to Bell Cove in a public way.

Just then, he heard a horn toot. Glancing to the right, a short distance away, he saw his old pickup truck. *God, the thing must be twenty years old by now.* Sally hadn't sold it, as she'd threatened many times over the years. *Why?*

But then the truck door opened, and there she was.

Her hair . . . the long, luxurious chestnut hair he'd loved . . . was super short and spiky now. Not unattractive. Just different. She wore a red tank top and white shorts and athletic shoes. Her body was average to her, perfect to him, but gave the appearance of being petite because she was so fine boned and delicate. Childbirth, three times round, hadn't changed her much, although her breasts had gained a cup size, to his delight and her embarrassment.

He knew every inch of that body . . . every ticklish spot, every erotic trigger point.

Or he used to.

Jake was different now.

Sally would be, too.

He was still in the open doorway of the seaplane, watching her walk closer. The shoreline was rocky and uneven; so, she didn't rush. Maybe she wouldn't anyhow. Maybe she had as many mixed feelings as he did about this "reunion."

Now, only a few yards away, she stopped. He could see a few freckles on her bare arms and her fresh-scrubbed-looking face. Sally was twenty-eight years old, or would be soon, but she could pass for a teenager, or the college student she had been when they first met. As for the freckles, which she hated and he adored . . . he'd dreamed about those damn freckles more than once these past three years.

At just that moment, the bells began to sound out the hour, the bells having been a feature of many

of his POW dreams, too. First, Our Lady by the
Sea Catholic Church. *Bong, bong, bong, bong, bong,
bong, bong, bong!* Then, St. Andrew's Presbyterian
Church. *Ding-dong, ding-dong, ding-dong, ding-dong,
ding-dong, ding-dong, ding-dong, ding-dong!* And finally the clock in the town hall tower. *Clang, clang,
clang, clang, clang, clang, clang, clang!*

Sensing his predicament, Ethan came around
the side of the plane to help him out. Even with a
cane, Jake would need to jump down the few feet
into the shallow lapping waves. A jarring exercise
in torture that would no doubt result in his falling
flat on his face, sucking salt water. With Ethan's
hands under Jake's elbows, practically lifting and
lowering him, Jake managed to steady himself in
the thigh-deep surf. He was wearing athletic shoes
with no socks, and cargo shorts with a T-shirt; so,
the wet didn't bother him. Then, using the cane
Ethan handed him, he hobbled up onto the rocky
shore. He waved Ethan off, after he dumped Jake's
duffel bag in the back of the truck, mouthing
"Thank you," knowing Ethan needed to return to
the mainland for some business. Only then did he
glance over to Sally again.

She was staring at him with horror. Or was it
pity? Either one was equally unpalatable to Jake.

*I knew this would happen. I knew it, I knew it, I
knew it.*

Thus it was that the first words out of his mouth
were: "So, Sally, how soon do you want a divorce?"

Still an ass! . . .

Sally was shocked at Jake's appearance.

She'd been warned, but somehow she must have expected the same old Jake, with a few bruises and, of course, the eye patch, which was actually kind of appealing. She hadn't expected him to be so thin . . . and . . . and . . . so helpless. At least twenty pounds lighter, which made him appear almost gaunt. And the limp . . . well, that wasn't just a limp. My God! He couldn't get out of the plane on his own. He wore some kind of soft brace that ran from his thigh to his calf. And he needed a cane! How would she ever get him into his pickup truck with its high chassis? And up the stairs at home?

She was not prepared for this!

Most shocking of all, of course, were his words to her. A divorce? Really? That's the way he wanted to greet her after all this time? Really? *Once an ass, always an ass, I suppose,* she thought. In the later years of their marriage, he'd often blurt out such nonsense in the midst of an argument, or for no apparent reason.

She would have smacked him upside his fool head, if it weren't for the dark circles under his eyes and the expression in his beautiful eyes. Beautiful eye, she corrected herself. She wasn't sure what that expression was . . . pain, regret, fear, anger, or a combination of all those.

Three years!

What happened to him?

Was he as broken inside as he appeared on the outside?

And did she care?

Acting on instinct, she launched herself at him, almost knocking them both over, and hugged him tight around his shoulders. Until she felt him relax and hug her back, so tight she could barely breathe.

Against her ear, he whispered, "You smell like sugar."

"Well, I knew you were coming. So, I baked a cake," she sang, a play on that old fifties song, "If I Knew You Were Comin', I'd've Baked a Cake." Then, she added, "Gracie Fields, 1950. Eileen Barton, 1950." It was something she'd done throughout their marriage . . . bursting into old songs and then edifying him with some interesting facts about the background of the tunes from her music education days.

Usually he rolled his eyes at her silliness. She leaned back and smiled at him. No eye rolling now, with his one eye. He did make an effort to smile back but was having trouble shaking his dark mood.

What was wrong with him?

Well, she knew what was wrong with him. Sort of. He'd gone through three years of hell, the details of which she was still clueless about. He had physical injuries, the extent of which she was also clueless about. And he might very well be suffering from PTSD, although no one had mentioned that to her.

"Let's go home," she suggested and they started walking toward the truck. She slowed her pace down to accommodate his limp. "Your dad's so nervous he started smoking again after being nicotine-free for more than a year. And the kids are dying to see you. They made a surprise banner for you. Make sure you act surprised, and pleased."

He groaned.

She darted a glance to see why that upset him, but his face was set into emotionless mode. She hated when he did that.

"Won't a banner alert the neighbors that I'm coming home? I thought we agreed that there would be no fuss."

"The banner is inside."

"Oh. Okay."

The Grinch! Too bad he wasn't around Bell Cove last Christmas. With his frowny face, he'd have been a contender for Grinch of the Year, for sure.

They'd arrived at the truck and she hesitated before asking, "Do you want to drive?" The question was, could he drive?

He shook his head. "I can drive, but I've been sitting for roughly twenty hours, and my leg can only take so much."

She nodded and tried not to watch or offer to help as he struggled to lift himself up onto the seat using the grab bar and his cane for leverage. Once they were belted up, he said, "I'm surprised that you didn't sell this old truck."

"It comes in handy for hauling supplies for the store, or for delivering oversized cakes for special events, like weddings."

He chuckled. The truck had been his dad's fishing vehicle before he handed it off to Jake.

"What's so funny?"

"Nice to know that *eau de* fish is covered by *eau de* sugar now."

She grinned. "On a damp day, I can still smell fish."

They rode in silence for a short distance as she left the bay and entered the residential section of Bell Cove. She could tell by the stiffness of his body and the fists resting on his thighs that he was nervous about anyone seeing him, until he was ready. "You should know, there are blockades set up at the end of our street so that cars can only pass through if they have a neighborhood pass. This is to prevent the press and nosey folks from coming to our house." Luckily, the other end of their street was a dead end, which meant access to their house from only one source. "Guards are posted there, day and night. I'm not sure if they're FBI or police or private security. No one will say, although they just arrived, without notice, following the visit from that general and senator. I don't know how long they'll be there, but for now, they've been a godsend." She was babbling but felt like there was so much she needed to tell him, to prepare him for, and only a fifteen-minute ride in which to do so.

"Don't the neighbors mind?"

"Nah. They think it's exciting." They were silent for a few moments, and Sally almost asked him what he was thinking, but she knew Jake hated that question. Most men did. Instead, she told him, "You have a couple of appointments set up for next month, according to some reminder cards sent in the mail. One at the Hospital for Special Surgery in New York City, and one at the Johns Hopkins Wilmer Eye Institute in Baltimore. I made note of them on the calendar on the kitchen wall. September 27 and September 30. I assume you know what they're all about."

He just nodded, as if he already knew this.

She would like to know what the prognosis was for his injuries. Heck, she'd like to know exactly what those injuries were. But he didn't seem inclined to clue her in, at this point.

So, she went on, "And some psychiatrist from the VA hospital in Richmond left a message for you to call him for an initial consultation." She assumed it might be related to some PTSD issues.

He made a snorting sound, but again said nothing.

Sally was trying to be tolerant of Jake's silence, which was kind of offensive, but then this return home had to be traumatic for him. She told herself to be patient.

Just then he swore and accused her, "I thought you said no one knew I was coming today."

"They don't."

"Then what's with all the friggin' yellow ribbons?"

He seemed to have just noticed that every residence had a yellow ribbon, some bigger than others, tied around a tree, or mailbox, or on a flagpole. Miles Gallagher, who had been Jake's football coach in high school, had dozens on all three.

"And how did they know we would be following this route?" Again the accusatory tone in his voice.

"These ribbons started going up the day after the press conference announcing your rescue, and they're all over town, not just on this street. They're on businesses and churches, and the town hall. Everywhere. The bow on the town square gazebo is big enough to gift wrap a boat. The church decided to put yellow roses on the altar the first Sunday you came home, with congregants paying for one rose each, at two dollars a pop. Within hours, they had two thousand roses on order. The money will go toward new bells for the children's choir."

"Son of a bitch!"

"Nice!" she commented on his response. "And I'll tell you right now, Jacob, you better soften that attitude. People care about you, and you have no right to insult them for that. Watch your language, too. You have sons who idolize you and will copy everything you say and do."

He sank down in his seat and muttered something.

"What did you say?"

"I never wanted any of this."

"Do you think I did?" Immediately, she realized how he might misconstrue what she'd said.

Which of course he did.

"It would have been better if I didn't come back, if I had actually died."

That would have sounded pathetic, whiney, as if he was looking for reassurances. But she could tell he meant his words.

She didn't get a chance to explain herself, though, because they'd arrived at their street. The guard, who wore nondescript clothing, no particular uniform, gave Jake a surreptitious salute as he passed them through, thus indicating to Sally that he probably was military. And then they were in their driveway and three boys barreled through the front door and stopped on the wide, covered porch only because their grandfather held them back.

Jake glanced at her with panic and whispered, "Help me."

Any hard feelings she'd been harboring at his attitude evaporated then as she asked, "How?"

"I don't think I can get out of this truck without falling on my face. I don't want my kids to see me like that, like a cripple."

She nodded, got out of the truck, and yelled, "Everyone back in the house. Wait for us there." She hoped her silent signal to Joe—his father—was accepted without explanation.

It was. Joe stared at her for a long moment, then shooed the boys back inside, cautioning, "Don't forget to hide. Remember . . . it's a surprise."

She went around the back of the truck and to the passenger side, where Jake had already opened the door. She was prepared to help him out when she noticed something that she'd somehow missed so far.

His one hand was on the frame of the door and his other hand was on the cane he'd set on the ground. And he had no fingernails. None at all, except for the beginning of new nail just starting to emerge.

She looked at his hand, then looked at him, tilting her head in question.

He just shrugged.

Her brain tried to understand. A person didn't lose all their fingernails hiding in a cave, that was for sure.

Suddenly comprehension came to her. The fingernails. The eye. The injured leg. And God only knew what else.

Jake hadn't been in hiding for three years.

But where had he been?

And what had the bastards done to him?

Chapter 6

Motherhood and apple pie . . . uh, chocolate cake . . . that's what it's all about . . .

*J*ake watched as Sally went into the house, leaving him alone for a few moments, at his request. "Don't worry, I'm okay," he'd assured her. "I just need a sec to regroup."

She'd looked worried, but left him alone anyhow, thank God. He wasn't sure how he'd react if pushed too hard, too fast, even by her. Especially by her.

Coming home to Bell Cove had been more of a shock to his system than he'd expected, and he'd expected plenty. This felt more like the g-force shots to the gut that jet pilots suffered, except his were hitting his heart. *Zap, zap, zap!*

But he *would* be all right, dammit. *Buck up, chin high, soldier*, he told himself. *I will survive. Even this.*

But, shiiiit! The problems just kept coming. He'd seen the question in Sally's eyes when she'd noticed his fingernails, or lack of fingernails. Such a little detail, but often it was the little overlooked fine point that blew a whole operation. He couldn't wait to tell Major Butt-inator, who thought he had all the angles covered, about his boo-boo. Then again, the less conversation with the asshole the better. They'd almost come to blows at their last meeting when the jerk had mentioned an "image consultant" he might want to meet.

Leaning back against the hood of the truck, he surveyed his surroundings. His house was one of a dozen Craftsman-style bungalows that had been built for Bell Forge workers a hundred years ago, each with a separate detached garage, and offered to them on a rent-to-buy basis. Six on each side of a residential street within walking distance of the once-booming factory, known for its high-end bells. Too far from Bell Sound on one side and the Atlantic Ocean on the other to be prime waterfront or water-view real estate—at least one mile either way—but they were still considered unique dwellings on a barrier island and had gone up in value dramatically the last few years. Or the last that Jake had checked, when he had been here more than three years ago.

His father's cottage, across the street, catty-corner, had belonged to his mother's family from the beginning. Jake had purchased his a year after he'd married Sally, when Matt was still in a crib, and Mark already a bun in the oven. Then, their three-bedroom home had seemed plenty big enough. Now, not so much. Cozy would be an understatement.

Am I ready for cozy?

Oh, fuck!

He noticed that the slate gray paint with darker gray shutters on his cottage was faded and peeling in places. The salt air and wind of the barrier island was brutal on wood. He would need to repaint. Maybe they would go back to the original white with black shutters, as Sally had always wanted, and he'd resisted. He couldn't remember why now.

But wait. His thinking about painting implied his having conscious or unconscious plans to stay on the Outer Banks, long-term.

Do I?

Hell, no!

Well, maybe.

I can't think about this now.

He studied his house again, looking for other improvements that would have to be made.

Yeah, he was procrastinating, putting off the big dreaded reunion. *Hope I don't trip over my feet and fall flat on my face in front of my kids. Hope there are no tears. From anyone. Especially from me. Hard to wipe at tears under an eye patch. Ha, ha, ha! I should have worn dark sunglasses instead of the patch, but then people would expect me to take them off indoors. Oh, God! Why is this so hard?*

Back to his delays, he looked around some more. Over the years, the twelve bungalows that started out identical had changed colors, put on additions, patios, and unique landscaping. As a result, each was distinctive now. You'd never know they'd originated from Sears, Roebuck and Co. kits. Overall, his cottage had held up well, the whole neighborhood had, considering its age, probably because they'd used quality materials to start.

He loved them.

Is that another indicator of my plans, or nonplans, to stay on the Outer Banks?

No, it was just an observation.

Or was it?

So many decisions! So many problems!

Maybe I do need a shrink. An Outer Banks Dr. Sheila. Like that will ever happen! I am not going to bare my soul to a townie.

With a deep inhale and then exhale, he pushed away from the truck and went around to the back of the cottage, where there was another deep covered porch, which they used for barbecuing in the summer. He'd never gotten around to the patio that Sally had always wanted. Maybe . . .

No, he was not going to think of anything beyond the moment. And a momentous moment it was, too.

He opened the back door and stepped into the kitchen . . . and gasped. Sitting on the center of the oak table was a chocolate layer cake on a milk glass pedestal stand. He didn't have to look at the stove to know crab chowder was simmering in the old cast-iron pot; the delicious smell filled the room. A new addition was a loaf of fresh-baked bread, instead of biscuits. Something from Sally's bakery?

His eyes filled with tears. He couldn't help himself. His mother wouldn't be here, but Sally had made an effort to make her absence easier to bear. How did she know that these little things mattered to him so much when coming home after an active op?

He blinked several times to get rid of any evidence he was so emotional, but then noticed Sally standing in the doorway to the living room. She put a forefinger to her lips, cautioning silence, before saying, louder than necessary, "Welcome home, Jacob. I don't know where the boys are. They must have gone over to your dad's house to help with his garden."

"That's too bad," he said, also louder than necessary, playing into her game, "I was really looking forward to seeing my boys after all this time. Oh, well. Gardening must be more fun for them than meeting their old man."

"I'm sure they'll be back soon." Sally winked at him. "C'mon into the living room and rest a bit. I'm sure you're tired after your long trip."

He followed her and pretended to be shocked when he was greeted with balloons and a huge handmade banner that read in less-than-perfect kid crayon lettering, "Welcome home, Daddy" and shouts of "SURPRISE!" from his three sons. The boys launched themselves at him, hugging him around his waist and thighs. He would have liked to hunker down to their level, but his knees and the soft brace he was wearing would not allow that.

They were all talking at once and asking questions, but not waiting for answers.

"I made the sign."

"I did, too."

"But I blew up the balloons 'cause PopPop's got no wind."

"That ain't nice."

"*Ain't* ain't in the dictionary."

"It's still not nice."

"Stop bein' so bossy."

"I am the boss. 'Cause I'm older."

"Anyways, that's what PopPop says all the time about bein' windy, usually after he sneaks a ciggie."

"Mark!"

"What? It's the truth, Mom."

"Do you smoke ciggies, Daddy?"

"Mikey Dunaway smoked a ciggie and coughed up a lung."

"That wasn't a lung, dumbhead. It was a loogie. Throat spit."

"I'm tho happy you're home, Daddy. Can I have a horse?"

"You can't have a horse, pea brain. We don't have a stable."

"Maybe Daddy could build a thable. No one uthes the garage anyway. That would be a good thable."

"A dog would be better. A German shepherd. Or a collie."

"But not a pit bull. Mommy says we'll get a pit bull when donuts fly."

"I like cats."

"A cat and a dog."

"Yay!" they all agreed, as if it was a done deal.

He didn't even try to get a word in as each talked over the other and tried to hug him tighter. In their enthusiasm, the inevitable happened. He fell backward to the floor. Which turned out to be better. Yeah, his leg hurt like a bitch, but now he was down to the kids' level and they were crawling all over him, giggling and laughing, and he found that he was the one doing the hugging now—tight, tight hugs that allowed him to nuzzle their necks, relishing the scent of little boy sweat and one of them must have been rolling in grass somewhere. Also, he managed to surreptitiously sneak a few kisses to the bristly hairs of their short summertime haircuts. They felt thin to him, and at the same time they were compact, squirming bodies of lively muscles. Like big puppies. Even Matt, who was only a little bit more reserved, being the oldest, in his wrestling with him on the floor.

Finally, Sally intervened. "That's enough, boys. Let your dad get up now. PopPop, can you help me?"

His father came over, and the two of them, taking one hand each, helped him to stand. It was only a little embarrassing. But then, it was the first time he'd had a chance to greet his father, with all the mad rush of the kids.

His father was the same six feet tall as he was, though wiry thin, always had been. With all the weight Jake had lost, he probably more closely resembled the old man now than he had in the past.

Sally had released his hand to go herd the boys over to the sofa where they sat with perfect precision, for the moment. But his father hadn't let go of his other hand.

Jake got his first good look at his father then and couldn't help but notice how he'd aged these past three years. As always, his skin was brown and leathery from thousands of days fishing under the hot Outer Banks sun. But there were more wrinkles creasing his forehead and bracketing his eyes and mouth. His blue eyes, which Jake and his sons had inherited, appeared rheumy, or maybe it was a mist of tears that were about to overflow.

The blasted tears he'd so wanted to avoid!

"Son," his dad choked out and tugged him into an embrace that involved his alternately clutching at him and patting his back, like he had when Jake had been a little boy and skinned his knee or some other body part. But no, Jake must have been mis-remembering because his father had been more inclined to tell him it was no big deal, to be a big boy and get over it. But then he noticed that his father was shaking, and then Jake was the one patting the old guy's back.

Son of a . . . this has got to stop before I start bawling.

He stepped back and said, "Hey, Dad, would you mind getting my duffel bag out of the truck? I think there might be something in there for boys who like to play games, but maybe kids here on the Outer Banks prefer to read books, or . . ."

It took his sons a moment before they realized he was referring to them and that there might be presents involved, ones that involved games. With a whoop, the three of them jumped up and ran outside with their grandfather, each of them offering an opinion.

"I knew he would bring us something."

"Maybe ith a dog."

"It's not a dog, Luke. Dad said it was in his duffel bag."

"A dog could be in a duffel bag."

"No. He said something about games."

"Hope it's not Monopoly or some dorky board game."

"I like Monopoly."

"That's because you always win."

"Corey's dad brought him a Rubik's Cube when he came back from a business trip."

That announcement was met with silence. Apparently, the handheld puzzle device would not have been a big hit.

"Jason's uncle went to France and bought him a stinky T-shirt."

That, too, was met with silence.

As their voices petered off, Jake glanced over at Sally, who was watching him from where she stood leaning against the doorway to the kitchen. "Good thing I didn't buy them Rubik's Cubes or clothing, huh?"

"I warned them to be appreciative, no matter what you brought, and I also warned them that you might not have had time to buy anything at all."

"Bet that went over big." He shoved a balloon aside and sank down into an easy chair by the large multi-

paned leaded window that fronted the house. Like
everything in a Craftsman house, there were added
details. In this case, a line of small square stained
glass windows across the top depicting Outer Banks
scenes. He didn't know much about antiques, but
he would bet the windows were worth more than
the whole house. But that was neither here nor there.
He looked at Sally, who still stood in the doorway,
and asked, "How did I do?"

"Perfect."

"Really?"

She nodded.

"I was worried."

"I could tell."

What did that mean? Had he been acting all Nervous Nellie? Pathetic?

His father and the kids were back, with the kids
doing all the carrying of the heavy bag, which they
dropped at his feet with a thud. They stared expec-
tantly as he unzipped the bag, slowly, just to tease
them. He could tell they wanted to tell him to hurry
up. First he pulled out a large box, about the size
of a laptop but thicker. There were also six smaller
packages. All of them had been gift wrapped by the
nice lady at one of the gift stores in the Ramstein
Air Base exchange. She, being a grandmother, was
the one who'd advised him on what to buy for boys
their ages. He might very well have opted for Rubik's Cubes or stinky T-shirts.

The kids quickly ripped at the bigger package and
then just stared, at first. Stunned, really.

At first, he wasn't sure if it was good stunned or bad stunned.

But then Matt exclaimed, "Nintendo Switch! Wow!" and his brothers agreed with echoes of "Wow, wow, wow!"

"How did you know they wanted this?" Sally asked him.

He shrugged. "I just asked myself what I would have wanted at that age." And got advice from a seventy-year-old grandma.

"Well, you hit the jackpot. They asked for it last Christmas, but I told them it was too expensive."

After examining the console and accessories in their hard protective case, the boys made quick work of the six smaller packages. Games, of course. Minecraft. Super Mario. Dragon Ball. Starlink. Mega Man. Donkey Kong.

He'd gone with his instinct not to buy any blood and guts, or zombies, and knew he was right when Sally went over to check them out before giving him a thumbs-up. She'd probably expected him to get a special ops terrorist-fighting game with fancy weapons and the number of kills determining the winner.

Okay, yes, he had looked at one like that.

"They had a game on fishing simulation that I almost bought so that you could play with the boys," he told his father, who sat in the other easy chair, on the opposite side of the window. With the morning sun coming through the stained glass, framing his father, it could have been an oil painting, he thought with what was probably hysterical irrelevance.

"Hah! I get all the fishing I want out on the water, thanks just the same."

The kids wanted him to set up the game right away.

He glanced to Sally to get her approval.

She nodded. "You could put it here, or upstairs in their bedroom where they have a small flat-screen TV."

"Uh, how about here for now?" He was going to make only one trip up and down those stairs each day, for the time being. His leg couldn't take much more than that. Thank God there was a bathroom on this level, even if it had only a toilet and sink.

Another nice thing about Craftsman homes was all the fine woodwork and the built-ins. Like the corner cabinet that was never intended to hold a television in its day, but worked perfectly for the set that was there now with several of the shelves removed and stored down below. He soon had the game system set up and ready to go, but Sally insisted that they all eat first, despite the moans and groans from the kids, especially since she made them wash their hands first, which they considered torture.

I could tell them a thing or two about torture. Or not. No, I will not let my mind go there.

He saw that Sally had set the table in the dining room, instead of the kitchen, making this a sort of special event. He sat at one end, his father and Matt

•

on one side, and Mark and Luke on the other. Sally stood at the other end of the table about to serve the steaming chowder from a tureen in front of her. Bread and pats of butter were set at each place setting.

She hesitated, then asked him, "Will you say grace, Jacob, or would you rather your father do it?"

He would have liked to refuse, but that would sound like he was no longer the head of his family, or that he'd lost his faith, which was still up in the air. "I will," he said, making it brief. "Thank You, Lord, for this good food. And for my family." He paused. "And thank You, God, for bringing me home."

"Amen," they all said, even the kids.

Everyone dug in then, and the food, simple as it was, was excellent. He had two helpings before the cake was served with ice-cold milk. That, too, was excellent, even better than his mother's, he had to admit.

Mostly, things weren't awkward, as he'd expected, because the kids talked nonstop. About everything.

Boy Scouts. "Those darn knots!" Jake was reminded by Luke.

Bicycles . . . Mark's needed a new chain.

Fishing . . . Mommy's friend K-4 had taken them, Matt revealed, causing Sally's face to pinken.

The upcoming Lollypalooza, in which Mommy was going to sing, which caused Sally's face to grow even pinker.

"It's just for fun," she explained.

"Uncle Kevin is gonna play the guitar while she sings," good ol' Matt added.

Uncle Kevin? Okaaay. Jake arched his brows at Sally.

But she was looking the other way.

Deliberately?

And the kids were off and running in another direction.

"Are you still a captain in the Army?" Mark wanted to know, speaking around a mouthful of cake.

"Sort of."

His father and Sally gave him pointed looks.

"They want to make me a major." *If I take their freakin' DC job.*

"Is that bigger than a captain?" Mark wanted to know.

"Um, sort of. It's a higher rank, son. That's the correct word, not bigger."

Mark ducked his head, and Jake could tell that he'd embarrassed him by correcting his language. Hadn't Sally mentioned that Mark was the sensitive one?

"It's a mistake lots of people make," he elaborated.

And Mark's head went back up.

"Do you have an eyeball, or ith there juth a hole there?" Luke wanted to know, pointing at his eye patch.

"Yes, I have an eyeball."

"Is it a glass one?" This from Matt. "I saw a video on YouTube where a guy could pop out his glass eye. It was so cool."

"Matthew Dawson!" Sally chided. "What did I tell you about watching YouTube videos without my permission?"

"It was a long time ago. At Bobby Allison's birthday party, and everyone else was looking. I couldn't not look and be a dork."

"*Dork* is not a word we use in this house, young man," Sally said.

Jake listened with amusement at this exchange between mother and child. Then answered Matt's question. "No, I don't have a glass eye. I wear the patch so I don't creep people out, although I should probably keep it off more often so I can force the eye to exercise. In fact, the doctor suggests I wear the patch over my good eye sometimes to force my injured eye to work, in an attempt to regain mobility. That's its main problem. The injured eye doesn't move up and down or to the sides the way it should."

"You can exercise an eye?" Mark honed in on the least important part of what he'd said.

All three of the boys pondered that idea then as they did a pretty good version of the Three Stooges attempting to roll their eyes in various directions, including cross-eyed.

His father was chuckling, and Sally was shaking her head with resignation at their antics.

Jake figured it was now or never. He couldn't hide it forever. "Here goes," he said and flipped the eye patch upward. To his surprise, no one gasped or looked like they were about to vomit.

"It's still blue," Sally remarked.

What? As if the eye color were important! But she said it in a nice way—he knew how much she'd always liked his blue eyes—so, he forgave her.

His dad was more practical. "Can they make it any better?"

Jake shrugged. "There are some experimental surgeries I might try. Later."

"I don't think it's creepy," Matt concluded. "I was 'spectin' blood and gooey stuff, like snot."

Sally put her face in her hands for a moment with dismay.

But Jake was okay with his kids' observations. He wanted them to say what they thought. Better that than folks who pretended not to notice his bum eye, like they had back at the hospital before he'd started wearing the patch.

Luke got up and came over to give him a closer look, even touching the scars that had yet to fade from the stitches. "Kin you thee me at all, from that eye?"

"Not really. Just a shadowy form. But that's better than it was before my last surgery. Before, everything was all black," Jake explained.

"How many surgeries have you had, son?" his father asked.

"On my eye . . . two." *On my leg, three.*

"Jake is scheduled for appointments next month at the Hospital for Special Surgery in New York City and one at the Johns Hopkins Wilmer Eye Institute in Baltimore," Sally told his father. "I checked on the internet and they are the best places by far for eye and orthopedic surgeries."

Really? That was news to him. That Sally had bothered to see if those facilities were up to par for her "ass" of a husband. *Hmmm.*

With the kids' curiosity satisfied, Jake flipped the eye patch back down, and the boys were off in other directions.

"Do you know how to play batheball, Daddy?" This from Luke.

"Yeah. It's been a long time since I've played, but . . . yeah."

"I can't hit the ball worth crap," Luke told him. The kid had more chocolate on his T-shirt than in his mouth, where, yes, his two front teeth were missing.

With my one eye, I probably can't hit a ball worth crap, either.

"Luke! That is not a word that little boys use," Sally reprimanded.

"Ith what Coach Thutter thaid."

Sally looked at Jake and told him, "Coach Sutter is the T-Ball coach. You remember Ted Sutter, don't you?"

Yeah, he remembered Ted, and when they were in high school Ted had a foul tongue with which *crap* was the least of what he would have said. To Luke, he offered, "We can work on your batting, if you want. That, and your knots. No, I didn't forget, buddy." Almost immediately, he wished he'd kept his mouth shut as the expression of what could only be described as adoration hit his kid's face.

Shiit! He didn't intend to be around any longer than he had to.

"Do you wear that eye patch all the time?"

"I'm gonna be a doctor when I grow up. Maybe I'll be able to fix your eye for you then."

"I'm gonna be a fisherman like PopPop."

"Maybe I'll be a doctor and a fisherman."

"Can I have another piece of cake?"

"Why do you have that thing on your leg?"

"Does it hurt?"

"I broke my arm one time and it hurt soooo bad."

"Did you really live in a cave, Daddy?"

"My scout troop went on a field trip to Crystal Cave over on the mainland. There was thousands of bats hangin' from the ceiling. Yeeech!"

"Bats are good. They eat bugs. Miss Lindy said so, in science class."

"Can I be excuthed, Mom. I hafta pee."

"Mr. Baxter says you're a hero. Are you a hero, Daddy?"

"What's a hero?"

"Can I go to a birthday sleepover at Danny Stewart's tomorrow night? He's gonna have tents in the backyard and a wienie roast and ghost stories and everything."

"I doan like ghosts."

"You're a scaredy-cat."

"Am not!"

On and on the conversation went, most of which required no responses from the adults, except for an occasional reprimand from Sally. Eventually, while Sally cleared the table, Jake went in with his father to watch the kids go to town with the games. The squealing and laughter and arguments reached a fever pitch and might become annoying later, but for now they were a joy to his ears.

"Well, I'm going to head home," his father announced suddenly. "I'll see you later at the barbecue."

"The barbecue?"

"Didn't Sally tell you—"

"No, I haven't had a chance yet," Sally said, coming into the living room.

His father was obviously relieved to leave the explanation to Sally.

"It's just a little get-together for the folks on this street, to thank them for being so accepting of the inconvenience . . . you know, of Forge Street being blocked off."

"And as thanks I'm being offered as an exhibit?"

"Jacob, don't be an . . ." She glanced over to see if the boys were listening. They weren't. ". . . an ass. Whether it's tonight, or tomorrow, or next week, you're going to have to face people sometime."

"I can cancel for tonight if you want, son," his father offered. "I was just going to grill burgers and hot dogs. Everyone else was going to bring a dish. We can postpone."

"The barbecue is at your place?" At his father's red face, Jake said, "No, tonight is fine. Sally's right about my having to face people. I was just surprised."

His father left then, and Sally scooted into the

kitchen before he could give her hell. He sat down on the low sofa and watched the boys play. It was sometime later that he woke up with no memory of having stretched out or fallen asleep. It was the silence that awakened him.

Opening his eyes slowly, he saw that the boys were gone, and Sally was sitting on the floor in front of the sofa watching the Food Network with the volume muted, some kind of kid baking championship. A tablet and pen sitting on her lap indicated she'd been taking notes.

"Where is everyone?" he murmured.

"The boys are over at your dad's, helping him prepare for the party," she said, turning to look at him, after setting the tablet and pen on the floor.

"A party is it now?" he teased.

"Don't be an . . ."

". . . ass," he finished for her.

When she realized he was teasing, she made a tsk-ing sound and went to swat at him.

"C'mere, babe," he said, grabbing her hand and rolling onto his side, making room for her to lie down beside him. He knew she would fit. This battered old sofa had been one of their first purchases when they'd gotten married. If sofas could talk!

She stiffened for only a second, then settled on her side facing him.

"Shouldn't you be at work today, at your bakery?" he asked as he rubbed a palm over her hair, wondering if it was still as soft now as it had been when it was long. It was.

"I have an assistant who took over for me today." She tilted her head into his palm which was now cupping her jaw. "Why would I go to work on your first day home?"

"You were pissed with me when I left."

"That was three years ago! Did you think I held on to that anger all this time?"

He shrugged as if he didn't know.

"Idiot!"

He nuzzled her neck, then leaned back a bit and said, "I'm going to like this bakery gig of yours if you smell so sweet all the time. I was going to buy you some perfume at the exchange, but this is lots better."

She was running her hand over his shoulder and chest and arm, relearning his body, which he knew was the same, and yet different. Leaner, certainly. But could she feel some ridges under his T-shirt? What would she think when she saw the scars? There would be questions, for sure.

His conjecture proved true when she asked, "Jacob, what happened to you?"

He blinked several times to mask any bleakness or horror that might be revealed in his one eye that was exposed, and said, "Shhh." Then he did what he'd wanted to do from the instant he'd seen her. For three friggin' years, actually.

He kissed her.

And the kiss was sweeter than any item she might offer in her bakery. The chocolate cake he'd just devoured came to mind.

And the kiss was sweeter than hot sofa sex. The many times they'd rocked this very furniture came to mind.

And the kiss was sweeter than anything his dreams could conjure up. Three years of sexual fantasies came to mind.

In fact, when he was being interrogated, endlessly, or tortured, brutally, he'd found a way to enter a dream state where he'd made a game of picturing kisses with his wife, all different kinds, seventeen in all. And caresses . . . who knew there were fifty-four ways of touching a woman, or being touched by a woman? Then there was the sex itself. Forget all those pseudo experts in men's magazines, Jake was the king of sexual fantasies, featuring his ten favorites.

And forget all that SERE training soldiers, especially Special Forces ones, were given under the Army Code of Conduct for "surrender, evasion, resistance, and escape" of POWs. When it came right down to it, each man had to dig deep and try whatever worked for him to keep faith, whether in God, country, or family, or a combination of all three, that he would eventually be saved.

In Jake's case, for some crazy-ass reason, it was Sally's kisses that had helped him most through some of the worst times. Maybe it was the simplicity, the honesty, of a kiss, compared to the evil he'd been facing. Or maybe it was the fact that a kiss was often the prelude to something else, a signal of hope, and he'd been pretty much without hope back then when he'd been told that everyone back home thought he was long dead.

And so he surrendered for the moment to the sheer bliss of kissing his wife. It wasn't a trick to make him reveal secrets. No one would beat him bloody for failing to show his pain. He could show his emotions without words. He could feel human for as long as the kiss lasted.

Gentle and seeking.

Shaping.

Ah, there, the perfect fit.

Sweet.

But, no, this is better.

Hot.

Wet and open.

Gentle again.

Oh, Lord, thank You for this small blessing. A willing woman. My wife.

For the first time in what seemed like forever, Jake was glad he'd survived.

Suddenly, he heard a buzzing noise. Not a doorbell, or any of the usual Bell Cove bell sounds. Was it in his head? Oh, Lord! Was this to be another effect of his torture, a new feature of PTSD . . . a buzzing signal when he got turned on? Red tide and now erotic buzzing. What next?

But wait. Sally was pushing away from him and laughing. "It's the oven buzzer. I'm making brownies for the barbecue," she explained. Standing, she straightened her clothes and looked down at him, all blush-faced cheeks and kiss-swollen lips, her short hair tousled as if she'd just engaged in a bed romp. In other words, sexy as hell.

As she walked away, he thought, *Saved by the bell . . . uh, buzzer.*

But he remembered a time when they wouldn't have let any damn bell, or buzzer, or an Outer Banks hurricane, for that matter, keep them from rocking the sofa.

Chapter 7

*The benefits of a hurricane
(Does IKEA know about this?)* . . .

(Bell Cove, seven years ago)

The hurricane had been downgraded from a Category 3 to a Category 1, but still Jake's mother and father decided to take part in the voluntary evacuation of the Outer Banks recommended by the North Carolina governor, and they were taking Jake's one-year-old son, Matthew, with them. They would ride out the storm at Aunt Tillie's house in Richmond.

Jake and Sally, on the other hand, had decided to stay put, guarding the cottage they'd bought last year, as well as his parents' place across the street. Even though they were located a mile in either direction from the Atlantic Ocean and Bell Sound, storm surge flooding was unpredictable and could be devastating. They weren't about to risk damage to the hundred-year-old cottage in which they'd invested every bit of their savings, including the bonus he'd received for reupping.

"Good thing I was home on leave," he told Sally as they continued to board up the windows with plywood that was kept in the garage for just such emergencies. It might be an unnecessary precaution, but the old leaded windows, especially the ones with stained glass on them, like the one here fronting the house, were too precious to take a chance on damage. There were also a dozen sandbags sitting in the bed of his pickup in case they were needed.

"What? You think I wouldn't have been able to handle an emergency by myself?" she asked, sucking on the thumb she'd just hit with a hammer.

Oh, boy! She is in one of her moods. Picking a fight.

When he didn't react to her question, she said, "That is so sexist."

Yep, mood central!

Probably still brooding over my reup.

Or maybe it's good ol' PMS.

That would mean she's horny as hell, as well as moody. Her hormones always go haywire before her period.

But, man, I better not say that out loud.

He just grinned, which annoyed her even more.

The humidity was about a hundred and ten percent, and sweat was pouring off both of them as they continued to batten down their home. Sally wore only a little halter top and shorts. With her long brown hair pulled into a high ponytail, she still had strands plastered along the edge of her face. He was no better, in running shorts and nothing else, though his hair, of course, was military short. A blessing in this heat wave, which would soon break when the rain finally hit. Which it was starting to do.

"You would have evacuated if I weren't here," he contended, putting in one last nail, then stepping back to observe his work. Good enough, he decided, then glanced at Sally who hadn't responded to his remark. "Wouldn't you?"

"I don't know. Maybe. Maybe not." She had the cutest little ski jump nose, which was raised obstinately at the moment.

He leaned down and kissed the tip of it. "Don't even think about trying to hunker down on your own during a hurricane. You're not used to storms on the Outer Banks."

She shrugged. "You're the one who plopped me down here after our quickie shotgun wedding and then went off to war or war games or whatever the hell it is that you do in that Special Forces unit. You have no idea what this city girl has learned while you've been gone."

It was a running argument they'd been having since their marriage almost two years ago.

Jake sighed. "A shotgun wedding without the shotgun," he pointed out, not for the first time. "If our nuptials were quick and without the usual hoopla, it was because your parents were horrified to see you marry a soldier. Our wedding was a sword to their pacifist hearts."

"Good point, but that doesn't alter the fact that you dropped this city girl in the boonies, so to speak, then jitterbugged . . . rather shagged your way off to more new and exciting places."

Shagged? Now there's a thought. And he wasn't picturing the dance step. "Sal, you knew I was a soldier when we hooked up."

"Yeah, but I didn't know it was for life. Or that I wouldn't be going with you. Other soldiers' wives go."

Not Delta Force. Or at least not this one, who hasn't been stationed in one place for more than three months at a time these past four years. And not to the places I've been.

He would have continued the argument, or not, but the rain was beginning to come down now in torrents. Putting his hammer on the windowsill, he stepped down off the porch and let the cool pellets wash over him. He stretched his arms out and looked upward, eyes closed, momentarily. "This is heavenly."

"You're crazy," Sally said, smiling as she watched him.

"C'mon. Join me," he encouraged, holding his hands out to her, beckoning with his fingertips. "Take a ride on the crazy train."

"Not a chance."

"Don't you have a song for this . . . something about singing in the rain?"

"Gene Kelly, *Singin' in the Rain*, movie, 1952. Broadway musical, 1985." She began to belt out the lyrics then and with a mischievous grin, she jumped off the porch and into his arms. Within seconds, she was soaked to the skin, but then her halter top was tossed aside, and he'd shrugged off his shorts. And she'd miraculously lost her shorts, as well. Her legs were wrapped around his waist.

And she continued singing and laughing, her head thrown back with sheer joy.

Until he kissed her.

And then she kissed him.

It didn't matter that they were naked in their front yard. Everyone on their street had evacuated, or if they hadn't, neither he nor Sally could care. But then he picked her up and made his way inside, kicking the front door shut with his foot. They landed on the sofa.

"No, we have to dry off first." She tried to shove him off her. "We'll ruin the new sofa."

"It's only water," he insisted, spreading her legs with his knees and settling himself into Happy Land. "Remember what Mom said when we bought this thing. Buy the best. Quality will out. Cost almost as much as a house payment."

It was amazing that he could talk and make love at the same time, but he did, grunting out the words as he worked her ears with tongue and teeth and hot breaths, one of the most sensitive erotic spots on Sally's body.

She moaned and arched up for more.

He rolled so that she was on top, sitting on his belly, staring down at him with caramel eyes already glazed with passion. Her hair was plastered to her head where beads of water still ran down her face. Freckles dotted her cheeks and shoulders, even her breasts, which were slightly larger now, post-childbirth. And the nipples were darker, more rose-colored than light pink.

She should have looked like a drowned rat, or a freckle-faced mouse, but, instead, she was the picture of wholesome, sexy womanhood. And he loved every bit of her. So much it scared him sometimes.

"Sally, do you know how much I love you?"

His question startled her. For a moment. But then she wiggled her butt on him and said saucily, "No. Show me."

She'd heard experts talk about "riding out a storm" but was this what they meant? . . .

Sally had been watching the Food Network while Jacob slept on the couch behind her. She was worried about him and wanted to stick close by. Even as he slept, he was restless and subject to sudden starts and occasional groans. But then he'd awakened and pulled her up onto the sofa, kissing her. Oh, how she had missed kissing! His kissing.

Luckily, the oven buzzer had gone off. She wasn't ready to dive into lovemaking with Jacob. Not yet. And she suspected he wasn't ready, either, despite the quick start of arousal on both their parts. There was so much that needed to be cleared up between them first.

Still, as she rose and made her way into the kitchen

and the persistent buzzing, she glanced back at her husband half reclining on the sofa, up on his elbows, and wondered if he remembered how they'd christened that piece of furniture, back before their marriage hit the rocks.

Memories . . .

*D*o you know how much I love you?"

Sally was perched on Jacob's stomach, with her sopping wet hair dripping water down her face, off her chin, and onto his chest. Being naked as a newborn and not looking her best, she was startled by his question for a moment. Even when her hair was blow-dried and her face made up artfully to hide her freckles, Sally knew she was no beauty.

Yeah, she had insecurities. Yeah, she'd always been amazed that a man as hot as Jacob Dawson would be attracted to a woman who was at best average, let alone love her. Although they didn't talk about it, she'd always been hung up on the idea that he'd "had to" marry her.

But then, in this instance, Jacob was a man and they hadn't done the deed since his return from a three-month deployment last night. From the moment he'd arrived, he'd been busy helping his dad secure his fishing boat and his house before their evacuation. To Jacob, love probably meant lust. She'd long stopped believing he was as madly in love with her as she was with him. Or had been. Oh, she still loved the man, but madly? Not so much.

It was an interesting question, though. *"Do you know how much I love you?"* she repeated his words in her mind.

Well, no, I don't know that. How could I? In the twenty-three months, or seven hundred and one days, we've been married, we've been together a total of seven weeks . . . only forty-nine days. And, yes, I bothered to count, Mister I-Am-Off-to-Save-the-World.

And yet here she was, pregnant, again, although GI Clueless didn't know yet. A new baby meant that she was further trapped in her situation. Not trapped by children. Never that! She loved Matty and was looking forward to the new baby. But she didn't want to be raising them alone.

How could Jacob have reupped without consulting me first?

How could he think his long absences would be okay with me?

How could he claim to love me, and then leave me, again and again and again?

On the other hand, if there was one thing she'd learned as a soldier's wife, it was to "pick your battles." Besides, there was nothing to do while the storm raged. Who was she kidding? She hadn't made love in a long time, and Jacob knew how to push all her buttons, literally.

And, so, she wiggled her butt on Jacob and teased, "No. Show me."

"Sassy today, are you, sweetheart? Sassy Sally?"

"You have a problem with that, *big boy*?" she inquired, putting emphasis on those last two words with her voice and a backward thrust of her butt against said "big boy," which was flush against the crease in her behind.

"Are you kidding?" he choked out.

She was the one who was going to make love to him then, she decided, employing all the tricks and techniques that he had taught her, the things he liked best. Sally had never had much sexual experience with anyone else before Jacob, and certainly none after. So, he'd been her teacher.

Now, she would teach him a thing or two. Why should he be the one calling the shots about everything?

He put his hands on her hips, about to lift her onto his erection.

She tried to slap his hands away and said, "No. Let me."

But he had different ideas. "Uh-uh. You told me to show you how much I love you. That's what I'm gonna do."

He succeeded now in lifting her up and sliding her slowly down his shaft until her pubic bone rested against his pubic bone. They both let out a long groan at the sheer, almost painful pleasure, especially as her inner muscles were already grasping at him. Not surprising was the slickness of her channel; the man could turn her on with a mere look when he wanted to.

And he knew it.

As he did now.

Those blue eyes of his—like the summer skies over Bell Sound—were surely weapons in his sexual playbook. When he gazed at her with erotic intent, she was caught in his hypnotic scope, as surely as a sniper's target, and would do anything he asked. Anything.

His thick dark lashes lowered, then opened slowly, lazily, as he regarded her.

Was there anything sexier than a dark-haired, blue-eyed man? Especially a blue-eyed man with wicked intentions?

While she was studying him, he stuffed a throw pillow behind his head so he could see her better. Then he put his hands on her thighs and spread her wider so he could actually see her engorged clitoris. After that, he raised his hands up to her breasts and strummed the nipples until they stood out like sentinels of arousal, creating a direct pulsing line between her breasts and her female parts. Then, putting his hands on her elbows, he pressed her arms to her sides so that she couldn't reach for him.

"Look at you," he rasped out. "My sweet Sal." She must have appeared skeptical because he continued his observation, "Hot as summer sand on the Outer Banks, like sugar on a hungry man's tongue."

Now she did arch her brows with skepticism. Since when did her husband get all poetical?

He laughed and added, "And this man is huuuunnnngry."

Before she could react—heck, her lower body was

reacting on its own by spasming around his cock, which she could swear was growing inside of her even as he forced her to remain still—he leaned up and took her breast into his mouth. Her whole breast! And, yes, she was a cup larger since Matty's birth, and still he managed to take her all in. He chuckled at her gasp of surprise, even as he slowly released his suctioning hold on her breast until he reached the areola, which he sucked on hard, then soft, then hard, before flicking the nipple with his tongue until she was unable to forestall the climax which hit her suddenly.

Bam!

Then, bambambambambam . . .

Even then, he didn't stop his ministrations, just moved his mouth to her other breast.

She tried to move on him, but still he wouldn't let her. His hands were on her hips now, preventing any movement, except that inside of her. Slowly, she opened her eyes and glanced downward. Her breasts were wet from his laving and there were drops of moisture on their blended pubic hairs. It certainly wasn't from his ejaculation because he was still rock-hard inside of her, still unmoving.

"How embarrassing!" she murmured.

"How sexy!" he disagreed.

She looked at him then and saw the intensity of his arousal in those gorgeous blue eyes. It was a sign of his discipline, which made him a good soldier as well as a good lover, that he could be so excited and not go trigger-happy.

"Are you convinced yet?" he asked, framing her face and pulling her down to him.

"About what?"

"How much I love you?"

"Hah! That doesn't prove anything."

He grinned. "Are you challenging me?"

Was she? "Sure."

He kissed her then. And caressed her. And murmured wicked words of praise for her body. And thrust and thrust and thrust. Then stopped. And started all over again. Meanwhile, the wind whistled outside now and the house shivered on its foundation, but she barely noticed. By the time he released himself into her with a roar of triumph, his neck arched back over extended tendons, after she'd finally surrender with a cry of "I believe, I believe," he'd brought her to climax two more times.

It took a while for their heaving breaths to slow down to mere panting. He was flat on his back. She was on her side, her butt and shoulders against the back of the sofa, with her face on his chest, listening to his heartbeat.

"I do love you, Sally," he said, kissing the top of her head. "The question is, do you love me?"

"You know I do. Why would you even ask?"

"You haven't said so since I've been home. In fact, you've been in a bad mood from the get-go." He chuckled then.

"What's so funny?"

"God bless PMS," he said irrelevantly. "I love how horny you get before your period."

She raised her head and glared at him. He knew how women . . . how *she* felt when men made remarks about women on PMS. "You are such an ass sometimes," she said, not entirely upset with him, still basking in the afterglow of good sex.

"Why am I an ass for liking my wife to be horny, whether due to PMS or my remarkable talents?"

She slapped a hand on his fingers, which were toying with her breast again. "I'm not having PMS, and I'm not about to have a period, you idiot. I'm pregnant. Again."

He grinned. He actually had the nerve to grin. "Really?"

Men! They viewed pregnancy as a reflection of their virility. "Oh, yeah. Three months." The exact time since his last leave.

He continued to grin.

"You're happy about this?"

"Yeah. Aren't you?"

Actually, she was, but that didn't mean she didn't have issues related to her having babies and his being gone.

"In fact, I have an idea. We should name this new baby Mark. Then, the ones after that could be Luke and John. We could call them the four little apostles. You know, instead of the Little Rascals . . . And, hey, maybe someday they would all play on the same NFL football team, and commentators would name them the Bible Brothers. Not that I'm religious or anything. Just a thought."

"Well, think about this, bozo," she said, giving

him a hard shove, which caused him to fall off the couch.

He was laughing so hard, he didn't even bother to get up.

"Have you lost your mind?" Leaning over the side, she looked down at him. "You want four sons? And what if some of the babies are girls?"

"We could have an equal number of each."

"Eight kids. What alternate universe are you living in?"

He was probably kidding, but still . . .

Once he wiped the tears of mirth from his eyes with the back of his arm, he sat up and teased, "Still love me, baby?"

"Not so much," she said, getting up and going off to the bathroom to see if she could get a comb through her tangled hair. But she did. Love him. And that was her downfall, and why she would probably stay in the upcoming years.

The storm lasted for two days.

Would she ever look at that blasted sofa in the future and not remember that this was probably the beginning of the end for them . . . or the end of something?

Chapter 8

Who needs internet matchmaking?

Joe Dawson's heart was full almost to bursting, like a big old puffer fish, as he watched his son at the barbecue that evening.

Oh, not a heart attack approaching or anything like that. Not after what had happened to his precious Marge last year! He knew the signs now. And he kept his ticker in good shape with healthy food and regular checkups and exercise, though he didn't need any fancy-pantsy exercise regimen with his hardworking job as a fisherman.

No, this was joy like he'd never felt before, not even when he'd seen his son for the first time, all red faced and pruney skinned when he came into the world thirty-two years ago. And it was a sadness that only a father would recognize when he knew his son was hurting real bad and could do nothing about it.

If only Marge had lived long enough to see her son come home! She'd been shattered when he was declared dead and lived in silent grief for two years afterward until last year when she'd died, too, thinking she would be meeting him "up there." Well, she knew now, wherever she was "up there," looking down on them.

Joe sighed. He was sitting on a glider on his back porch with Old Mike, the two of them nursing cold bottles of beer. Mid-August on the Outer Banks could be sweltering hot, and the temp had barely dropped below ninety all day. Even now, in the early evening, it was a humid eighty. Storm coming, for sure. Which could affect their planned five a.m. start to spend the day fishing stripers about twenty miles out at his favorite spot.

Mike had been renting a room from him ever since Marge died of that sudden heart attack. Mike had asked if he could move in because he was about to lose the lease on his trailer, but Joe suspected that Mike, good friend that he was, had just wanted to help Joe as he mourned.

Just then, Karl Gustafson walked into the backyard with his mother, Vana, who was carrying a bowl of what must be her famous, or infamous, Norse potato salad, which was heavy on salted herring. *Don't ask!*

Gus was an impressive figure at six foot three or four, having been a professional football player at one time. Quarterback for the Dallas Cowboys. He now ran a convenience store on the island known as Gus's Gas and Goods, and seemed content enough with his noncelebrity status these days. His mother, a longtime widow, had an equally impressive figure, Joe had to admit . . . as had half the male population in Bell Cove over the age of fifty. At six feet tall, still wearing her hair long and blonde at sixty-plus years old, she had a body that could only be called statuesque, if one were being polite. Va-va-voom, if one were being less than polite.

He and Mike exchanged a look, then sat up straighter when Vana noticed them on the porch and gave a little wave. She was wearing tight white jeans with a floaty kind of see-through top and wedge-heeled sandals that probably made her six foot three. If Joe were standing in front of her, which he had no intention of doing, his eyes would probably be planted dead center on her boobs.

"Lordy, Lordy!" Mike muttered under his breath.

"Yep!" Joe agreed.

Vana took her dish over to the folding table where food was being set out by Sally and Francine Henderson, owner of Styles and Smiles, a beauty salon on the square, and immediately began an animated conversation. From the minute Jake and Sally had arrived at Joe's cottage this evening, Jake insisted on manning the barbecue, probably so he had something to lean on to relieve the obvious pain in his leg. And Sally went over to set up the food table. A mere twenty feet apart which might as well be twenty miles, Joe observed with a sigh.

In any case, Francine was sporting one of those old-fashioned beehive hairdos which she was attempting to bring back in style, apparently. Hopefully, to no avail. Was a time, years ago, when rumor had it that creatures took up residence in those hair nests, and he didn't mean bumble bees. Francine was married to Sheriff Bill Henderson, who was at the back end of the yard supervising his daughter Mary Anne and Joe's three grandsons in a game of badminton, which involved much giggling and shouting and barking. The barking coming from Joe's mutt, Goofus, who considered the birdie his personal chew toy. Mary Anne, who was about ten years old, had a mini version of her mother's bee-hive hairdo, most of which was falling down due to her energetic movements.

Back to the food table, which Joe intended to visit real soon, not having eaten anything since lunch, he noticed that Sally had put on a pretty peach-colored sundress before walking over with Jake an hour ago, a slow and obviously painful process that his son had insisted on. No walker or wheelchair for him! He was wearing dark sunglasses tonight, which were almost as jarring as the eye patch, considering the sun was no longer so bright.

Gus grabbed a cold beer from the cooler and went over to shake hands with Jake, who had to tug off one of the blue vinyl disposable gloves he'd donned to handle the meat, or was it to hide those nailless fingers? *And what was that all about anyhow?*

Joe didn't know what Jake and Gus were talking about, but there was laughter involved; so, Joe relaxed, despite being on pins and needles, worried that someone might say something to Jake that would offend him or cause him to feel uncomfortable. Yeah, Joe was being overly protective. Came from being a father, no matter the age of the kid.

"Whattaya s'pose happened to the boy?" Mike asked out of the blue.

"What? You not buyin' the cave hidey-hole story?"

"Hell, no! What about you?"

Joe shrugged. "Hard ta believe, but then him just survivin' for three years, that in itself is unbelievable. A miracle."

"Thank the Lord," Mike said. And Mike wasn't even religious.

"Amen," Joe agreed. And he wasn't very religious, either, although he might become more so with the "miracle" of his son's return.

"We gotta do somethin' to help those two," Mike said.

Joe nodded. He didn't need to ask what Mike meant. Jake and Sally hadn't been within two feet of each other since they'd arrived. They pointedly avoided even looking at each other. It was obvious, at least to Joe and Mike, that Jake and Sally were as skittish around each other as strangers. And it wasn't just the usual getting-acquainted-again that soldiers and their spouses faced every time they came home after a long deployment. And it wasn't just that Jake had been MIA for three years and carried baggage Joe couldn't imagine. And it wasn't because Sally was an independent businesswoman now, who'd been about to hook up with a new man. Nope, these two had bigger problems than all that, ones that had been festering before he'd ever gone

missing. Joe knew how devastating it had felt when
Jake had chosen not to stay home and run the fishing business with him. It had to be doubly devastating to Sally that her husband chose, over and
over, to stay in the military, on top of that, a branch
of the military that had him constantly on the go to
some dark and dangerous places, rather than stick
in one place with her to raise a family.

And, yeah, there was patriotism and loyalty and
bravery and all that. And, yeah, he was proud of
his son. But still, he understood. That didn't mean
he was gung-ho for Mike's suggestion that they fix
Jake and Sally. "Oh, no! I'm not getting involved in
my son's marriage," Joe said. Then asked, "What'd
ya have in mind?"

"Those two need time alone ta work things out,
even an ol' bachelor like me knows that. How 'bout
we plan a weekend fishin' trip with the boys? We
kin take them out to where the yellowfin will be
hittin' in a week or so. Eat and sleep on the boat."

"Oh, Lord! I have a headache already just thinkin'
about the noise. Those kids don't talk when they
can shout. All at the same time. The last time I took
them out, and it was only for a few hours, Matt
caught a hook in his thumb, Mark almost fell over-
board, and Luke released all our bait because he
felt sorry for the little fishies."

"Do ya want that K-4 fella ta be takin' Sally *fishin'*,
if ya get my meaning?"

K-4 . . . that would be Kevin Fortunato, a new guy
in town who'd been sniffing around Sally. Nope,

Jake didn't need any competition. Not that his son couldn't handle the challenge. And deep down Joe knew that Sally loved his boy, and vice versa. There was a legend in his family that the Dawson men fell hard and fast for the women in their lives, and that it lasted. It certainly had for him and Marge. But could he just assume that Jake and Sally would get their acts together? Wouldn't that be tempting fate? And it seemed to Joe that fate hadn't been treating Jake very well in recent years.

"It'll be fun," Mike insisted.

Joe arched his brows. "Since when did you become Mister Matchmaker?"

"Don't be so grumpy, or they'll be votin' you the Grinch of Bell Cove come Christmas."

"I'm not grumpy. You're the one who's grumpy."

"Anyways, those two need some time alone together."

They both took long draws on their bottles of beer and looked at Jake, who was alone for the moment. He drew a kitchen counter stool over and leaned his butt back on it with a long sigh. Being on his leg for this long was taking its toll, but Joe knew without making the suggestion that his stubborn son would decline pain meds or any obvious fussing over him.

But then Jake's attention seemed to be caught by something across the yard. Sally was welcoming Jeff Hale, the new doctor who'd taken over the local medical clinic. A single doctor! As they talked, Jeff put his hand on Sally's forearm and leaned in to whisper something in her ear. She threw her head back and laughed out loud. The hand on the fore-arm remained.

Not good!

Jake stiffened.

Definitely not good!

On the other hand, good, if he's finally dropping that mask of "I don't give a shit" emotional detachment that he's been wearing like a shield since he got home.

Bad, if he's going to react in some public way.

"Okay, I'm in," Joe said.

Yep, blue eyes—or a blue eye— can still turn green . . .

*T*he barbecue wasn't as bad as Jake had expected. In fact, it was kind of nice to meet up with neighbors, some of whom he'd known his entire life.

What made it more palatable in this small crowd— about fifteen people so far—was that they acted as if he was back from a routine deployment. None of them grilled him about where he'd been the last three years and what exactly happened to him. Yeah, he had the canned dickhead responses that his dickhead liaison had fed him for practically every question. Luckily, he hadn't needed to use any of them.

He wasn't sure if his father and Sally had pre-pared the way for him by warning folks not to ask those kinds of questions, but more likely these were just good, sensitive people—friends—who knew how to be polite. That didn't mean they wouldn't be gossiping about him when they got home. It was Bell Cove, after all, where everyone minded everyone else's business.

"Hey, buddy!" Karl Gustafson said, coming up to shake his hand. Jake had to remove one of the vinyl gloves he was wearing to handle the raw hamburger, and, yes, to hide his nailless fingertips, before taking Gus's clasp. Gus didn't stop there, though. The big blond giant of a man, whom he'd known from grade school, pulled Jake into a bro hug.

Jake almost fell, but caught himself just in time, regaining his balance with a hand on the side shelf of the barbecue.

"Gus! How you doing? Still playing football?" He'd been drafted right out of college by the Dallas Cowboys—which prompted much teasing by the sports pundits because a guy of Norse descent had been expected to go with the Vikings.

"Hell, no! I retired more than two years ago when my knee got torn up *again*. Shortest career in NFL history!"

That wasn't quite true. As Jake recalled, Gus had been playing pro for several years before Jake had left on his last deployment. Four years in the pros was nothing to sneeze at. "And now? You left the limelight and you're back in Bell Cove?"

"The limelight isn't all it's cracked up to be. Home

is where the heart is and all that shit." He grinned and took a long swig of beer.

"Doing what?"

"I have a convenience store on the outskirts of town," he said. At Jake's snort of disbelief, he added, "And more recently, I joined up with Bell Cove Treasure and Salvaging. That's a new operation started up by a former Navy SEAL, Merrill Good. You'll meet him soon enough. Your wife and Good's wife, Delilah, are best friends."

Really? That's news to me. First, the SEAL she'd been dating, and now BFF with another SEAL's wife. Just how many SEAL connections does my wife have?

Like that matters!

Jake flipped the burgers and turned the hot dogs as they talked. "I heard about that company. Izzie—Isaac Bernstein, you remember him, don't you?—sent me a bunch of old Bell Cove newspapers. A big shipwreck discovery, huh?"

Actually, that was the operation that Sally's ex-SEAL, K-4, or Kevin Fortunato—*Uncle-Fucking-Kevin*—was involved in, as well. Not that Jake was going to ask Gus about that.

"Yeah. Beginner's luck!"

"So, you married? Have any kids?" he asked as he moved the burgers and dogs that were done onto a warming rack, and placed fresh meat on the grill. He'd wait until he had at least two dozen of each before the first serving, he decided.

"No kids. I was married for a blip of a second to a trophy wife who wasn't too fond of my return to

Bell Cove, out of the media spotlight and all that hoopla. Now, being the only celebrity hereabouts, I'm looked at as a potential trophy husband. Every woman I meet seems to view me as a stepping-stone to something bigger."

Jake shook his head at Gus's self-deprecating humor.

"Hey, you're a celebrity now, too. You could say you're already a trophy husband."

Hah! Sally would have something to say about that. Probably, "Some trophy!" But wait . . . his father and Sally had promised him that only neighbors were invited to this barbecue. That meant . . . "You aren't still living at home with your mother, are you?" He glanced across the yard to where Vana Gustafson was chatting up Frank Baxter, who owned Hard Knocks, a hardware store on the town square. Good ol' Frank still sported the world's worst comb-over, or rather comb-forward, to hide the bald spot on top of his noggin. Vana, on the other hand, was seriously hot, and always had been—the source of many a Bell Cove boy's, and man's, wet dreams.

"Just temporarily . . . until my house is finished."

"Oh?"

"I was living in an apartment over the convenience store, but then I had this special needs boy working for me, and the authorities found out he was living in his car and were gonna force him to go live in some crappy halfway house in Myrtle Beach. So"—he shrugged—"I offered him my digs and started building a house I'd been planning for some time. It's out on the Sound near the cove. This all happened about the time we discovered the shipwreck, but I had money left over from my football days, too. So . . ." His words trailed off as he realized how much he'd been talking. He grinned and said, "Sorry. TMI. I had a few beers before I got here. Needed something to cushion the shock. I just found out my mother, who's been a widow for twenty frickin' years now, has suddenly decided to sign up for some half-assed senior citizen internet dating site, and when I saw her profile, well . . ." He fanned his face and rolled his eyes.

"Bell Cove soap operas! This place never changes."

"You got that right. Did you hear about that sexy seniors club over at the Patterson house? Supposedly a dance club, but I don't know." He grinned at Jake.

"Why didn't your mother just join that club if she was looking to hook up?"

"Please! Don't use *hook up* and my mother in the same sentence," Gus said, still grinning. "Actually, I made the same point, and she said she's looking for a younger man. Can you believe it? My mother, a cougar?"

Half of what Gus said was, no doubt, bullshit, but Jake found himself laughing, which was probably Gus's goal.

"By the way, I recognize a fellow partner-in-pain." Gus used his beer can to point at Jake's leg where a soft brace could be seen below his board shorts, then pointed to his own knee where old scars marked his numerous surgeries. "I can recommend a rehab place over on Hatteras that has not only primo licensed physical therapists but a whirlpool to die for. I can give you the number if you want."

"I may take you up on that." Jake was surprised that he wasn't offended by Gus's mention of his injury. Probably because he hadn't asked any questions that would force him to spew out the military version of his POW experience, or rather, MIA experience, and how he'd gotten said injury. *Shiiit! Lying is damn hard work, or rather being discreet about covert activities is hard work!*

Gus went off to referee the badminton game, and Abe and Rachel Bernstein, Izzie's uncle and aunt, came up to give him warm hugs. They both had tears in their eyes as they looked him over. Jake wasn't sure if it was because he looked so pitiful, or they were so emotional over his return, knowing that their nephew might very well have been in the same kind of situation. Probably both.

"Still making your famous Reubens?" Jake asked Abe.

"Of course."

"I've suggested a fat-free version, but will he listen to me? No," Rachel said with a laugh.

"Every good Jewish butcher knows there has to be a little fat on the corned beef for flavor. Skinny meat, skinny women, pfff!" He pinched his wife's ample behind for emphasis.

"Oh, you! Behave!" Rachel chided her husband, though not offended. For as long as Jake could remember, these two, a childless couple, had been bickering playfully with each other. "Have you heard?" Rachel addressed Jake now. "Izzie is coming for a visit over Labor Day. His mother and father are coming from Seattle, too."

No, Jake hadn't heard that, but then he hadn't been reading any email or text messages that were nonessential the past few days. "A regular family reunion," Jake remarked.

"For sure, but also to take part in your Welcome Home celebration," Abe said, beaming at Jake. "I'm thinking about offering red, white, and blue sandwiches. Rare roast beef, white sour cream and horseradish sauce, dotted with blue cheese, all served on fresh kaiser rolls from Sally's bakery. What do you think?"

Jake bristled and asked, "What 'Welcome Home' celebration?"

"Shhh!" Rachel elbowed her husband.

"What? It's not a secret," Abe responded.

"It's not a secret and it's not going to happen," Jake asserted, vowing to contact Mayor Doreen Ferguson himself to put the kibosh on any events involving him. "Not that I don't want to see Izzie and his parents again."

After that, Ina Rogers came up. She also gave him a welcoming hug, which involved him bending over at the waist since she was about five foot two. Ina had been the secretary at Our Lady by the Sea Church for as long as Jake could remember.

"Jake, honey, you can borrow my walker, if you

want. I bought it when I had hip surgery last spring and don't need it anymore."

"Um . . . I'll think about it." Seeing as how Jake had about ten inches in height on her, he couldn't see himself ever using her walker, but then he had no intention of using a walker, period. He didn't say that, though. "Thanks for the offer, Ina."

"I assume I'll see you in church on Sunday," Ina said.

Some assumption, he thought, and was about to say so, in a nice way, but she was already heading for the porch where his dad and Old Mike had been sitting on the glider, watching him to make sure he didn't trip over his size twelve flip-flops, or something. Without saying a word, just keeping an eye on his every move, they were acting like overaged babysitters and he was the unpredictable toddler.

His attention was caught by something else. A man, one he didn't recognize, went up to Sally, and he put his hand on her forearm as he talked to her. It couldn't be the ex-SEAL, whom he would expect to be super buff. Not that this guy was in bad shape. Just ordinary build in khakis and a golf shirt. But not military-looking. More like nerdy. Besides, the K-4 fellow didn't live on this street, as far as Jake knew.

But then the nerd-with-a-death-wish not only kept his hand on her forearm but leaned down to whisper in her ear.

Sally was looking hot tonight in a thin-strapped sundress, which cupped her breasts like a bra, hugged her abdomen and waist, then swirled out to just above the knee, leaving her suntanned arms and shoulders and legs bare down to strappy, flat sandals. He wondered idly how she'd gotten so sun bronzed if she worked in a bakery all day, but that was a question for another time. Although an image flashed in his brain for a moment of Sally lying on a beach blanket somewhere next to a stud in Navy SEAL shorts. She had long hair in that image. In reality, her short hair had been spiked up today with mousse or gel or some hair product, making her look elfish. A sexy elf! The sundress was peach-colored, like the one she'd worn the first time he met her in New York City all those years ago. Was that deliberate? Probably not.

It shouldn't matter to Jake. He'd decided before he ever got on that plane in Germany that Sally was better off without him. She was already halfway there with that SEAL dude. His plan had been to come home, get his affairs in order, sign the divorce papers she clearly wanted and had prepared more than three years ago, then take off for some solitary place where he could heal. He didn't need this kind of complication in his own recovery.

Frankly, he didn't care anymore.

Or he'd thought he didn't.

The conflict was driving him nuts.

And still the guy's hand remained on her arm—her *bare* arm—as they chatted. Jake blinked and saw a flash of red behind his eyelids. No, no, no! No red tides! Not now! What was it that Dr. Sheila said he should do when he felt a rage coming on . . . that mindfulness crap. *Just breathe.* That was it.

So, he inhaled, and exhaled, and chanted to himself. *Breathe. Inhale. Exhale. Breathe. Inhale. Exhale. Breathe . . .*

I am one screwed-up sonofabitch.

Just breathe.

I shouldn't have come home.

Breathe, dammit.

If it hadn't been for my last deployment rocking off into a three-year goat fuck, Sally and I would be divorced by now. No doubt about it.

Breathebreathebreathe.

So, what do I do within five hours of coming home? Practically jump my wife's bones. Pathetic, that's what I am. She probably only kissed me back because she felt sorry for me. A pity fuck, that's what it would have been if we hadn't been saved by the buzzer.

Don't knock it, pal. A fuck is a fuck is a fuck.

I can't breathe.

I need to get out of here.

Just then, the town bells began to toll the hour. The two churches and then the town hall. *Bong, bong, bong, bong, bong, bong, bong! Ding-dong, ding-dong, ding-dong, ding-dong, ding-dong, ding-dong, ding-dong! Clang, clang, clang, clang, clang, clang, clang!* By the time they were finished, he was grounded back in reality.

"Daddy?"

It took Jake a moment to realize that his son Luke was tugging on his shirt, trying to get his attention.

He looked down and asked, "What's up, buddy?"

"I hafta pee," Luke said.

He frowned with confusion. "Don't you know where Grandpa's bathroom is?"

He nodded but was still tugging on the hem of his shirt, then his arm, indicating that he wanted him to lean down. Then, into his ear, Luke whispered, "My zipper is stuck."

Jake's lips twitched with a grin. "An emergency, huh? Okay. Lead the way." Jake tossed off the other vinyl glove, grabbed for the cane he'd placed against the grill, and took Luke's little hand in his big paw and proceeded to walk with him up the stairs to the back porch. When he got there, he told his father, "The first batch of burgers and dogs are ready. Can you serve them and turn that new batch?"

"Sure," his father said, and both he and Old Mike started down the steps.

In the bathroom, he stood Luke on the closed toilet seat and worked out the snag in the zipper, then waited while the boy took care of business. Afterward, they both washed their hands. Luke looked up at him and flashed a gap-toothed grin at him. "I love you, Daddy," he said.

And Jake's heart about cracked with emotion. "Love you, too, short stuff," he said, ruffling his bristly hair.

"Chow's ready!" they heard his father's shout from outside.

And Luke ran off.

Instead of returning to the backyard, Jake headed

down the hall toward the front door. On the way, he hesitated and went into the living room, which was similar in layout to his own home. On the fireplace mantel and on the built-in shelves on either side, he saw a series of framed photographs which drew him closer.

On the mantel, there was his parents' circa-1970s wedding picture, his dad in a formal black suit and his mother in a big fancy white gown and veil, standing outside Our Lady by the Sea Church. His dad had a serious, nervous expression on his face as he stared ahead at the camera. His mother's head was tilted toward her new husband in a teasing, intimate manner, the way it often was when his father was all grumpy after a bad day on the water.

Next to it was a photo taken outside city hall in New York City, Jake in his full dress uniform and Sally in a white suit with matching high heels. She carried a bunch of daisies which he'd purchased from a street vendor on the way. Sally had been four months pregnant by then, but you'd never know it by her slim figure. The way she was looking at him in the photo clearly showed that the setting didn't matter to her a bit. She was happy. And in love.

Jake couldn't remember the last time she'd looked at him that way.

Over on the shelves, the framed photos were arranged by event. His birth: a newborn baby being held by his mother in a hospital bed with his father sitting on the edge of the mattress, beaming with pride. Then the birth of Jake's three sons. Sally and the newborns were featured in these three, of course. He was in one, wearing a blue hospital gown and cap, holding baby Matthew. Jake had tried his best but had been unable to make it home in time for the deliveries of his other two sons. A sore point between him and Sally, to say the least.

On other shelves were pictures of christenings, first communions, kindergarten graduations, Pee-Wee and Little League baseball, birthday parties, Christmases, first bicycles, fishing off the Bell Cove wharf . . . dozens of them. Jake had seen all these, or most of them, before, of course. Sally had been religious about sending him digital photos of his kids. Still . . . seeing all of these in one collection, he realized how much he'd missed of his sons' lives. And of Sally's, too. There was one particular one he noted showing her standing with a giant pair of scissors about to cut the ribbon on a storefront with a sign boasting "Sweet Thangs," the grand opening of her bakery.

All water under the bridge now. And, really, no different than any other soldier's wife or family.

"Jake? Food is ready," Sally called out, and then he heard her footsteps approaching.

"I'm in here," he said, not wanting her to think he was hiding out or anything pathetic like that. He was pathetic enough without being that kind of wuss, too.

She arched her brows when she saw him standing before the photos. "A walk down memory lane?"

she asked, leaning against the archway leading to the hall.

"Sort of," he said.

"You gonna come and eat?"

"In a minute," he said, sinking down into his dad's recliner.

Instead of taking the hint and leaving him alone, she sat down in his mother's rocker on the other side of the fireplace, facing him. "You've seen all these photos before," she reminded him.

"Not all. The one in front of your bakery is new," he pointed out.

"Right," she said. "Speaking of which, there's something I need to discuss with you." She rocked a little faster now. With nervousness?

Uh-oh. Was this the beginning of the uncomfortable questions he wouldn't be able to answer?

"This will sound really morbid, but I used your death benefit to buy the bakery. Will I have to pay it back now?"

Ah. He relaxed visibly. "Don't worry about that. Uncle Sam won't be knocking on your door looking for a payback. They owe me too much."

"Do you mean back pay?"

"No, I mean leverage." As soon as the word left his mouth, he knew it was a mistake.

"Leverage?" She pounced on the word.

"I mean, how would it look if they sicced a collection agency on one of its POWs—I mean, MIAs?" *Man, I am screwing up here big-time.*

He could tell she wasn't convinced but, luckily, she moved on to another subject. Well, unluckily, considering the subject.

"Are you still in the military, Jacob? I know you reupped for another four years before your last deployment, but does that mean you're still considered active duty?"

"I'm on medical leave at the moment, and with all the rehab I need, my term of duty will end in March, like it would normally. It will be up to me to decide whether to reup again then."

Shock appeared on her face for a moment before she masked it over. Still, she glanced at his leg and his eye, and Jake knew what she was questioning. How could he ever engage in battle again?

He couldn't.

"They want me to work in the Pentagon, some kind of public affairs position." *In other words, a propaganda puppet.*

The shock was back, or was it anger now? "Please don't tell me you accepted without discussing it with me first." She'd said almost those exact words when he'd told her he reupped for four years before his last deployment.

He shook his head. "No, I didn't accept, and I have no intention of moving to the capital."

The expression on her face revealed nothing about her feelings at that news. "What *will* you do?"

His head was beginning to hurt, along with his leg. "Do we have to discuss this now?"

He could tell that she wanted to, but she conceded. "No. But we do need to talk sometime, Jacob."

And she wasn't just referring to his career plans. He knew that.

For a few moments, there was just silence between them as they looked at each other. The pretty peach dress was hiked up to her thighs and he noticed once again how bronzed she was, all over, or at least what he could see, and that was a lot. "How is it that you're so suntanned, Sal? Don't you spend your days indoors at the bakery?"

"The bakery doesn't open until eight, but I usually go in at about four to start the ovens and begin baking. I stay until after the lunch hour, and then I leave the bakery in the hands of one of the clerks who work for me. The rest of the day I spend with the boys, usually on the beach over by the lighthouse if the weather is nice. I go in again, after the kids are in bed, to prepare the breads and rolls so they can rise overnight."

He nodded, though he had to wonder how she juggled so many hours. Very efficient, his wife had become. Maybe she always had been, and he'd just never noticed, or hadn't been home to notice.

His bad!

Or more of his bads!

As if she'd read his mind, she added, "Your dad, and your mom when she was alive, helped me a lot. Your dad still does. He, or Old Mike, come over in the evenings for those few hours I'm gone. I don't know how I would have survived without them . . . all of them. And the townsfolk, too. Your mother probably instigated the help from that quarter, everything from volunteer cleaners and painters when I first bought the bakery to, yes, the yellow ribbons. Your mother's rosary society came in for coffee and donuts every morning after mass, religiously." She smiled at her pun.

The pain of his mother's death hit him with a sharp stab to the heart. The loss was still new to him.

"Your mother prayed for you every day, you know. And she was always doing novenas for 'special intentions,' but everyone knew they were for you."

That shocked him, for some reason. "Because she thought I was still alive."

She shook her head. "No. The military was definite in declaring you dead. She just prayed for you, wherever you were."

"In hell," he muttered.

"What?"

"Nothing." He used his cane to help propel himself up out of the chair. When he stood, he said, "C'mon. Let's go outside before everyone starts speculating about what we're doing in here."

"No one would think *that*."

"Are you kidding? They're probably taking bets on how many times I need to boink you to make up for three years in a cave."

"Boink?" She laughed. "Just out of curiosity, how many boinks would that be?"

"Five hundred, at least."

She had nothing to say to that, but she did blush, which he kind of liked. *Nine years of marriage, and I can still make my wife blush. How about that?*

As he began to walk beside her down the hall toward the kitchen, he said, "I'm sorry about what happened earlier."

She frowned and gave him a sideways glance.

"On the sofa. I practically jumped your bones."

"Please! You weren't the only one jumping."

There were a dozen remarks he could have made to that, ranging from raunchy to only slightly inappropriate. He chose to keep them to himself. "It was a mistake. We have issues."

"Tell me about it."

He thought about asking her what she meant by that. He knew what he meant, but were they on the same page? Instead, he remarked, "I like your dress."

"I thought you would."

Whaat? "My favorite color."

"I know."

So, it was deliberate. Or am I reading too much into a simple statement? And do I want her trying to entice me? Entice? Where the hell did that word come from? I've been living in a cave too long, apparently. Ha, ha, ha!

Talk about ping-ponging emotions! I am a regular whack, whack, whack job. Really, he had to stop this back-and-forth banter with Sally with its sexual undertones. They *did* have issues, probably insurmountable ones, and engaging in sex would only complicate them, not solve them.

Although it was an *enticing* prospect.

He had to ask the big question that had been nagging at him for weeks now. Hell, probably for more than three years. "Do you still have the papers, Sally?"

"What papers?"

"The divorce papers. The ones you told me that you got from a lawyer."

She stopped midway down the hall to stare at him.

He stopped, too, and stared back at her.

She didn't back down, like she used to in a stare-off. "You idiot!" she said finally. "There were no papers."

"But you said . . . I specifically recall, just before I left for my last deployment, you saying that you met with a lawyer and got some divorce papers to look over, and . . ." He let his words trail off.

"Idiot!" she repeated. "I lied. It was intended to be a wake-up call for you."

He didn't know if he was angry or happy at her ploy. One thing he did know: he might not have been awake back then, but he sure as hell was now.

Chapter 9

*There were many steps on the
road back home . . .*

Less than twenty-four hours home, and Jake was
driving her crazy with his flip-flopping actions.
She was trying to be sympathetic because of all
he'd been through, but he made it hard. Not that
she knew exactly what he'd been through because
he clammed up every time she asked even the sim-
plest question, like, "Did the locals help you with
food and stuff while you were hiding in the cave?"

Nope. First thing out of his mouth on seeing her
for the first time after more than three years had
been to mention divorce. Then he'd kissed her into
a melted pool of hormone hotness on the sofa. After
which he practically ignored her at the barbecue.
Then tugged at her heartstrings when he revealed
that all the time he'd been missing he'd been under
the impression that she'd seen a lawyer and didn't
want him anymore, thus explaining the earlier divorce remark.

Why couldn't he just say what he was thinking?

And now, ever since they'd returned from the barbecue, he'd gone all silent and brooding. Dark and brooding might be great for a romance novel hero, but not for a real-life hero. After she'd glared at him a time or five for his one-word responses to the kids' incessant questions, he went out to the garage where he was still prepping his "go-bag," the backpack that had to be "wheels up" ready on a moment's notice when a soldier was called to active duty. The go-bag, also known as a grab-and-go or Go-to-Hell bag, included a seventy-two-hour supply of everything from clothing to first aid kits to MREs. Plus weapons and ammo, which was why it was kept in a locked chest under the tool bench.

Like he was going to need a go-bag anytime in the near future! Not with his injuries! Although what did she know? Maybe, with his skill set, limping, vision-impaired soldiers were a prized asset in the field today.

She could accept that his detachment was just the way he was when only she was involved. But the boys were confused and hurt by his actions, as well, and that she couldn't tolerate. After the barbecue, following quick showers and teeth brushing, they'd finally gotten into their beds, despite their moans that they wanted Daddy to tuck them in tonight.

Yeah, well, Daddy was too busy with nonessential crap out in the garage. Not that she told them that. Instead, she said, "Not tonight, sweeties. Daddy has important business to take care of right now. He'll be here when you get up in the morning."

Bottom line: really, sometimes Jacob could be such an ass.

So it was that she went, with a mother's ire, stomping down the steps and out the kitchen door to confront the insensitive brute. She found him sitting on the back steps. By the light coming through the kitchen door and window, she could see clearly. He'd removed the soft brace and was massaging his extended leg.

She stopped dead in her tracks, and all the anger seeped out of her at the sight of the uncovered limb. It had been shaved, unlike the right leg which was covered with black hairs, and there was clear evidence of old and new scars from midthigh to midcalf. Lots of them.

"Are they from injuries or surgeries?" she asked, sinking down to the top step beside him.

"Both."

"Jake, the kids are disappointed."

"I know."

"They're little. They don't understand. You have to be careful—"

"I'm trying, Sal."

"Would it have hurt for you to go up and tuck them in?"

"Actually, it would have. More than you can imagine."

Was he talking about physical hurt, or emotional hurt? She frowned at him in confusion.

"I couldn't have made it up the stairs tonight unless I crawled, and even then it would probably have to be backward, a butt bump up the steps, bracing myself on my arms." When she didn't say anything, he elaborated, "I'm going to get better. Eventually. I mean, my leg will improve with rehab over time. Probably never back to normal, but better than this mean mess that it is presently. For now, though, I'm in excruciating pain. Bear with me if I don't act the way you think I should."

Wow! Was that a kick in the gut or what? Guilt me out, why don't you? That was probably why he'd bathed in the cold outdoor shower before going to the barbecue tonight, instead of using the full shower and bath upstairs. She had wondered at the time, figuring he'd just wanted to leave that bathroom for her and the kids to get ready. "The pain is that bad?"

"Oh, yeah."

"Don't you have pain meds?"

"I do, but I don't like to take them."

"The opioid addiction thing?"

"That and the fact that they dull my brain, make me sleepy."

She nodded.

"I'm gonna take one in a few minutes," he said, then looked directly at her. "Don't take this the wrong way, babe, but I'm gonna sleep on the couch tonight."

She wasn't sure if he meant because of the stairs, or because of the mistake they'd made earlier with the "almost sex" on the sofa. She wasn't sure she wanted to know, or to engage in that particular discussion tonight.

He was still looking at her. Was he expecting her to argue with him, or offer to sleep on the couch with him? Which would be tight, and therefore involve more than sleeping. He was, after all, still an attractive man, and she had been celibate for a very long time, and he was her husband. Instead, she said, "I'll get you a pillow and sheets."

He was the one who nodded now, and then was back to massaging his leg and staring straight ahead.

She thought about offering to do the massage for him. Perhaps with some warm oil. No, no, no! That would lead in the same direction as sharing the sofa. She felt the need to say something else, though. "Jacob, I am glad to have you home. I hope you know that."

He didn't look at her when he said, "I'm glad to be home." It was almost as if he was surprised to be "glad," that perhaps he hadn't wanted to come back here.

Maybe she wasn't the only one who'd been thinking about divorce three years ago. Or even now.

Later that night, she awakened suddenly, disoriented. She wasn't sure what had drawn her from the deep sleep she'd fallen into the second she hit the mattress. It had been a long, long day. For all of them.

Any mother—especially the mother of three boys—was alert to the slightest disturbance in the air during the night, even when asleep. She looked at her bedside clock. Almost two a.m. She slipped out from under the sheet and coverlet and made her way down the hall.

First, Matt's tiny bedroom where she saw that he was spread-eagled out on his back, uncovered, snoring slightly. Because he was prone to throat infections, he would probably need to have his tonsils removed next year. She covered him, kissed him lightly on the forehead, and left the room.

Next, she checked the second bedroom where Mark was on the top bunk and Luke on the bottom. Both fast asleep. She kissed them, too, and was about to leave the room when she heard a shout from downstairs, "No!"

It was Jake.

That must be what had awakened her.

Had someone entered the house? An intruder bent on theft? Or, more likely, a reporter? But, no, she was about to grab for Mark's metal baseball bat when she heard Jake muttering, "Name: Jacob Lloyd Dawson. Rank: captain. Identification number . . . No! Oh, Jesus, please, not the knife again!"

She dropped the bat and ran down the stairs. In her bare feet, she approached the living room unnoticed. But maybe Jake wouldn't have heard her anyway. The television was still on, some old war movie, and she could see by the lighted screen that he was flailing about on the floor, wearing nothing but a pair of boxer briefs.

Because of all the weight he'd lost, she could see

his ribs. And scars. Many, many scars. Not just on his leg.

She stopped and leaned against the door frame. *Oh, my God! Look at him! Oh, my God!*

He was moaning now, clutching frantically at his injured eye. The eye patch was on the floor beside him, along with the balled-up sheet and blanket and the pillow that she'd laid out for him earlier. He must have rolled off the couch in the midst of this nightmare, or whatever it was. Sometimes Mark suffered from night terrors. Was that what this was? Or something more?

"Jacob," she said. "Are you all right?"

He jackknifed to a sitting position and then, in one fluid motion, up into a low crouch. The sound that came out of his mouth was almost feral.

"You're just dreaming, Jacob. It's not real," she said softly, the same way the doctor had told her to approach Mark when he was still in that half-sleep state. She stepped forward, intending to help him up and onto the sofa. That position must be killing his leg muscles.

He was looking at her, but she could tell he wasn't really seeing her. He was seeing something, though.

"You vicious bastard!" he yelled and tackled her to the floor. Instantly, he had her pinned down with his hands against her shoulders. "Tables are turned now, motherfucker."

She was able to free her own hands, but, instead of attempting to shove him off, she framed his face with her palms and said, "Jacob, honey, it's me. Sally. Your wife."

He blinked at her, still not awake, but disconcerted. She noticed that though his injured eye didn't appear to move, his eyelid did when he blinked, which seemed odd to her.

And then the town bells rang the hour. *Bong, bong! Ding-dong! Clang, clang!*

He blinked some more, staring down at her with shock as he realized what he must have done. "Jesus," he whispered, and it sounded like a prayer.

"It's all right, Jacob. Really. I'm all right. You're all right." She pulled his face down and took his full weight on top of her as he released a breathy exhale of relief.

When she felt a wetness on her neck, she knew that there was something else his bad eye could do, besides blink. It could weep.

There was hope in that, wasn't there?

Back to square one . . .

*J*ake stuck close to home for the next few days, but he was as busy as if he had a full-time job. With Sally gone from four a.m. to one or two p.m., the empty house (except for three loud kids) became his office.

He spent as much time as he could getting to know his boys. Giving all their bikes a tune-up. Hitting balls and showing them how to pitch. (Luke was as bad as his coach had said, but he was improving.) Teaching them all how to tie knots, especially Mark, who was trying to earn the badge and was excited for his next meeting when he could show the scoutmaster what he could do.

This latter project called attention to his nailless fingers which fascinated his sons. Actually, the nails were one-quarter grown back by now. He didn't want to lie; so, he just told them, "Sometimes bad things happen, but don't worry. The good thing about fingernails is that they do grow back."

Yeah, right. "Bad things happen." What a hokey thing to say. And, man, what I could tell them about bad things in this world! Which he wouldn't, of course.

"Just like your second teeth, which are growing in, short stuff," he said, giving Luke a playful jab in the chin.

Luke flashed him his gap-toothed smile, and Jake's heart about melted. The kid was adorable. They all were. And they were so accepting of his just bouncing back into their lives after all this time.

"Will your eye grow back . . . better?" Luke wanted to know.

"Probably not, but it might get better than it is now, if I decide to have more surgeries."

"Are you afraid?" Matt asked.

Jake wasn't sure what he meant. "Of what?"

"Surgery. I might have to have a surgery. On my tonsils," Matt revealed in a shaky voice. "Cecily

Dolan says they cut you open with a sharp knife and there's blood everywhere and it hurts real bad. Sometimes they miss and take out the tongue, too. Her daddy is a doctor."

"Cecily is full of sh—shells. They put you to sleep and you don't feel a thing. Afterward, you can suck on cherry popsicles till your tongue turns red and eat as much ice cream as you want."

Matt smiled, while Mark and Luke frowned with concentration. Jake could tell the other two were wondering if they should ask for an operation, too.

But today the boys were off for a previously scheduled all-day scout field trip to the Graveyard of the Atlantic Museum in Hatteras. Sally had offered to cancel their participation since Jake had so recently come home, but Jake had been adamant in wanting them to resume their normal lives, or as normal as they could with the media spotlight still hovering over him, and therefore their lives, too.

Jake spent the morning at the kitchen table culling through the dozens of text and voice mail messages that had accumulated, taking notes along the way. Using a special military-secure app on his phone, he forwarded the list of media ones to his liaison, Major Durand, who was in daily contact with him. To Jake's shock and dismay, he was informed via text message today from Durand that he would be coming for a Labor Day weekend visit, just to make sure Jake was doing as well as he claimed to be. Not that he said so in those specific words.

Immediately, Jake called Durand at his DC office and said, "You can't come here. There's no place to stay."

"Not to worry. Lieutenant Bernstein has offered me a room at his uncle's home."

"Izzie?" *The traitor!*

Jake had already called Mayor Ferguson declining any attention being paid to him during the holiday festivities. In addition, he'd told her that he wanted the townsfolk to remove all those bleepin' yellow ribbons.

Even though he'd thought he was being polite using *bleepin'*, rather than the more graphic word he was thinking, Doreen was offended. "Why don't you tell them yourself? They're only trying to show their love." She didn't add Sally's usual tagline of "ass," but she was probably thinking it.

"I know that," he conceded, "but it's embarrassing."

"Live with it, boy. You're a hero."

He could have argued that point, too, but instead he'd agreed to make nice with the elderly mayor by being one of the judges in the Lollypalooza talent contest. Not that he had any intention of doing so. Maybe he would skip town by then.

And now he had to deal with this pole-up-the-ass military dude. He suspected that Durand was going to show up like Jake's rucked-out guardian angel. "You're just going to call more attention to me," he complained.

"No. I'll be in civilian attire. Just a weekend of

R & R. I even bought a Hawaiian shirt and surfer shorts."

Oh, my Lord! "Since this is supposed to be a vacay-type visit, is your wife coming with you?"

"I'm not married."

Surprise, surprise. Who would have you?

"But still looking. Ha, ha, ha."

Suddenly, an image of Gus's hot-cha-cha mother came to mind, and Jake cringed. *Note to self: warn Gus to keep his mother under wraps.*

"We can just say I'm a friend of Lieutenant Bernstein's."

Yeah, like anyone's going to believe that! On the other hand, maybe you and Izzie can cruise the singles bars. I can't wait to make that suggestion to the traitor. "You better start calling him Izzie if you want to pull that off."

"Roger that," Durand said.

To which, Jake rolled his one eye.

"Also, I'll have a team of agents incognito around the town. The media will be there in droves trying to get at you."

That was just great! In a town that thrived on gossip and minding each other's business, there was no way they wouldn't recognize strangers in their midst. Yeah, it was tourist season, and there were bound to be the usual strangers, but Bell Cove-ites had a nose for strangers with ill intent . . . their words, not his. And, yes, they put newshounds in that category, unless it was publicity they were seeking.

"I still say we should schedule one carefully or-chestrated media event where you can answer a few questions and say that that is the only inter-view you will be granting."

Carefully orchestrated, Jake repeated to himself. He could imagine what that would involve. A love fest for Balakistan and Nazim bin Jamil.

Not gonna happen! "Sorry. I'm not ready for that. I *am* going to talk to Laura Atler, the editor of the local weekly tabloid this afternoon, an old friend. Nothing political. Just a glad-to-be-home vanilla feature."

"Whoa, whoa, whoa! Wait. I'm not sure that's a good idea. You need more prep first."

"No. I can handle this. Don't worry. I won't up-set your political applecart." *Not yet anyway.* Where that last thought came from, he wasn't sure. He had no inclination to become a hot football between the US and some foreign nation.

After that, he called Izzie. "What the hell? You're coming to Bell Cove? And becoming bunkmates with the asshole? Why? Is the Army making you come to babysit me? Or do you and Durand have something going on?"

"What? I can't come to sip a few suds with my best bud?"

"Bite me," Jake said. "By the way, I'm meeting Laura Atler for lunch today. She asked me if 'that loser Izzie Bernstein' is coming to Bell Cove any-time soon. Says she has something to return to you."

"Uh-oh."

Izzie and Laura had had a thing going on in high school and even into college, but something had come up to break off their relationship. And later Laura got engaged to some other dude. As far as Jake knew, that engagement had ended rather dramatically, or so Jake had heard on one of his leaves. "Any idea what she wants to return to you?"

"No idea," Izzie said.

He was clearly lying. "Well, well, well. Do I smell a relationship brewing?" Jake teased.

"Not a chance!" Izzie declared. "Maybe I won't come to Bell Cove, after all."

Jake laughed.

But then Izzie turned the tables on him by asking, "Speaking of relationships, has this been a commando week for you and Sally?"

Jake had made the mistake years ago, soon after his marriage, of confiding in his best friend—okay, bragging—that he and his wife had enjoyed a unique "commando" game week while he'd been home on leave. As in, they'd gone commando the entire time, him without briefs and her without panties, so that they could have sex anywhere, anytime. And whoo-boy did they ever! Jake still had dreams about the porch swing, and the outdoor shower, and the bed of his pickup truck on Lookout Cove, and the lighthouse restroom, and . . .

Which was nothing compared to the time that he'd heard that chewing cinnamon gum before engaging in oral sex could produce really amazing results on the receiving party. That leave home had been remarkably hot, in more ways than one.

Enough of that! "No, Izzie, we are not going commando with three kids in the house." *And, frankly, the sex has been nonexistent, period.* But Izzie didn't need to know that.

"See, all the more reason why I should never get married and breed a bunch of Mini-Mes. The commando game, though. I'm saving that for a special babe, minus the wedding ring."

"Good luck with that."

They both laughed, and that's how they ended the call.

Jake took a shower in the outdoor stall then, and hardly thought about those other times with Sally. Who was he kidding? He got turned on just thinking about them and took care of business in the only way that had been available to him in recent times. He dressed in black running shorts, a plain white T-shirt, and sockless athletic shoes. His hair, which had been shaved when he first arrived at the hospital in Germany, was growing out and would soon need a cut if he was going to keep it military short, which was debatable at this point. Wearing the pirate patch today because the eye felt irritated after spending too much time in the sun with the kids sans protection, he grabbed for his truck keys and prepared to go into town to meet Laura at the Cracked Crab for lunch. It would be his first foray out of his neighborhood in the daytime hours.

He left off the brace for the few hours he would be gone, but he did take the blasted cane with him. Although he didn't start formal rehab until next week at the facility Gus had recommended, he'd been working with his old free weights out in the garage, and the leg felt slightly better. Still, in the old days, Jake would have jogged the five blocks to the town square, easy peasy. He loved to run. Unfortunately, that might not ever be an option again. Although there were vets with more severe injuries who managed to run marathons, he reminded himself. He was playing it one day at a time.

He waved to the security guard who set aside the barricade for him as he drove down the street. Tentative plans were for the barricade to go down after Labor Day, but that depended on Durand and his Pentagon cohorts and whether the media would have given up by then. As it was, he was pretty sure those were news vultures following him in a plain panel truck and a black sedan. Just in case, he zigzagged through the neighborhood and down some alleys. He lost whoever they were.

If he had turned left at the end of the road, he would have shortly been at Bell Forge, but a right turn went past the Rutledge Christmas tree and landscape business, through the residential area, heading toward the town center. He cut through the back of the Rutledge property and reemerged onto the main road for town. On a man-made bluff along the way stood Chimes, the mansion built by the Conti brothers, original founders of the bell-making factory, and now owned by one of their descendants, Gabe Conti, an architect. When he got to the town square with its central parklet and gazebo he saw that it remained the same, and yet was different. There was no longer any on-street parking, but instead vehicles were directed to two parking lots one street over on either side of Beach Road, or Highway 12, that passed through the entire Outer Banks. And while the old standbys were still there—the two churches, a hardware store, Abe's deli, a quilt shop, Sally's bakery, several restaurants, including the Cracked Crab, and gift shops—there were some new boutiques and specialty stores.

After parking, he walked with his cane along the side street and came out on the side of Our Lady by the Sea Church. The handicap ramp there seemed like a sign to him, pretty much saying he had no excuse to avoid going in.

The church was empty as he slid into the back pew. Even if he'd lost his religion, he had to admit there was something peaceful about being in a church, and this was an especially beautiful one with its marble pillars and stained glass windows. There must have been a wedding recently because the altar was decorated with numerous baskets of red roses and fluffy white baby's breath. He recognized the latter because his mother had a huge bush of the stuff planted in her backyard. She'd always said that anyone could make a beautiful bouquet in a vase, no matter the flowers, as long as you used baby's breath as filler.

What an odd thing for him to recall!

But then he also noticed a huge yellow ribbon
tied around the feet of St. Michael the Archangel
in a recessed side altar where his statue was fighting a dragon. St. Michael was the patron saint of
warriors—all fighting men and those serving in
dangerous situations, whether they be soldiers or
policemen, or mariners since this was an ocean-
related church. His mother had given him a St. Michael medal on a heavy chain when he was last
deployed. Fourteen-karat gold, she'd emphasized
at the time.

More memories of his mother!

The jewelry was probably sitting in a bedroom
drawer of Nazim's villa, or wherever the hell he
was living these days now that he had a cabinet
position in Balakistan. Or else he'd melted it down
with all the Balaki treasure he'd pilfered over the
years. Men in that part of the world, even in remote
tribal villages, tended to shower their women with
gold and silver and precious gems, considering it a
form of portable wealth, which could be taken with
them on the spur of the moment whenever the terrorist du jour hit their villages.

He thought about going up and removing the yellow ribbon from St. Michael's feet, but wasn't sure if
the ribbon was there for other lost servicemen, not
just him. Plus, he wouldn't want to be caught in the
act. Talk about a media circus. He could just see the
headline, "Long Lost Soldier Steals from Church."

Despite his lack of religious fervor, old habits

died hard, and he bowed his head, praying silently, *Thank You, Lord, for bringing me home.*

Glancing at his watch, he saw that it was almost one o'clock. He should get going if he wanted to be on time for his lunch appointment with Laura. When he came out of the church, though, he saw that his "stalkers" had caught up with him. The truck which now somehow sprouted a satellite dish and the sedan were blocking the side street. Knowing Bell Cove, Sheriff Henderson would be here soon with his ticket pad in hand.

One guy with a bald head and a salt-and-pepper beard, wearing a golf shirt and dark slacks, motioned to a camera guy behind him and stepped in front of the ramp. "Carl Brandt from CNN. Welcome home, Captain Dawson. Can you tell us how you survived for three years in Balakistan? Did you have help from the Qadir tribal leaders? Do you resent the fact that they didn't send you home sooner?"

Jake schooled his face not to show any reaction to that incendiary question.

A thirtysomething woman, who looked harried and not too happy to have been sent to the Outer Banks, probably because she'd been sitting around for days, twiddling her thumbs as she tried to get an interview with him, said, "Celeste Novak, *Time Magazine.* We'd like to do a cover story on you and your family, tentatively titled 'Hero Comes Home.' I'm sure you're familiar with the importance of our magazine and its international circulation."

She said that as if he should be honored.

He ignored both of them and continued down the ramp, about to go around them, not an easy task when he had to rely on his cane to keep his balance.

"Hey," the CNN guy inquired, pushing a microphone in front of his face. "What are you hiding?"

"Yeah," Ms. Important Magazine Reporter added. "Why are you blocking all our calls? We're not out to do a hatchet job. We just want to know about your experience."

"Why are you wearing an eye patch? And that leg looks gnarly." Back to CNN guy. "How did you get those injuries, Captain? And how about the two soldiers who traveled with you to Afghanistan? How did they die?"

Jake gritted his teeth and refused to say a word. He was out on the street now, as a means of getting around the newshounds, and they were beginning to draw a crowd. Luckily, Sheriff Henderson showed up then, as expected, and, yes, he was carrying his yellow ticket tablet when he exited his police car.

"Are these folks bothering you, Jake?" the sheriff asked.

"Nah. I'm all right," he said.

"But we can't have people parking willy-nilly on our streets, creating a traffic hazard. Didn't you people see that sign? Maybe you folks speak a different language up there in New York City." The expression on his face when he made reference to the Big Apple made it sound like another world, a distasteful one. He glanced at Jake and, with a straight face though he was clearly joking, *an inside joke*, remarked, "City slickers!"

"We were only here for a few minutes," CNN guy protested. His cameraman was already packing up his gear.

But Henderson was not to be deterred. He was writing down the license numbers of both vehicles. "Let's see your licenses and registrations, please. And be quick about it. There are cars behind you that can't get through. The fools are backing up, probably more city slickers, and those idiots could very well cause an accident, which would be your fault. Then I'd have to arrest you." The doleful expression on his face at that prospect wasn't fooling anyone. "Of course, we don't have a jail here in Bell Cove. So I'd have to lock you in the basement of The Honey Hole, Delbert Brown's fish shop, until the magistrate hits town on Monday. Hope you like the smell of mackerel."

The woman muttered something about small-town crooks posing as crime stoppers.

"What did you say?" Henderson asked.

Jake mouthed "Thank you" to Henderson as he passed by and made his way to the Cracked Crab. Hopefully, the word would spread among the news media about how these two were treated by an overzealous local sheriff, and the rest of the horde would be more cautious in crossing the line.

Along the way around the square, Jake was stopped repeatedly by folks he'd known his entire life, but hadn't seen for more than three years. They all wanted to shake his hand and thank him for his service, but then added a few words. Some offered sympathy on his mother's death. Others expressed a wish that he would be sticking around for good. Still others gave him news on sons or daughters or nephews or nieces that he knew from high school or earlier—marriages, births, divorces, new jobs.

He would have liked to stop in Sally's bakery, which was only a few doors down from the restaurant, but he was already ten minutes late because of his stop-and-go walk. When he went inside the Cracked Crab, Laura was already seated at a far table. She stood and waved for him to come in, bypassing the hostess. Once again, along the way, his progress was stopped repeatedly by people greeting him warmly. Not one of them asked an uncomfortable question. Yet.

He shook hands with Laura, who wasn't satisfied with that. She took his face in hand and gave a quick kiss to one cheek, then the other. Then, leaning back slightly, her hands on his upper arms, she perused. "Hey, big guy! Looks like you been through the wars."

"You could say that," he replied and dropped down into the chair, with his back facing the room. Laura sat down, too, opposite him.

She, on the other hand, looked good. A platinum blonde with masses of wavy curls, a petite body shown off in a white sleeveless blouse over tight black calf-length pants, and white sandals. In fact, she looked lots better than she had back in high school when she'd been shy . . . a bit pudgy and plagued with the usual teenage acne. He couldn't wait to tell Izzie about the transformation. Izzie must have seen beyond the physical appearances back then because he sure as hell had been crazy about her. Somehow, somewhere, post–high school, the love connection had been broken. Maybe just a case of absence not making the heart grow fonder when they'd been separated by the distance of different colleges.

He noticed right off that there was a recording device sitting on the small table.

"Do you mind?"

He thought a moment, then said, "As long as you turn it off, if I ask you to." Frankly, he didn't intend to divulge anything that might be newsworthy, or objectionable to the higher-ups at the DOD.

After they placed their orders—the restaurant featured a mix of Italian and seafood cuisine—and exchanged a few pleasantries, Laura clicked on the device.

"Captain Dawson, welcome home and thank you for your service."

He nodded.

"Where've you been the last three years?"

Talk about blunt. "Afghanistan."

"In a cave? Doing what?"

"That's classified information."

"How did you get those injuries, and exactly what are they? I can see that your eye and leg have sustained some damage. Are there other injuries that we can't see?"

"Whoa, that's a lot of questions. The eye and leg are the most serious. As to how . . . shit happens when a soldier is on a live op."

"How about PTSD?"

What? "Why would you ask that?"

She shrugged. "Just that it appears to be the norm for POWs, doesn't it?"

"I believe the official news release from the Pentagon mentions that I was MIA, not POW." Was that ambiguous enough to save him from telling an outright lie?

"So, how does it feel to be home? Were you surprised at all the yellow ribbons the townsfolk put up for you?"

"It's wonderful to be home. And, yes, I was surprised by all the yellow ribbons. I didn't realize so many people cared." Well, that answer should satisfy Sally, at least, and nullify her disgust at his previous reaction to the yellow ribbons. "It's time to take them down, though. Time to look for another hero."

"Oh, not until after Labor Day weekend, at least. I hear that the Army is sending its marching band to take place in the parade."

What? That was news to him. He would have something to say to Durand about that as soon as he got home. Holy crap!

"And you'll be riding in the lead convertible with the honorary parade marshal, Phillip Franklin."

"Who?"

"That World War II vet who was a POW for five years before becoming a US senator. I think he retired about ten years ago."

"Are you kidding? That dude must be ninety years old."

"Ninety-one." She smiled. "We tried to get Bradley Cooper who played Chris Kyle, that Navy SEAL in the movie *American Sniper*, but Cooper is a hot commodity these days since he was such a hit in *A Star Is Born* last year. We couldn't even get through to his agent."

On and on the interview went, mostly with general questions about what he was doing now that he was home, his family's reaction to his homecoming, what his plans for the future were—mostly a local view of a returning hero, rather than a gotcha-type journalism piece about the military involvement in Afghanistan or his opinion of the new Balaki government.

When they were done, Laura turned off the recorder and looked at him directly. "I'm no idiot, Jake. I might be the editor of a small-town paper that looks hokey to the outside world, but I know when I'm being snowed. Promise me this, old friend. When you're ready to spill your guts, give me first dibs on the story."

He thought about denying her assertion, but then he nodded. "Okay, here's a headline for you. The bells of Bell Cove played a key part in getting me home, or at least helping me to survive until I could come home. When I was at my lowest, I seemed to hear these damn bells in my head—the two churches, the town hall tower—all of them distinctive and clearly Bell Cove. They pulled me up and made me stronger. Hokey, huh?"

"Oh, my God!" Laura actually had tears in her eyes. "The Sounds of Bell Cove Brought Hero Home."

He would have rolled his eyes if he had two eyes to roll. Somehow, rolling one eye didn't have quite the same effect. Trying for a lighter tone, he said, "So, Izzie is coming home for Labor Day. I gave him your message."

"And? Bet he was overjoyed. He probably threatened to change his mind about coming home." At Jake's heated face, she hooted. "He did! The idiot!"

"Mind telling me what it is that you want to give him?"

"Not a chance! I'm relishing the prospect of seeing his face when he gets my 'gift.'"

Jake was surprised when he left the restaurant to find that he'd been there for an hour. He was feeling good about the way the day had gone. His first foray into the public hadn't been as bad as he'd expected. Thus, he was smiling when he entered Sweet Thangs, Sally's bakery.

He just looked around at first. It was the same space as the bakery he'd grown up seeing here on the square, but totally redecorated. A sunny mural depicting the lighthouse beach scene covered one whole wall. There were a half-dozen small ice-cream-parlor-type tables and chairs. A long glass case showcased the bakery items of the day—all the monster cookies that Sally had mentioned, some artisan breads and rolls, cakes, and such. Another cold case held six flavors of homemade ice cream, including the local flavor of the month, Peach Passion, with fruit directly off the trees from a Rutledge orchard over on the mainland.

There were only a few customers in the shop at the moment, the lunch-hour rush being over, and one clerk, who looked about high school age, manning the counter. No sign of Sally. Maybe she'd gone home.

Jake waited his turn, and before he could introduce himself, the girl said, "Captain Dawson! Your wife thought you might stop by after your lunch with Ms. Atler. She's in the kitchen. You can go through this door."

He was smiling at the look of awe on the young girl's face, a sort of hero worship that he in no way deserved and was really kind of embarrassing, when he went through the swinging door.

And saw Sally leaning against the frame of the open back door leading to the alley.

Staring up into the eyes—*two of them, dammit*—of a buff guy in a T-shirt and sweats. He wasn't touching her, but then he didn't have to. His gaze said it all.

Jake didn't feel the red tide of rage rising, like it had at the barbecue when the doctor had touched her arm. This was more of a sadness. A soul-deep acknowledgement of how far apart he and Sally had grown.

Sally looked over then, noticing him, and the guilt on her face told him more than any words could who this guy was.

He turned on his heels and limped through the shop and out the front door. He heard Sally call after him, but he didn't stop. He inhaled and exhaled several times once outside, his chest so tight he could hardly breathe.

Through the open door of the shop, he could see Sally had been stopped inside by a customer who wanted to place a special order. Which gave Jake time to head for home.

Oh, God! Do I even have a home anymore? he thought.

But then he reminded himself that he was a soldier, a man taught to fight the hardest battles. Was he really going to give up so easily? Wasn't Sally, and his marriage, worth the effort?

On the other hand, if Jake wanted to be a real hero, he would let Sally go. She deserved better than what he'd become, better than what he'd been before, for that matter.

But there was that legend about the Dawson men. One love, for life. What a sad future he'd have without her! Or his kids—oh, God!—his kids!

Jake had a lot of thinking to do.

Chapter 10

Honey wasn't home . . .

Sally was in the kitchen after the lunch-hour rush, making a list of supplies to be replenished, the baking menu for the next day, and a work schedule for herself and her four employees: José, an assistant baker; along with one full-time clerk, the indispensable and always reliable Mary Lou Tonelli; and two part-timers, college students at home for the summer. Plus, she needed to plan for special bakery items to provide during the Lollypalooza weekend, the theme of which seemed to waver from pirates, celebrating the recent shipwreck gold discovery, to patriotic military, celebrating her very own reluctant hero.

The OBX oldies station on the sound system that played both in the shop and back here was featuring 1970s beach music this afternoon. Suddenly, Sally had an image of a summer day in Central Park and two bands warring over whether West Coast or Southern girls were the best. It was where she'd first met Jake.

She smiled, sadly, at the memory and found herself singing along. She still had a good voice, as evidenced by José, who glanced her way and raised two flour-coated hands from the massive bowl where he'd just set aside several rounds of sourdough to prove for a special event later today, giving her two thumbs-up.

Under ordinary circumstances, with the boys being gone all day on a field trip, she would have spent the extra hours on-site getting caught up. But with Jake being home, she felt pulled in several directions. A million things to do! So many worries! She would need to hire another clerk and perhaps another baker if she was going to be away from the shop as much as it appeared she would have to be now that her husband was home. So far, Jake had been understanding, but it wasn't fair to him.

She heard a light tapping on the back door, which was open to let out some of the heat. Stepping inside was Kevin, whom she hadn't seen or talked to since Jake got back. Supposedly, he'd been out on the salvaging boat searching a new site in the Atlantic for shipwreck treasure.

She got up and went over to greet him. "Kevin, how are you?"

He gave her a quick hug and a kiss on the cheek before saying, "How are *you*? I've been worried."

"I'm okay. Surviving."

"That doesn't sound too promising."

She shrugged. Oddly, this man, whom she'd been about to have an intimate relationship with—this good-looking man—seemed no more than a friend to her now. Maybe fate had intervened at just the right moment. "Can I ask you something in confidence, Kevin?"

"Sure."

"As ex-military, trained in survival scenarios, how could a man end up with no fingernails?"

He frowned at her. "Other injuries?"

She nodded. "A damaged eye and badly injured leg. Lots of old and new scars."

The alarm on his face was telling.

"Yeah, I'm thinking the same thing."

"The eye and leg injuries could have happened when he landed or crashed or in any number of circumstances. But the nails . . ."

"I know."

"Do you want me to talk with him?"

"Oh, my goodness, no!" She suspected that Jake had been told of her dating Kevin. What would he think—how would he react if Kevin approached him? "He has all the help he needs, I think. Tons of appointments coming up, doctors, hospitals, therapists, rehab, and he's on the phone every day with someone at the Pentagon."

"The Pentagon?" Kevin arched his brows at her. "Seriously? The Pentagon?"

"Yeah, a Major Durand."

"Do you want me to look him up for you?"

She thought about his offer and was tempted, but then shook her head. No, Jake would not appreciate her going behind his back.

Kevin had to be wondering why she didn't just ask Jake herself. Hah! He clammed up at the least questions about his experiences of the last few years. Somehow, it seemed traitorous of her to mention this to someone who was a stranger to Jake. And it was embarrassing to her, as well.

"Anyway, how's the treasure hunt going?" she asked, going for a change of subject.

"Slow. We're just setting up the new site. Farther out in the ocean than the last one. About seventy-five miles."

"Is it still the Three Saints that you're looking for?"

"Yep."

There was a reason why the Atlantic Ocean off the Outer Banks was known as the Graveyard of the Atlantic. Because of the treacherous shoals and frequents storms, some hurricane strength, thousands of ships had gone down out there. Among them were the Three Saints, a Portuguese convoy that sunk in the 1850s. Their cargo was worth millions. The Three Saints had been the initial target of the salvaging company Kevin worked for. The treasure they found belonged to an entirely different shipwreck, which left the Three Saints still undiscovered.

Just then she heard the swish of the door to the shop and there stood Jake. Despite the cane he held in his one hand, he looked almost like his old self, wearing running shorts and a white T-shirt. He was still too thin, but she could swear he'd already regained some of his old weight. He even had some color from being outdoors with the boys so much. The happy expression on his face, something that had been absent since his return, faded suddenly to questioning, then grim.

It was obvious what he was seeing and what he was thinking.

"Jake," she called out, but he'd already turned and was going back through the shop.

She followed after him, but Nancy Dreyer, one of the planners for the Lollypalooza festivities, wanted to talk with her about an order involving a cake in the shape of a treasure chest with gold coin cookies. By the time Sally was able to get away, Jake was gone.

"Oh, shit!" Kevin said, joining her on the sidewalk outside the shop. "This is my fault. I shouldn't have come by here. Let me go catch up with him and straighten him out about what he saw—or thought he saw."

"No, it's not your fault. Don't worry. I'll clear it up myself. No biggie."

But was it?

After Kevin left, she finished up her work at the shop and told José that she would be in that evening to prepare all the bread doughs for tomorrow morning, thus relieving him to spend time with his visiting daughter, who lived in Nags Head with his divorced wife and her new husband.

When she got home, she was surprised to see that Jake's truck was missing. Still, as she went inside, she called out an idiotically hopeful "Honey, I'm home." He was hopeful that, after calming down, he wasn't as upset by what he'd seen with her and Kevin as she expected. But a quick look around showed that he hadn't returned after his trip to town. His laptop, various notebooks, and a calendar were strewn about the kitchen table where he must have been working this morning.

She called Jake's cell number, but it went directly to voice mail. It was three o'clock, and the kids didn't need to be picked up in the school parking lot until five; so, she decided to make a special dinner, one Jake used to love in the old days. He'd ordered it every time they went out to eat in a restaurant. Back then, Sally hadn't been much of a cook. It was linguine with white clam sauce and a crusty baguette she'd brought home from the bakery for dipping in the rich, garlicky juice. Joe had given her a bag of fresh clams last night.

While she prepared the meal, stopping every few minutes to make notes on a tablet sitting on the counter for Lollypalooza monster cookie ideas, she kept calling Jake's cell. To no avail.

Finally, around four, she got a text from him. I'll pick up the boys.

Immediately, she texted back, Where are you? I've been worried.

She got no return text. Instead, Recipient Unavailable.

Was Jake out of the area, so soon after texting her? Or had he blocked her?

The ass!

Dinner was ready by five; so, Sally set everything on warm and waited. And waited. And waited.

At five fifteen, she expected the truck to pull into the driveway and the kids to come barreling into the kitchen bubbling with excitement over their excursion. The school was only three miles from here. At five thirty, she figured the bus might have been a little late. By five forty-five, she grew worried. At six, when she finally heard the roar of the truck's motor and the shouts of the kids, she was alternately relieved and angry.

They came running into the kitchen, giving her a quick hug, then rushing into the living room for their two-hour video game fix. They were permitted only two hours per day during the summer, and there would be a one-hour limit come fall on school days, after homework, according to the rules Sally insisted upon. In the midst of their chatter, she caught the words *burger and fries* and *The Bay Shack*. When Jake sauntered in, he carried a doggie bag with The Bay Shack imprint on it.

"You took them out to eat? Without letting me know?"

"We brought you some food, too," Jake said, plopping the bag on the table, as if she should be happy at the surprise. Just then, he took a look around the kitchen, saw what she'd prepared, and said, "Uh-oh!"

"Listen up, oh, clueless one," she said, trying to keep her voice down to control her fury. She put her hands, which were shaking, on the table and leaned forward. "I get that you were upset, but you didn't give me a chance to explain. Kevin just stopped by to see if I was all right."

"No, you listen," he said, seething back at her, his hands on the opposite side of the table, leaning forward, too. Their faces almost met in the middle. "I don't give a damn if you want to continue your affair with good ol' Kev, but at least have the decency to do it in private."

"Affair? Affair?" she sputtered.

"Shhh!" Jake cautioned, looking toward the living room where the creepy ambient cave sounds of Minecraft could be heard at a high volume.

"Don't you shush me," she said, although she lowered her voice. "Where were you all afternoon?"

"Driving around."

"For three hours?"

"Yeah. I was pretty upset, but I calmed down. That's why I took the kids out to eat and brought you food. A peace offering. Some peace, huh?"

"Here's a news flash, Jacob. I never had sex with Kevin or any other man since we've been married, but, if I decided to, I sure as hell wouldn't need permission from you."

She could see that she'd startled him, and he started to apologize. "I'm sorry if I overreacted—"

"*If?* I'll give you *if*, Mister Ass-of-the-Month!" With that statement, she went over and lifted the pot of linguine with clam sauce and dumped the contents in the sink. "Thank you very much, Sally," she said in a fake male voice, "for preparing my favorite meal, even though you were scared to death when the kids were an hour and a half late. Thanks for the fucking phone call. And, oh, thanks for worrying that I might jump off a cliff. Like I ever would! Ha, ha, ha."

"Are you crazy?"

"Maybe. Or maybe I'm just regaining my sanity. By the way, who's Major Durand from the Pentagon?"

He had been gaping at the mess in the sink. The pasta and sauce could go down the disposal, but the shells would have to be picked up. His head jerked up suddenly as he realized what she'd asked him. "How do you know that name?"

"It popped up on the caller ID of your phone a few days ago when that oddball ring came on. You know, brr-ing, brr-ing, brr-ing."

"That brr-ing, brr-ing, brr-ing caller ID doesn't come up automatically," he replied with a decided note of sarcasm. But then he tilted his head in question and stared at her suspiciously, as if she'd been deliberately invading his privacy. "His calls are on a private, secure app."

A private, secure app with the Pentagon. Interesting. "Yeah, well, you were out in the garage lifting your stupid weights, and the phone kept buzzing, and I thought it might be important, so I punched a bunch of buttons till it stopped and the caller ID came up. Big fat hairy deal!" She glowered at him.

"And you never bothered to mention it to me?"

"So sue me!"

Jake hated that expression. It was what people said when they lost an argument. "Calm down."

"No, you calm down, you clueless moron. And don't worry. I didn't read any of your precious secret messages."

"Good."

Sally felt as if the threads that had held her together the past few weeks were frayed and beginning to unravel. Any minute now she would start bawling. And so she picked up her car keys and purse and headed for the door. "I'm going back to the shop where I'm wanted and needed *and* appreciated. See you later. Maybe."

"Sally, don't go. Let's talk."

But she was beyond talking now. She slammed the door after her.

Even clueless men know that a slammed door makes a statement . . .

Jake let Sally go.

And he didn't follow after her.

Or call to check up on her. He trusted that she was at her shop. At this point, if she'd remained celibate for three years after he "died," like she'd said, then she wasn't about to hop in the sack with a guy just to spite him. He hoped.

Instead, he let the boys play an extra hour of video games, despite his wife's rule. "So sue me!" he murmured, reiterating Sally's lame exclamation. He actually didn't disagree with her TV and video game limits, but sometimes rules were made to be broken. This was one of those times.

If anyone disagrees, they can friggin' sue me.

While the boys played, he started to clean up the mess in the kitchen, thinking the whole time. In some convoluted way—*a clueless man's brain works that way at times*—Jake decided that Sally's bombshell reveal about her celibacy had been like throwing down the gauntlet. Yeah, they had a million problems, foremost being his wavering thoughts on Bell Cove and on his marriage and on his future in the military, which raised two million questions that needed to be answered, but her never taking a lover, not even once, well, that threw a whole lot of other questions into the mix.

Like, did he still love Sally?

Hell, yes!

Did she still love him?

Up in the air.

Did he want to stay married to Sally? No, the overriding question in that regard was: Would she be better off without him?

Probably.

But if he gave up on his marriage, what about the kids?

He was just getting to know the boys and loved them with a ferocity that made his heart ache at just the prospect of giving them up.

On the other hand, if he and Sally were to separate or divorce, that didn't mean he would sever all connection with his children, did it?

A fly-by father, that's what I'd be. Nope. No way!

Then, fight for your wife and your family, dammit.

Which brings us to my military career. My being assigned away from home, whether DC or the Middle East, was the bone of contention that splintered my marriage from the get-go.

So, give it up. Stay in Bell Cove. Work on what's most important.

And do what? Become a commercial fisherman like my dad?

There are worse things.

Yeah, I can see it now. A one-eyed cripple hauling nets.

Stop the pity party. Wounded vets are doing amazing things in the workplace. Find something you can love, or at least live with, to save what's most important.

Easier said than done.

Suck it up, soldier, and fight for what you want.

So many questions! So few answers!

Blah, blah, blah.

Where's Dr. Sheila when I need her?

Maybe it's time to contact that local shrink.

Maybe I'm losing my friggin' mind.

Unfortunately, his father dropped by in the middle of his convoluted thought process.

"Uh," his father said, taking in the slop in the sink and the clam shells he was dropping into the trash bin he'd pulled over. "An accident?"

"You could say that."

"Trouble in paradise?"

"You could say that." Jake turned on the disposal three times to handle it all. Then he pushed the now-closed trash bin with his right foot over to its spot by the door. "What's up, Dad?"

His father blushed.

Which caused Jake's brain to go on red alert. *Last time Dad blushed was when he told me about condoms. I was twelve at the time. Oh, Lord! Do I have to do that with my boys?*

"Mike and I have an idea."

"Okay." *Not the condoms then. Whew! But this oughta be good.*

"We'd like to take the boys for an overnight . . . actually, a weekend out on the boat. Fishing. Cooking fresh fish on board. Swimming in the coves. Board games. That kind of thing."

"You and Old Mike? And three kids?"

"What? You think me and Mike are too old?"

"That's not what I said." Although, as his dad stood there, wearing ratty old fishing pants and a plaid shirt with one of the buttons missing, Jake noticed how tired he looked. Jake knew that he and Old Mike had been up since dawn, fishing for blues. Maybe it was time his father cut back. Had he considered retirement? He was sixty-two, after all. Did he need the money? Would he sell the boat? Or was he still holding out for Jake to take over?

More questions!

"You implied it."

"Huh?" Jake had lost track of their conversation.

"You implied that I'm too old to take care of your three boys out on the boat for one blasted weekend. You don't trust me."

"It's not that. I just find it kind of strange. Your timing and all that."

"Actually, it's all about timing. Labor Day is coming up soon, and the boys will be busy. The scouts are going to be in the parade, you know, and they have a float to prepare. Then, after Labor Day, they'll be busy with school. Plus, the weather starts to get iffy after September. Yep, it's all about timing."

Jake stared at his father, not at all convinced. The old man was up to something. But he didn't have time to argue with him now. He had too many other issues on his plate. "Discuss it with Sally. She's the boss when it comes to the boys."

His father smiled. "Good. Sally told me to discuss it with you."

"When did you talk to Sally about this?"

"Tonight. I stopped in the bakery when I saw the light on out back. I was dropping off some fish at The Honey Hole."

So, Sally really was at the bakery.

Not that he'd doubted her.

"Another thing," his father said, and the blush was back. "Vana Gustafson offered to come out with us. So, three adults to keep an eye on three kids."

Jake's eyes about popped out at that news—well, his one good eye. The sexpot senior had offered to go boating with his father? Was this a senior version of a dirty weekend? But no, Old Mike would be there, too, and three mini chaperones.

A grin twitched at Jake's lips as he thought, *Maybe I should be having the condom talk with dear old Dad.* "That's just great. Let me discuss it with Sally first, though."

After his father left, he made the boys a big bowl of microwave popcorn because they were hungry again. They were always hungry.

"Okay, Minecrafters, time to shut off the TV and play the butt game," he announced to the boys a short time later. It was nine p.m. and Sally wasn't home. Looked like he was going to have to put them to bed. Which was not going to be a pretty scene.

"What's the butt game?" Luke asked. He was the first one to meet Jake in the hall at the bottom of the stairs. The other two soon followed, coming to a skidding stop. Aside from always being hungry, his boys were always on the move. They never walked when they could run.

"Is the butt game like the fart game?" Matt wanted to know, smiling widely. "I can do three in a row."

"Especially after he eats beans," Mark agreed.

"But Binky Jones ith the champion. He did one really loud at the mutheum today," Luke said.

Matt nodded. "Yep. He cut the cheese *real* loud. And Mr. Allen, the assistant scout leader, made him go sit in the bus for an hour."

Jake had discovered that little boys loved anything involving body noises, whether they be farts or belches, as well as body emissions, like poop or piss. "No, my butt game has nothing to do with farts," Jake said. "I need to go upstairs to get you guys to bed. I'm gonna need a little help. On my butt."

"You're coming upstairs?" Mark asked.

Even if it kills me.

"Sorry. That was a silly question," Mark added.

Not a silly question since Jake hadn't been upstairs since he'd gotten home.

"What about your leg?" Matt wanted to know. "Won't it hurt?"

Like a hot iron, which I am ironically familiar with.

"Will you read uth a bedtime thory, like Mommy doth?"

"Dads don't read bedtime stories," Mark chided Luke.

"Besides, I'm too old for bedtime stories," Matt contended.

Luke ducked his head.

"Actually, dads do read bedtime stories. And you never grow too old to listen to a good story. You wouldn't believe how much the guys in my unit love to tell and listen to stories when we're out on a live op."

They all stared at him, amazed. Like they didn't think men liked books? He had obviously been gone too long, for more than the apparent reasons.

"My favorite book when I was your ages was *Sneetches*. Later, your grandfather and I read *Moby Dick* together. Did he ever read it to you?"

The three of them shook their heads slowly.

"*Dick* is another word for your dangler," Matt pointed out.

Whaat? Does he mean what I think he means?

"Mom says we're not supposed to call it a cock or a peter or a prick or a pecker," Matt elaborated.

"How about just penis?" Jake asked, choking back a laugh.

"That's okay," Matt told him, very seriously.

"Anyhow Moby Dick is the name of a whale and the story is about the captain who tries to catch him."

"PopPop likes to talk about fishing," Mark said with a nod.

"Anyhow, butts on the stairs," Jake said. "Watch me and follow suit."

Then, with sheer upper body strength and a lot of pain, he propelled himself up one step at a time, backward. When he got to the top, the kids followed after him, ten times faster and with way more ease.

"Can we do it again?" Luke wanted to know.

"Maybe tomorrow."

After showers and tooth brushing and gargling that left the bathroom in a godawful mess which he would have to clean later, Jake led the kids into the master bedroom with his queen-size bed which should hold them all, unlike the kids' rooms with twin or bunk beds. Jake hadn't been up here in more than three years and was surprised to see the bedroom he'd shared with Sally looking almost the same, right down to the blue-and-white star quilt his mother had given them for a wedding present. Sheer white curtains hung at the windows, which were open to the slight evening breeze. The furniture was an old tiger maple set passed down from his grandparents, a golden color that had mellowed over the years. It was a pleasant room with mostly good memories.

Dressed in only underpants, in deference to the heat, identical white briefs, the trio hopped on the bed like rambunctious puppies and cuddled up next to him in the center. Each had been told they could bring a favorite book. They started with Luke's shyly offered *Sneetches*, which Jake read twice, at their urging. Mark's pick was one of the Diary of a Wimpy Kid books, this one titled *Dog Days*, which of course prompted the three of them to beg him to get them a pet dog . . . or else a horse. Finally, a somewhat embarrassed Matt handed him *Charlotte's Web*, probably fearing his choice was too childish for an eight-year-old.

"Hey, bud, how did you know this was one of my faves? Ya gotta love that Wilbur."

Which prompted them to ask for a pet pig, in addition to a dog and a horse.

Matt smiled at him and cuddled closer.

The phone rang out in the hall—the landline that they kept because of the occasional weak mobile signals, especially during storms on the Outer Banks—and Matt jumped up to go answer it. "It's Mom. She always calls to make sure we're in bed."

Jake could hear half of the conversation from the bedroom, where the other two imps moved in, filling Matt's space.

"Yeah, yeah, Mom, we did all that. And Dad read us three stories. Well, not three whole books. He said *Charlotte's Web* was too long to read all in one night."

"Uh-huh, Dad came upstairs with us.

"The butt game. That's how.

"We're reading in your bed.

"Okay, I'll tell him." Banging the phone down, Matt raced back in and made a flying dive for the bed, barely missing Jake's bad leg which was extended and vulnerable. "Mom said to make sure you lock the doors. She'll be late. One of the ovens broke, and she's waiting for the appliance repairman."

Jake didn't like the idea of Sally being alone in her shop this late at night with some strange repair guy. Yeah, it was Bell Cove, but you never knew. And the things Jake had seen around the world made him super cautious. Still, she would not like him showing up at her shop like a Clueless Knight with a Limp, waving a cane, instead of a spear.

So, he waited. And then the kids asked him to tell them a real story about something that happened to him.

"Well, I'm not saying this really happened," he began and proceeded to spin a wild yarn about a man who lived in a cave for years and years and became friends with the spiders, one of whom was coincidentally named Charlotte, and the bats, one of whom was named Wimpy.

Jake hadn't intended to let the kids sleep here, but they lay waiting for Sally to return, talking softly about the books they'd read, including his fantastical tale, about their summer activities, what they wanted to do the next week and next month. On and on. Jake really didn't need to speak. They did all the talking, sometimes talking over each other.

And, really, Jake was just enjoying the coziness—at some point, he'd pulled the quilt up over them all—and the closeness of warm live bodies—he hadn't realized how much he'd missed that human touch—and the smell of newly bathed little boys, except for Luke who must have used a half bottle of pine-scented body wash and smelled like a Christmas tree.

Gradually, of course, feeling a bit like the Big Bad (Clueless) Bear and its three cubs, they all fell asleep. What would Goldilocks make of them?

Chapter 11

Pillow talk is the most revealing . . .

*I*t was eleven o'clock before Sally got home, having spent two hours and eight hundred dollars with an appliance repairman who had a bad case of BO. At least she'd been able to make a half-dozen extra loaves of artisan bread while she waited, including an experimental ginger-peach country loaf with a crème fraîche glaze and pecan crackles.

She took idle notice as she pulled into the driveway behind Jake's truck that there were lights on all over the house, upstairs and down, but she couldn't be mad about that. Same went for the back door being unlocked. According to her phone conversation with Matt, his father had experienced quite a painful time getting up the stairs on his butt. He probably wasn't too anxious to rush back down to turn off the lights.

The kitchen was surprisingly spotless. Even the floor had been mopped. Jake's visible form of apology, she supposed.

When her stomach growled suddenly, she realized that she was starving, not having eaten since lunch, and was pleased to see that the doggie bag from The Bay Shack was in the fridge. She warmed the soft crab sandwich and the curly fries in the oven and poured herself a glass of sweet tea. After she ate, she turned out the lights, except for a lamp in the living room, which Jake would need when he came down to sleep on the couch. Or maybe she would need it if Jake was in her bed. Only then did she tiredly make her way up the stairs.

She almost tried going up on her butt, just to see how it felt, and grinned at the embarrassing prospect of being caught in the act. Maybe tomorrow.

The bathroom was a mess of wet towels and globs of toothpaste in the sink and spit spatters on the mirror. Well, at least the boys hadn't crawled into their beds dirty, which was what they were inclined to do when not supervised.

She was too tired to clean up tonight, but she did brush her teeth. With a wide yawn, she entered her bedroom and stopped with a gasp. She'd fully expected to find Jake there, and he was. But she hadn't expected to see the three boys there, as well.

The room was warm since the air conditioner hadn't been turned on, and the quilt was tossed into a pile near the footboard. They all wore white briefs—the kids, the traditional Fruit of the Looms, and Jake, the boxer briefs he'd always favored. Mark was cuddled under one of Jake's arms. Luke was plastered over Jake's chest, his little hands around

Jake's neck. Matt was lying beside Jake on the opposite side from Mark, on the other pillow, in an identical pose to his father, but so close their bodies were aligned, arm to arm, thigh to thigh. Matt was also snoring lightly, like his father, in his case due to enlarged adenoids, an issue she would have to address soon.

Tears welled in Sally's eyes, and she took out her cell phone to memorialize the picture. This was what she'd always wanted when she imagined marriage and a family with Jake.

She thought about waking the boys to get into their own beds and Jake to go downstairs to the sofa, but that seemed unnecessary. Instead, she went into Matt's room and crawled into his single bed. There was the slight worry that Jake might awaken to one of those nightmares like he'd experienced the first night he'd been home. The kids would be terrified. But then, she was close by, and the nightmare had only occurred that one time. Within minutes, she was asleep.

It was still dark outside when she felt Jake slip into bed with her. She was on her side, and he spooned her from behind, pulling the sheet up over them both. He said nothing but she felt his breath against her neck. With her wearing only her usual bed clothes, a tank top and shorts, and him in only boxer briefs, she was more than aware of skin against skin. His chest, her back. Thigh to thigh, calves to calves. Erection to butt.

But it was a lazy kind of arousal, on both their parts. Nothing urgent. The kind of thing that said: this might happen, but maybe not.

"Are you awake?" he asked.

"Yes."

"I'm sorry."

"For what?"

"There's an open-ended question!" He laughed, and she felt the shot of breath in her ear.

The arousal, on her part, amped up a notch.

"I could say I'm sorry for everything," he explained, running a forefinger down her bare arm, from shoulder to wrist, creating a wave of erotic goose bumps, "but mainly for the way I overreacted today, when I saw you at your shop. For not thinking to contact you after I picked up the kids. For some of the things I said back here at the house."

She wanted to ask him if he really didn't care if she had sex with another man, as long as she was discreet, which was what he'd said, but instead she conceded, "I might have overreacted myself, by dumping dinner in the sink."

"Will you make it again for me sometime?"

"I don't know. Maybe."

He was still spooning her, but he adjusted himself so that one arm was over her head on the pillow, and the hand of the other arm laced fingers with hers, his hand on top of hers, resting on her abdomen. He might have kissed her shoulder, but she wasn't sure if that was her imagination.

There was nothing sexual about their position,

and yet it was utter sensuality. Pure and honest. Husband and wife. A couple long accustomed to each other.

"Jacob, what happened to you?"

He didn't ask what she meant. He knew. And said nothing.

"Tell me."

"I can't."

"Can't or won't?"

"Both."

"Will you ever?"

"I don't know." Somehow, his honesty made it okay. He said nothing for a long moment. She thought he might have fallen asleep, but then he told her, "Izzie is coming to Bell Cove for Labor Day."

"Uh-huh." There was nothing particularly new about that, and what it had to do with him telling her about the past three years, she had no idea. "I haven't seen him since his parents moved to Seattle."

"They're coming, too."

"Abe and Rachel will have a full house."

"You have no idea," he murmured.

"What?"

"My boss—well, my liaison with the military— will be coming, too, and staying at the Bernsteins'." He paused. "Raymond Durand."

"The major? Major Durand?" Now, this *was* news!

"You *would* remember that name, just from a caller ID!" He squeezed her lightly in reprimand. "Yeah. Major Durand is coming down from DC."

"Why?"

"Just to be friendly?"

"That's bullshit."

He laughed.

"Here's a news flash, buddy. My parents are coming that weekend, too."

He groaned and repeated her question, "Why?"

"Just to be friendly?"

"Bullshit!" he also repeated back at her.

She could hear the smile in his voice.

"Where will they stay? There's no room here. I suppose they could use the guest room at my dad's place."

She shook her head. "No. I was able to get a room for them at the Heartbreak Motel. My friend Delilah owns it, and she did me a favor by shuffling out one of the salvaging company employees who has a long-term rental. He'll sleep on the boat that weekend." She was pretty sure that Jake knew that person was Kevin.

"That's good then. Your parents can't stand me."

"It's not you. It's the military."

"Same thing."

Which was a telling statement, that he still considered himself a soldier. Did that mean he intended to stay in the Army in some capacity?

Before she could rag him on his future plans, he asked her, "Why didn't you go live with your parents in Manhattan after I was declared dead?"

"It's no place to raise kids, or at least not active ones like our boys." *Besides, this is my home now. Or I thought it was.*

"You could have resumed your music career."

"Jacob, I never had a music career. I was a Broadway music student, at best. I can't remember the last time I belted out a full song, not even in the church choir, which I gave up when I bought the bakery."

"Not even for a duet at the Lollypalooza?" he teased.

At least she thought he was teasing since he referred to the remark one of the boys had made about her and Kevin doing a guitar/singing twosome in the talent contest. "That was wishful thinking on the boys' parts. Nothing we—I—actually planned."

"I wouldn't mind, if you want to do it," he said.

And that hurt a little. He should mind. Just like he should mind if she had sex with other men, dammit.

"Back to your parents. I'm surprised that your folks are coming to the Outer Banks. They rarely leave the city, and they always looked down their noses at small-town life."

"Actually, they've visited a few times while you've been gone. In fact, they used their set-designing skills to paint that mural on the wall of my bakery. Did you notice it?"

"I did. So, they supported your idea to run a bakery, instead of heading back home with them?"

"Jacob!" she chided him. "That was never on my radar."

He shrugged.

Instead of arguing that point, she continued, "My parents did some Elvis-themed murals for Delilah, too, at her diner. That's probably why she was so amenable to making room for them at the motel on a busy holiday weekend. Not just as a favor to me."

Changing the subject of her parents, an unsavory one to him, he said, "Did you know that my dad and Old Mike are planning a ménage à trois with Vana Gustafson out on the boat, with our three sons as chaperones?"

"Whaaat?"

But Jake was burrowing closer to her, yawning aloud before slipping into slumber.

So, he probably didn't hear her say with just a hint of sarcasm, "Happy times ahead in Bell Cove." Nor did he hear her add, "Sweet dreams, sweetheart," before she, too, fell asleep.

There's good quicksand and bad quicksand, and then there's wicked-good quicksand . . .

The following days were so jam-packed with activities for Jake that he hardly had time to think about the fact that he'd been home for two weeks and hadn't yet made love with his wife. He'd started rehab on an every-other-day basis, which was improving his strength and dexterity tremendously. When his father's boat motor made a funny noise, Jake had helped repair it. The oil had been changed in both the truck and Sally's car, and (to Jake's dismay and Sally's horror) most of the used lubricant ended up on his three eager gremlin assistants. He practiced baseball with the boys, and they helped him paint the porch swing. (*Again, picture green gremlins.*) Every hour of the day seemed to be filled.

Therefore, he thought about sex only when Sally put on that tank top/shorts sleep outfit. (*Sweet dreams, for sure!*) Or when she pranced about in a bikini on those afternoons when they took the boys to the beach. (*Forget about knot tying. Did I mention I'm an expert at knot untying, too?*) Or when she donned her baker's apron. (*Oh, the ideas I get!*) Or when she bent over in a pair of jeans to pick up one of the boys' toys. (*More ideas!*) Or when she held out a new cookie for him to try with her fingertips touching his lips. (*Delicious!*) Or when she vacuumed (*All that bending again!*) Or kissed the boys good-night. (*How about me?*)

Okay, he thought about sex a lot.

But he wasn't getting any.

He was pretty sure that Sally knew about his discomfort, and she was playing him. No way did any woman need to bend over that many times, or wear jeans so tight they looked painted on, or bat her eyelashes when she asked him to apply sunscreen to her back.

And so he wasn't above tempting her right back. He'd gained ten pounds since he got home and was starting to regain his muscle definition. Sally had always liked his body; she clearly still did. If he brushed against her when passing behind her in the kitchen, that was an accident, right? When he asked her to help him get into the tub last night, her eyes had gotten big as saucers as she'd glanced downward. What could he say? It had been a *long* time.

Meanwhile, his boys had no filters, God bless them. When it came to whatever popped into their heads, they just let loose.

"Daddy, why don't you sleep in Mommy's bed?"

"Jimmy's grandpa has bleeding hem-her-oyds, and he has to sit on an inner tube."

"Mommy, why are your nipples so pointy under that shirt?"

"Daddy, why do you have a big bulge in your swimming trunks?"

"Do girls fart?"

"We should get a baby brother. Four is better for playing teams."

"Or else a puppy."

"What's a condom?"

"Why don't girls pee standing up?"

"Because they don't have danglers."

"Mommy says we should all join the bell choir this year, even Daddy."

"She did not."

"Well, she probably meant Daddy, too."

Jake was heading toward town now, with the three boys. Sally had asked him to come to the shop this afternoon so that she could get his advice on something. He couldn't imagine what expertise he would have regarding a bakery, but he was trying to be helpful. Besides, she might be wearing a baker's apron over shorts and a tank top that would make it look as if she was wearing the apron and nothing else.

Did I mention how horny I am these days?

When they got to the bakery, Jake planted the three boys at a window table with one monster cookie and a mini carton of orange juice each, warning them, "If any one of you moves, there will be no video games tonight for all of you."

"Aw, geez!"

"That's not fair."

"How long do we hafta sit here? What if I hafta pee?"

He gave them a look, one he'd perfected over the last week or so, and they immediately zipped up.

He found Sally in the kitchen where she was talking to her assistant baker, José, who gave Jake a wave. She wasn't wearing an apron (*Darn it!*), just an OBX T-shirt and yoga pants. He'd developed a particular affection for yoga pants in the highly amped testosterone quicksand he waded through these days. (*Yeah, aprons and tight jeans and bikinis are flags in that quicksand, too. Aaarrgh!*)

"What's up, Sally?"

"I need your advice about something. Come with me." She led him out the back door and into the gift store next door, which seemed to specialize in scented candles based on the myriad aromas that assaulted them. "Hey, Alma," Sally said, "this is my husband, Jacob." To Jake, she said, "Meet Alma Vemeer, the owner of this shop."

Jake shook hands with her and they exchanged a few words, mostly the usual "Thank you for your service," and him remarking on how nice the shop looked and how he remembered when it had been a Bell Cove fixture that specialized in nothing but kites.

Finally, Sally asked Alma, "Do you mind if I show my husband around?"

There wasn't much to see. It was pretty much the same size as Sally's adjacent bakery, including the front shop and kitchen, except in this case, it was all one space.

Jake was confused. "What am I supposed to be looking at?"

"The square footage. If that wall were knocked out, imagine what a great space would be created. I've been thinking about expanding into more breakfast and lunch fare, light things that utilize what I already make, carryout types of things for people headed to the beach or to take back to an office. Like fried eggs on bacon croissants in the morning. Gourmet egg salad on toasted sourdough bread. And at lunchtime, oh, so many possibilities! Ham and imported Swiss cheese with stone-ground mustard on pumpernickel swirl rolls. Individual baguettes filled with chicken salad, heavy on the crunchy grapes and walnuts."

"You make me hungry just describing those."

She smiled.

He loved when she smiled at him like that. He wished he could make her do it more. But he was about to rain on her parade. "It wouldn't just be a case of taking down a wall, though, would it? You're talking a bigger kitchen and additional appliances. More display cases and counters. Seating. Painting. Flooring. Windows. Doors. Lighting."

She nodded. "And that's just the start."

"Sally, you're already working a huge number of hours. Can you really take on more?" What he didn't say, but she had to realize, was that more time would be taken away from the boys. And him.

"I would need more staff, of course, but I could move José up to head baker with me, and add two other assistant bakers. Mary Lou Tonelli, who's been a full-time clerk, is perfectly capable of becoming manager, and then I'd hire additional staff, more in the summer than the rest of the year."

"You've really been thinking about this, haven't you?"

"I have."

"Any idea how much all this would cost?"

She shook her head. "Alma wants to sell me her store for a hundred thousand dollars, which is probably a bargain. She's given me until the end of September to decide before she puts it on the market. Then there's all those additional expenses I mentioned."

He blinked. "Do you have that kind of money?"

She blushed. "*We* don't have that kind of money. But *we* do have fifty thousand for a down payment. *We* would have to finance the rest."

Okay, he got the message with that "we" emphasis. This was something she expected, or wanted, him to engage in with her. A joint venture.

He also got another message. She was asking if he was going to be around long enough to see something like this through.

But holy shit! A business loan of upward of a hundred thousand dollars? "And that big of a loan doesn't scare you off?"

"No. Well, a little bit, but if the figures play out the way I think they might, it doesn't seem like too big of a risk."

Was this the same woman who'd lived with a malfunctioning fridge for a year because she didn't want to finance a new one? Debt had scared her.

"Sally, I know nothing about bakeries. I can't see myself kneading dough and selling baked goods."

"What do you see yourself doing?"

He winced. That was blunt.

He shook his head. "I don't know."

"Anyhow, all I'm asking at this point is whether you can investigate all this for me. Maybe hire an architect like Gabe Conti to draw up some plans. Look over my accounts and project how much additional income there might be. Whether the whole idea is economically feasible. You don't have to be an expert to do that."

He sensed a trap. Either way loomed a misstep. If

he said, no, he wasn't interested, she would take it personally. The repercussions would be more than "no sex." On the other hand, if he said yes, would he be making a commitment he was unready for?

"I'll try, Sally," he said finally.

She actually got tears in her eyes and gave him a quick hug. "Thank you. You are a godsend."

He wasn't sure about that. But he took her hugs wherever he could get them.

The two of them went to gather the boys, who were looking suspiciously innocent as they sat waiting for them in the shop. Jake's father called just then from his cell phone out on the boat to say that he and Old Mike were heading in early, having had a particularly good day fishing, including a huge yellowfin tuna, which he thought the boys might like to see them unload. Yellowfin tuna weren't nearly as valuable as bluefin tuna, which were highly regulated and made famous by that TV show *Wicked Tuna*, but they were still good eating. And impressive-looking.

Sally agreed to come with them.

As they drove toward the marina in his truck—he and Sally up front and their sons in the back on a bench seat—the boys chattered on, as usual, mostly about the upcoming weekend excursion planned by PopPop and Old Mike. (*Vana Gustafson had supposedly bowed out, thank God! Something about a blind date to go shagging. The dance, not that other.*) Somehow this grandfather/grandsons bonding experience on the water had become a fact without either Jake or Sally having given permission.

But then Matt asked the question that had been niggling at the back of Jake's mind for days (*Can anyone say testosterone quicksand?*), "Daddy, what are you and Mommy going to do when we're gone all weekend?"

Chapter 12

The gamble: knowing when to
fold them, when to walk away, or,
what the hell, when to stay . . .

*P*opPop and Old Mike picked up the three boys at
four p.m. on Friday afternoon. They'd been packed
and ready to go since nine, checking and recheck-
ing to make sure they had all the magnetic board
games handed down through the generations of
Dawsons that could be played in the wind and motion of a boat out on the open seas—such as, check-
ers, backgammon, cards—and enough live bait to
feed a small nation of hapless fish. They looked
adorable with the red OBX baseball caps and the
mini fishing vests, which also served as flotation
preservers in an emergency, that Jake had purchased for them at the town mercantile. Joe's mutt
Goofus sat on the front seat between him and Old
Mike, eager to be out on the boat, too.

By the time her father-in-law's packed pickup truck
left the driveway with the kids yelling goodbyes out
the back seat windows, Sally was exhausted. But not

so exhausted that she didn't notice the smoldering expression in her husband's eye. He'd been looking at her like that a lot lately.

And, boyohboy, did he look good himself these days! With the little extra weight he'd gained, the tan he was perfecting being in the sun so much with the boys, and his genetic hotness, the man was pure temptation. Instead of detracting from the eye candy package, the patch added an extra element of edginess to his attraction.

"Do you want to go out to eat tonight?" she asked.

He shook his head and continued to stare at her as they walked toward the back porch.

"You're not hungry?"

"Oh, I'm hungry."

Okaaay. Feeling suddenly awkward, she found herself rambling. "Two whole days without my boys! I don't think I've ever been away from them for that long. Well, there was that time I went to a bakers' convention in Myrtle Beach, but that was just overnight. Without them to care for, even with the bakery, there will be all that extra time."

"Maybe that's a good thing," he remarked enigmatically.

"Actually, there's enough food in the fridge to feed an army." Friends and neighbors throughout Bell Cove had been dropping off quick-fix meals and sides for days now. Ham and other meats, potato and macaroni salads, including Vana Gustafson's infamous Norse potato salad with salted herring. Fresh garden tomatoes. Pies, cakes, breads.

Did they forget she owned a bakery? Even a bottle of wine from Father Brad at Our Lady by the Sea Church. "You'd think it was a funeral or something. Do they think you and I are going to starve if we don't have the kids and your dad and Old Mike to cook for?"

He shrugged, though a grin twitched at his lips.

"In fact, without the boys here, I have no idea what I'll do with all that extra time."

Jake chuckled. He apparently had ideas.

They were on the porch now, and Jake leaned against one of the thick tapered square columns that supported the roof.

She leaned against the column on the other side of the steps, folding her arms over her chest, just in case a certain part of her anatomy revealed something embarrassing.

He folded his arms over his chest, too, but in his case, it was more a lazy attitude of cat versus mouse.

"You could take care of me," he said softly.

"Do you need care?"

"In spades."

She arched her brows. "Are you in pain?"

"Always."

"Would it help if I massaged your leg?"

He made a low choking sound before replying, "That would be a start."

"I have some scented bath oil."

"Even better." He smiled.

And Sally melted a little bit more.

The answer to whether they were going to have sex or not was a foregone conclusion. Nothing that had been discussed. Just something understood. There was no doubt in Sally's mind that Jake wanted it. She sure as sugar did.

Sally wasn't sure when she'd decided to give up her resolution to have a firm commitment from Jake, a clear-cut idea of their future together, before starting a sexual relationship. In some ways, it was like her reasoning for expanding the bakery business, taking on a huge loan. A risk. At some point, days ago, she'd decided to gamble that she and Jake had enough assets, enough promises of return on investment, to jump in headfirst. Yeah, they had a checkered P & L relationship statement, but nine years of marriage and three children had to count for something.

The big question, the big elephant looming between them, was love . . . or lack of love. Had that all-consuming love at first sight died?

She didn't know. She felt raw, exposed. If he'd come back a few months after his last deployment, she might very well have given him his walking papers. That's how disillusioned she'd been with her marriage. Now? She wasn't sure.

As for Jake . . . she hadn't heard any expressions of undying love on his part, either. Unlike his old cocky self, overconfidence personified, he seemed equally unsure of himself. He'd even been willing to let her go. Hadn't he told her in so many words that she could have an affair with another man, as long as she did it discreetly? *The clueless ass! Does he know me so little? Sex as a widow was one thing. Adultery was quite another.*

The thing was, Jake didn't talk much at all. About the things that were important. Maybe if she understood what he'd been through the past three years, she could bridge the gap between them.

Would sex provide that bridge?

It appeared that she was about to find out.

Jake pushed away from the column and moved the three steps closer to her. Tipping her chin up, he said, "Honey, I'm home."

And it was as if the last few weeks, the last three years, were wiped out. A new start.

Home is where the heart is,
and other body parts, too . . .

Thank God!" Sally said and leaned into the palm of his hand.

Jake's heart swelled in his chest at that mere gesture. He assumed she was responding to his remark about being home.

"So? Are we going to do this thing?" he asked.

She nodded, and there were tears in her eyes, turning them from chocolate to misty caramel. He didn't think they were tears of sorrow. More a surfeit of emotion.

He knew how that felt. The time for "Should we?"

or "Shouldn't we?" or "What if this?" or "What if that?" or "Maybe we should wait" was long past. The time for going for the flow of emotion was at hand.

Tugging her closer, with both hands on her hips, he leaned down to kiss her. She wrapped her arms around his shoulders and went up on tiptoes to meet his kiss and kiss him back.

It was sweet.

So sweet.

And then it was hot.

He sighed into her open mouth.

She groaned.

The kiss went on and on, a reshaping and relearning. His hands roamed her back and shoulders and behind. Her hands cupped his face, holding him in place.

Finally, he drew back and looked at her. Her lips were moist and parted. Her eyes half-lidded with arousal.

"Come," he said, taking her hand and leading her inside.

When he locked the kitchen door behind them, she arched her brows in question. "We don't want any friends bringing goodies to just walk in," he explained.

She giggled.

Lord, he hadn't heard her giggle in a long time. Years, maybe.

She had to help him up the steps as he leaned on

her shoulder, refusing to go up backward on his ass at a time like this. Which of course led to them stopping every other step to kiss and pet. Once, when she accidentally, or perhaps not so accidentally, brushed her hand across his erection, he almost tipped over backward. After that, there was no more stopping. Still, it took them fifteen minutes in all, to get from bottom to top, Jake figured.

In their bedroom, Sally turned down the quilt and sheets, then stood watching as he pulled his T-shirt over his head, toed off his athletic shoes, then shrugged out of his briefs and shorts, all in one swoop.

"You are so beautiful," she said.

"I am not!" And that was the truth. He was too thin, and covered with scars, and bent in places he shouldn't be.

"Yes, you are, Jacob."

He touched the eye patch and held out his one leg to display the vicious marks of damage.

"They make you more attractive." She raised a halting hand when he was about to disagree. "Really. They do."

Okay, if his broken body made her more amenable to sex with him—hell, if it turned her on, who was he to argue?

"Your turn, baby," he said and waved a hand for her to get naked, too. Meanwhile he arranged himself on the bed, propped by two pillows, to watch. He put a third pillow over his lap because, frankly, his hard-on was becoming rather embarrassing. Well, not embarrassing so much as distracting. To him, anyway.

"Is that an order?"

"Definitely an order."

She gave him a sharp salute. "Yes, Captain, sir!" Then, with a wicked gleam in her eyes, she kicked off her sandals one at a time. One landed on the bed next to him, way too close to vulnerable territory. Good thing he'd had the foresight to cover himself. He lobbed it back at her. The sassy wench caught it with a laugh and tossed it aside, over her shoulder.

Then, still being sassy—did he mention he loved when his wife became Sassy Sally?—she moved to the bottom of the bed and turned her back to him. She was wearing a loose sundress with wide shoulder straps. She dropped one strap, slowly, then the other, holding the dress up in front with both hands to her chest. Without turning around, she asked, "Is this what you had in mind?"

"Not even close."

She dropped the dress to puddle at her feet and just stood for a moment, letting him take in her nude form from behind. Then she wiggled out of her bikini panties. She had the cutest butt, leading up over the curve of her hips to a narrow waist. She glanced over her shoulder and asked, "Better?"

"We're getting there." Then he added, "Man, you've still got a perfect heart-shaped ass."

"You and your heart-shape nonsense!"

"Turn around now. Slowly."

She did, and he inhaled sharply. He always did when looking at his wife. She wasn't so cocky now. Instead, she looked downward, not meeting his eyes. She'd always been insecure about her body, apparently still was. Yeah, she was average in height and build, and she was far from voluptuous, but who wanted that? Her breasts were a little bigger, and she had light stretch marks on her belly, from three pregnancies. Pregnancies which he'd caused. So, in a way, they were his marks on her. Yeah, convoluted macho man thinking. In any case, Sally set the bar for perfect womanhood in his mind.

"You gonna just keep looking, soldier?" she taunted. "Maybe the flag can only go half-mast these days."

"If I were in better condition, I'd leap off this bed and show you just how high this flag can fly."

"Blah, blah, blah," she teased.

To her shock, and his, too, he did, in fact, launch himself forward and tackle her to the floor. He saw red blinking lights behind both eyelids at the pain, but then adjusted himself over her. Raising himself on his straightened arms, with his flag planted firmly between her legs, he said, "You were saying?"

"Are you crazy? I was just teasing." She tried to push him up and off her. "Move, you idiot."

No way was he moving now. "Isn't there a song you can sing about now, sweetheart? 'It's a grand old flag,' or something like that?"

"Idiot!" she said.

Leaning down, he brushed his lips across hers and murmured, "I don't think I can wait. Are you ready, Sal?"

"I've been ready for weeks."

With those words, he took himself in hand and worked his way slowly into her. Slowly, because he really was damn friggin' big today. And slowly, because her inner muscles were welcoming him every inch of the way with spasms that about caused his head to explode . . . or something else to explode. And slowly, because he was where he'd wanted to be for more than three years.

Once he was in, though, the agony in his leg caused him to cramp up, and he rolled to his side, his good side, and raised her leg up over his injured thigh. Then, carefully, he was able to begin the long, unhurried strokes that went deeper with each thrust. He didn't last long, and neither did she, especially when she grabbed his buttocks, hard—he would have fingerprints on his ass by tomorrow—and rocked against him, also hard. She arched her neck back and went into a full-blown orgasm that held his cock in a rhythmically clutching stranglehold, milking him dry.

"Oooooh!" she cried out at the end.

He didn't cry, but he felt like it, with the sheer joy of a torturously pleasurable climax of his own.

This was the time when he should say that he loved her, or she should say that she loved him. But neither of them said anything, perhaps both waiting for the other to speak first.

Finally, she got up and said, "I have to go to the bathroom. Do you want me to help you up?"

"Nah. I'll be okay." And he was, once she left the room, not wanting her to see the humiliating way he had to maneuver himself to get to his feet. As he sat on the side of the bed, trying to catch his breath, the cell phone, which she'd placed on the dresser, pinged a few times, indicating an incoming text message.

When she returned and he was about to go to the bathroom himself, he told her, "You had a text message. Maybe you better check to make sure it's not from my dad." *Though, if there was an emergency, he would probably call me,* Jake thought. *And my dad doesn't do text.*

She was in the bed with the sheet pulled up under her armpits when he got back and climbed into the bed with her. He'd taken half of a pain pill when he was in the bathroom. It should kick in soon. "So, who called?" He immediately regretted his words. If it was Kevin, for example, she might consider his question an invasion of privacy.

"It was José. He texted to say that I didn't need to come in tonight to prepare the breads for tomorrow. In fact, he said I should take off the entire weekend, that he and Mary Lou could handle everything." She frowned as she relayed that information. "Which is really odd."

"Why is it odd?"

"This offer, from him and Mary Lou, and all the food that people have been bringing over—I don't know—everything. They're being so nice. I mean the people in Bell Cove are always nice, but this is somehow different."

He began to laugh, first a chuckle, then a chortle, then full-blown belly laughter.

"What?"

"Really, Sal, you don't know why Dad and Old Mike offered to take the kids for the weekend. Why people have been bringing enough food to supply an army. Why your employees want you to stay away from work." When she still looked confused, he explained, "They want you and me to spend all of our time doing—" He threw his arms out to indicate the bed.

"Nooo!" she said.

"Yep. All of this so you could get laid and I could get my rocks off. Repeatedly."

She put her face in her hands. "I feel so stupid." But then she looked up and over at him beside her and slapped him on the upper arm. "Why didn't you tell me?"

"I thought you knew."

"Oh, my God! They're all sitting in their homes, or businesses, or walking down the street, speculating on what we're doing at the moment." She thought for a moment. "Even Father Brad. Oh, I'll never be able to look him in the face again. Any of them."

He just grinned.

"You're not upset?"

He shrugged. "It's Bell Cove. It's what they do."

"They've gone too far this time."

"Ya think? Wait till we go to town. They'll be checking me out to see if I walk bowlegged or have a loopy grin on my face."

"And me?"

"They'll be counting the days till they see a baby bump on you."

"Bite your tongue, boy."

"I have better uses for my tongue, *girl.*"

And he did.

"Blow the Man Down," or "Fire in the Hole"—either worked for these pirates . . .

The town bells rang eight times as Sally eased her way out of the bed, but even those sounds didn't awaken her husband, who lay splayed out on his back, arms thrown over his head, legs spread. She'd worn the man out, Sally thought with a smile.

With his eyes closed and his face relaxed with satiation, he looked younger and less battle worn. God only knew where the eye patch had flown! Possibly under the bed.

Sally didn't know if having sex with her husband was a mistake with all the baggage they both carried. Without a doubt, there were problems ahead for them, questions that would have to be answered, hurdles to overcome. Maybe insurmountable ones. But, for now, seeing Jake like this, she was pleased that she could do this for him.

Hah! Who am I kidding? It was for me, too.

She didn't want to make any noise by opening a drawer; so, she just drew Jake's T-shirt over her head. Its hem skimmed her midthigh, which should be okay, just in case a friendly Bell Coverite decided the two lovebirds didn't have enough food to sustain them through a dirty weekend. She tiptoed out of the bedroom and down the stairs.

It was still light outside, of course, so she didn't need to turn on any lights in the kitchen, which was a blessing. A light might have signaled a neighbor to come over.

After setting a handled tray on the kitchen table, she took a bunch of the donated items from the fridge. A meal for herself and Jake would be welcome about now. Neither of them had eaten since lunchtime. And there had been all that hunger-inducing "activity."

She started by buttering some of her very own slider rolls and filling them with paper-thin slices of roast beef from Abe's deli, with arugula and Eliza Rutledge's homemade horseradish sauce. Thick slices of beefsteak tomatoes from Elmer Judd's garden over at the Patterson house were soon glistening with olive oil and balsamic vinegar, heavy on the salt and pepper. Three small bowls of salads: potato, shrimp, and fresh fruit. (And, no, she was not using Vana Gustafson's lutefisk creation.) Deviled eggs from Ina Rogers. A plate of various pickles, olives, and hard cheeses with crackers, courtesy of Stu and Barb MacLeod of the Blanket-y Blank quilt store. Assorted cinnamon rolls from Delilah's diner. A pitcher of iced sweet tea.

A half hour later, she struggled to carry the tray up the steps without spilling anything. Jake was sitting up in bed, reading some message on his cell phone, when she came in. Immediately, he placed the device on the bedside table and made room for her to set the tray on the middle of the bed.

"You read my mind, babe. My stomach's growling as loud as those bells."

"You heard the bells? I thought you were asleep."

"I didn't want to let you know I was awake and miss the sight of your bare butt sneaking out of bed. Or you raising your arms to put on my T-shirt. Or you bending over to put on a pair of slippers."

She gave him a mock glower of disapproval and kicked the slippers off, moving onto the bed, carefully, to keep the tray level between them. "For the record, I wasn't sneaking. I was being considerate."

"Whatever you say. Please flash your 'consideration' at me anytime you want." He smiled at her.

And her heart melted. A little bit. A lot more when she noticed that he'd put the eye patch back on. He must be self-conscious about how he looked.

They both sat cross-legged on either side of the tray and dug into the feast. The whole time they talked. Comfortably. Which was a treat for Sally, who'd felt as if she had to walk on eggshells around her husband since he'd come home, never sure what would be a forbidden subject.

First they talked about the possible addition to her bakery.

"Gabe will bring some architect drawings over for you to look at next week," he told her. "Just preliminary stuff. Nothing too expensive or detailed until you decide for sure if this is what you want to do."

"Not just me, Jacob. This has to be a joint decision."

She could tell that he was about to disagree with her. He still wasn't ready to commit to a long-term sojourn in Bell Cove, maybe even to their shaky marriage. At least, that was her opinion on his hesitation. In any case, he stopped himself from arguing with her on the "you" versus "us" issue, and instead said, "Once I have the costs worked out a little more, I'll go to the bank for you."

"I appreciate your offer, but *we* will go to the bank," she corrected.

"Yes, ma'am," he said, and gave her another heart-melting smile. "Just so we're clear, I'm willing to do any grunt work you need to make this happen, but I still don't think I could be involved in the actual operation. It's just not me."

"Good enough! I'll appreciate anything you can do. I know nothing about construction. And this saves me time for other stuff."

"So, have you thought about your Labor Day bakery theme items yet?" Jake was aware that Mayor

Ferguson had been bugging her for days to tell her what she planned so it could be put in the Lolly-palooza brochure.

"I'll have the usual red, white, and blue frosted flag cakes and Mookies. In light of the secondary pirate theme, I found some oversized, pirate-ship cookie cutters online that might be nice, except it would take a lot more fancy piping than I might be willing to do, unless I charge double for them, which I don't like to do." She gave him a look, fluttering her eyelashes.

"Not a chance!" he said with a laugh. "Not unless you want anatomically correct pirates."

She laughed, too. "Then, there's the other secondary theme, the treasure discovery. For that, I'll do some kind of gold coin Mookies."

Another secondary theme was the "Hometown Hero" for which she was designing a palm tree cookie with a yellow ribbon tied around its trunk, but she didn't think she'd tell Jake about that. Best that it be a surprise, and, yeah, she feared he'd put the kibosh on it. Little did he know, the entire town would be welcoming their hero home in their own distinctive way, including Abe Bernstein at his deli which would be featuring Italian hero sandwiches. And Delilah was going to make her cinnamon bun of the day with blueberries, strawberry jam, and white icing. The mercantile ordered in a huge supply of flags for people to wave. The bookstore was planning an "American Heroes" window display.

"The good thing is that I can bake and freeze

many of my cookie recipes ahead of time, and do the decorating in the off hours."

"I'm gonna have to be in that stinkin' parade, you know," Jake said, wiping his mouth with a paper napkin. "I promised Doreen. It was either that or agree to be on a dumbass float with a replica of a Blackhawk jet and some military choir singing 'God Bless America.' Where does that woman get these ideas?"

"You got me! Did you know she helped plan a surprise wedding for Delilah and Merrill, complete with leftover Fourth of July decorations and a pirate-themed reception at Chimes, that mansion of Gabe's? And, of course, the Grinch contest last December was the absolute best, or worst, of her schemes for bringing more tourists to Bell Cove, the kind who spend their dollars here and then go home."

"I read about that. Izzie brought me a bunch of newspapers to read while I was in the hospital."

"By the way, that was a nice article that Laura wrote about you. Focusing on your family and Bell Cove. I saw Matt clip it out of the paper and put it in his desk for safekeeping. All of the boys are proud of you."

His face went blank at that. It was a trick he had for not showing emotion. Why would he feel that he couldn't show his feelings in regard to the boys? Or was it the boys' regard for him that made him uncomfortable?

"I'll check to see if your uniform needs to go to the dry cleaners," she said. "I assume they'll want you to wear that."

"Either that or dress like a friggin' pirate, which I could do with this eye patch and gimpy leg."

She knew he was sensitive on the subject of his injuries; so, she just teased, "You'd make a very handsome pirate. Sex on the (pirate) hoof, so to speak."

He grinned, but then asked her suddenly, "Should I have been using a condom?"

"Kinda late to ask that, Long John." She shook her head at him. "But, no. Not necessary. I'm on the pill."

He stiffened.

And she could read his fool mind. "Don't go getting bent out of shape. I got a prescription once I heard you were coming home."

He tilted his head at her. "So, you planned to have sex with me from the get-go, but made me wait these two weeks before taking the plunge?"

"No, Jacob. They were just in case."

He looked as if he wanted to discuss the subject more, but then he relented and said, "*Just in case* you're feeling partial to a salty dog . . . wanna help this pirate swab his deck? I'm thinkin' Long John Silver's boat is smellin' a bit like bilge water and needs a good shower after all this activity."

"Just so you know, this wench gives no quarter when it comes to Jolly Rogers," she said, entering the playful banter. She glanced meaningfully to his "flag."

A short time later, under a warm shower, she laughed and teased, "Not so much yo-ho-ho-ing now, is there?"

And Jake said, "Aar!"

Chapter 13

Ride, Sally ride . . .

The town bells might have been ringing in the hour, over and over, as usual, but it wasn't until they reached ten that Jake finally awakened to find himself flat on his back with Sally splatted half over him, her face nuzzled in the crook of his neck, an arm thrown over his waist, one breast on his chest, the other pressing his side, a knee thrown over his happy place. In other words, an invitation to morning sex.

Jake didn't move. Sex with Sally had been amazing. Having his wife back in his arms was a dream come true. Yeah, an impossible dream, one that might be over in a blip of a second, once she came to her senses, or if he managed to be a bit more noble and think about her and not his raging libido. Hell, for now, selfish bastard that he apparently was, he just wanted to freeze the moment, inhaling her sweet scent, memorizing the feel of her smooth skin against his rougher edges, cherishing the honesty of her lovemaking.

But then Jake muttered a swear word as he realized the implications of the ten bells. They'd overslept!

"Hey, babe, wake up," he said, kissing the top of her spiky hair. "I forgot. I have an appointment at two o'clock in Hatteras." A two-hour drive in the off-season could be up to four hours with tourist traffic and ferry delays.

"What?" she asked sleepily.

He was already up and pulling out clean clothing from the bureau drawers. A pair of briefs, athletic socks, sweat pants, and a T-shirt. "I have a rehab appointment at two o'clock in Hatteras. I need to get going if I'm going to make the Bell Cove ferry at eleven." Jake had been scheduling his appointments at the same time as Gus, whenever possible, and thus hitching a ride. But Gus didn't go on the weekends.

"Do you have to go today?" She was careful to pull the sheet up under her armpits as she sat up.

Which amused the hell out of him. Almost nine years of marriage and she thought to hide her intimate parts from him? What was it about a woman that she could engage in wild monkey sex all night long and then turn all virginal modest in the morning?

"I do," he replied. "The every-other-day routine is important if I want to improve. It's too easy to skip a session. Then it becomes two. And more. Come with me."

"Huh?"

"Come with me. It's a long drive, especially with the two ferry crossings. I could use the company. Plus, you can watch what the massage therapist does to my leg, and if I'm a really good boy, maybe you'll follow through with me here at home."

"A really good boy, huh?"

"Or a really bad boy." He waggled his eyebrows at her. Well, one of them. "And if you're a really good girl, I'll take you out to dinner somewhere nice along the way back. I can bring a change of clothes with me."

"And if I'm a really bad girl?"

"Even better."

"I really should go into the bakery and help out while you're gone."

He refused to beg, but he did give her a look.

"Don't smolder at me, you . . . you pirate, you!" she said with a laugh.

"Me? Smolder? With one frickin' eye?"

"I imagine that the other one is smoldering, too. Under the eye patch."

He shook his head at her silliness.

"Okay, I'll come with you, but you hit the shower first. I am not hopping the plank again."

"Blimey!" he said with a grin.

Within an hour they were on their way, taking Sally's Toyota Avalon, instead of his truck, for comfort. He drove, though. And, actually, the traffic wasn't too bad going north. On the other side of Beach

Road, going south, it was bumper-to-bumper. Hopefully, by the time they returned, the traffic wouldn't be so thick.

It was a balmy day and with the windows open, the scent of the salty ocean in the air, it was a pleasant drive. Reminiscent of many drives he and Sally had made along this road. So mellow was he that he sang a few lyrics from that old Wilson Pickett song "Mustang Sally." He wasn't much of a singer, unlike his wife, but it was a song with lyrics he used to tease her with as they drove along—or at *other*, more intimate times—urging, "Ride, Sally, ride!"

She rolled her eyes and said, "You should have been singing that earlier."

"I was more inclined to 'Lay Down Sally.'"

"You and Eric Clapton. Although . . ." She paused and grinned at him. "I did get laid."

He was surprised that his usually modest wife could make such a bawdy remark, but he liked it. This was one of many changes he'd noticed in his new, independent partner, not all of them as much to his liking.

They got out of the car on the first of the two ferry rides so that Jake could stretch his legs. He'd brought his cane, but hoped not to need it. The limp was a given either way. She was wearing the peach sundress and had to hold her hands over the lower portion to prevent the ocean wind from billowing under and giving any spectators a Marilyn Monroe–vent-type moment.

To help her out, he positioned himself behind her

with his hands on the rail, bracketing her within his arms.

"Thanks," she said.

He kissed the top of her head and almost said, "I love you." It would have been a spontaneous declaration, the kind of thing he wouldn't have thought about uttering in the past.

Now, he hesitated.

And the moment was lost.

"This is a really long drive for you to make several times a week, even if you do carpool with Gus," she noted. "Can't you find a place closer to home? Isn't there one in Ocracoke?"

He shook his head. "No, this one is the best for my purposes. Otherwise, I'd have to stay on base at Fort Bragg and work out there. Besides, these visits will taper off as I improve. Hopefully, I'll be able to do more of the exercises on my own."

"And I'll be able to take over for the massage therapist," she added, glancing back at him over her shoulder with a wicked gleam in her eyes.

"Promises, promises," he said, but he was pleased that she would even be willing to take on that duty with everything else she had on her plate.

As they stood at the rail, and the wind died down a bit, he encountered a few people he knew. Invariably, they shook his hand and said, "Thank you for your service." Luckily, they didn't ask any further questions.

"Do you mind when people approach you like that?" Sally asked.

"I don't look for attention, but I don't mind, usually. Most times it's more about them than me. They often have a family member serving in the military somewhere, or having bit the dust."

"Jacob, I noticed that your appointments at the end of next month at the orthopedic hospital in New York and the eye center in Baltimore are back-to-back. Does that mean you'll be out of town for an extended period?"

He nodded. "At least a week, for testing. As much as two or three weeks if they decide to go ahead with any surgery, which is unlikely."

"Do you want me to come with you? At least to New York. I could stay at my parents' apartment."

He was surprised at her offer. "Can you be away from the bakery that long?"

"I could, if I had to."

"And what about the kids?"

"They could come, too."

"Won't they be in school then?"

"Yeah, but I could get special permission."

"No. I don't want the boys hanging around a hospital. It's no place for kids. And it's not really necessary."

"How about me? Do you want me there?"

"Nah. It's really just a lot of hurry-up-and-wait crap. With the testing stuff anyhow."

"And if they decide for the surgery right away?"

"There's still just a lot of waiting around. I don't want you there." *Especially if there's bad news. I'd rather wallow in private.*

She looked kind of disappointed at his words. Did she think he meant that he didn't want her, period? How could she think that? Well, hadn't he used those exact words on more than one occasion when Sally had begged him to let her come live on one of a dozen different bases where he'd been stationed?

The last call came over the speaker system for drivers to get in their vehicles, and he didn't have a chance to correct her misconception. But he did lace his fingers with hers as they walked back.

They continued to hold hands as he drove the rest of the way. This felt a lot like dating, like those early days when they were just getting to know each other. When they couldn't stand to be apart, when just a touch could set their blood racing. The whole friggin' torturous bliss of the falling-in-love process.

Except that he'd fallen right from the start. Like a sledgehammer to the heart she'd been for him. And still was.

He would recover eventually from his physical woes, at least enough to get by; Jake was determined about that. But would he ever recover from loving Sally, if he needed to leave her, which was a very real possibility?

Hell with that!

I'm tired of thinking and rethinking every damn thing.

Forget about the Delta Force motto of De Oppresso Liber, *"To Free the Oppressed." I'm the oppressed one here. My new motto is going to be the universal* carpe *diem, or "seize the day." In other words, enjoy the moment while I can.*

Until I can't anymore.

And then the scales fell off . . .

*S*ally went into the white hospital-like room at the rehab center with Jake where he shucked down to his briefs and hitched himself up onto a metal table. He was wearing a pair of the black-and-silver-striped boxer briefs she'd bought him for Christmas before his last deployment. They made his butt look even better than usual.

Noticing her perusal, he laughed.

She was about to slap said butt when a tall, slim, extremely physically fit black man wearing rimless glasses walked in, carrying a clipboard. Jake introduced him as Martin Alexander, his massage therapist.

He wasn't at all what Sally had expected. Though she wouldn't admit it to Jake, she'd been half expecting some voluptuous blonde in a skintight, thigh-high nurse's outfit that would show a thong when she bent over.

Jake winked at her. *With his one eye!* And she knew that he knew what she'd been envisioning. Maybe that was one reason why he'd invited her to come with him.

Turned out that Martin, a fortysomething former marine, had a master's degree in physical therapy, and he specialized in injured military men. In fact, he was some high uppity-up in Wounded Warriors, which Sally found out about when he told them that the biker division of his organization planned to participate in the Lollypalooza parade.

First, Jake lay on his back, and Martin worked his thigh muscles. "I see changes, Jake. Do you feel any improvement?"

"A little. Going up and down the stairs still brings tears to my eyes—eye—but not as much as the beginning when I almost passed out."

Sally's heart went out to her husband because she knew he was making the effort mostly because the kids wanted him upstairs at bedtime. Yeah, having him in her bed this weekend was a bonus, but knowing Jake and his sexual creativity, they could have done the deed anywhere. And had, numerous times in the past.

"Sally, come over here and put this on," Martin said, handing her a white cotton over-the-neck apron that tied around the waist. "I want to show you what to do with some oil, and I don't want you to soil your pretty dress."

She stepped over and caught another of Jake's winks, which she ignored. He'd told her how he fantasized about her in a baker's apron and nothing else. She assumed he was imagining the same thing with this apron.

"Put some oil on your hands and use just your fingertips, like I am, on the thigh muscles. Can you feel the knots in there?"

She nodded. It felt like cords of hardened plastic under the skin.

"The goal is to work those muscles that have scar tissue on them until they soften up. Don't be afraid to knead hard. He may piss and moan, but, with massage and a structured exercise routine, he might eventually recover some of the tone and movement."

Sally noticed that he said "might." That had to be disheartening to Jake.

Martin showed her different ways to work the thigh and calf muscles, which were marked with odd one-inch scars everywhere. Dozens of them. She also gave a smaller amount of attention to the good leg, which had the same kind of scars, but way fewer. She wanted to ask Jake what had caused these scars but sensed that he wouldn't relish her asking in front of someone else, maybe not at all, the way he was so closemouthed these days.

In truth, Jake had always been secretive about his Special Forces work.

When he was home, he didn't want to talk about where he'd been, what he did, or with whom. It was only by chance that she occasionally learned something about Delta Force missions on TV. Once she'd made the mistake of Googling *Delta Force* and learned some things she'd rather not know. She'd had trouble sleeping that night.

After working his leg for about a half hour, and, yes, Jake did piss and moan, with good cause, Martin turned him over onto his stomach.

Sally gasped. She'd felt the ridges on Jake's back when they made love. She'd seen him naked since his return, of course, but she must not have noticed the extent of his injuries. In retrospect, she recalled that when they'd gone to the beach, he'd worn a T-shirt. To avoid the direct rays of the sun, she'd thought. Now, she wasn't so sure.

"Okay, Sally, the massage here will be pretty much the same as the legs. The scar tissue tightens up, and if Jake isn't careful, he could end up with a stooped posture to compensate for the pain. Watch what I do. I won't have you work on his back today because you're too short with him on this table. At home, it would be better if you straddle him to get maximum pressure. Like on the floor, or a firm mattress."

Jake, whose face was turned away from her, snorted back a laugh.

If they'd been alone, she would have smacked him on his very nicely rounded butt.

After that, when Jake was about to go into the weight room for exercise and then the whirlpool, Sally said, "I think I'll go out and hit some of the shops in the strip mall across the street. I rarely get to just browse."

"Good idea," Jake said. "I should be done in an hour."

Sally was troubled when she left the rehab center.

She wasn't sure why. Even so, she strolled through the different stores, buying herself some lingerie in a boutique and kites for the boys in a beach shop. Then, in a drugstore where she'd gone in to get some basic toiletries, she found something special for Jake at the checkout that made her smile. When she got back to the rehab center, Jake was still in the locker room getting dressed, so she sat near the front desk and flipped through a magazine.

One of the attendants, a college-age kid, came up to the girl working the front counter. "Hey, Diane."

"What's up, Andy?"

"Man, oh man! You shoulda seen that guy in the whirlpool. His back was a mess of stripes. You know what causes that, don't you. A whip. Someone whipped that guy but good. Musta been a bloody mess when—"

"Shhh!" Diane said, glancing toward Sally. "You're not supposed to talk about clients, you idiot. You're gonna lose your job."

"Oops," Andy said and slunk away through the employees' door.

"Sorry," Diane said to Sally.

"That's okay," Sally said.

But it wasn't okay. And not just because of the un-professionalism. Sally wasn't dumb. She'd known that Jake was hiding something from her. The lack of fingernails. The nightmare. What she now realized must be stab wounds all over his legs. And now the whip marks on his back.

It was like she'd had scales on her eyes—on her mind—and they were falling off now.

MIA, my ass! Sally thought. *More like POW.*

Torture!

Three years of torture?

Where?

He hadn't been sitting in a cave eating grubs, that was for sure.

Oh, Jacob!

Sally swiped at the tears that filled her eyes. She didn't want Jake to see her upset. She needed time to think about this, what it all meant. And why he couldn't or wouldn't tell her about it.

She managed to be composed when he emerged a little later, looking hot in a blue golf shirt that matched his eyes, and which was tucked into belted black pants that accentuated his wide shoulders and narrow waist. And, yes, she meant eyes, as in plural, dammit! *Oh, my Lord!* she thought suddenly. *Did whoever captured him deliberately damage his eye? How? The monsters!*

"You okay?" she asked, standing to walk out with him.

"Sore, but good. How about you?" He was looking at her suspiciously.

Did she have tear tracks on her face, or something? "Great," she said cheerily.

"You went shopping." He pointed at the half-dozen bags she carried.

"Yep. And I bought something special for you."

"Ah, you didn't have to," he said, taking a small bag from her. Glancing inside, he let out a hoot of laughter.

It was a six-pack of cinnamon chewing gum.

Taking her free hand in his, he laced their fingers, and squeezed. "Maybe we should skip the dinner out on the town, and go home to make use of all those leftovers. A shame to let all that food go to waste."

"My thoughts exactly."

"You don't mind?"

She shook her head. All she could think as she looked at him was, *Torture, torture, torture.*

He leaned over and gave her a quick kiss. "How's my breath?" he whispered against her open mouth.

She forced herself to smile and said, "You might need a stick of gum, or two."

Chapter 14

They gave new meaning to car games . . .

*J*ake could tell that something was wrong with Sally, but she wouldn't tell him what it was, claimed she was just tired. He suspected that she was repulsed by his battered body and what she would have to do to help him regain some mobility.

She wouldn't be the first woman unable to deal with a partner's war wounds. A pilot back at Landstuhl, who'd been badly burned in an explosion, mentioned in a group therapy session one day that the first time he got naked with his wife to have sex, she vomited all over him. A sexual buzzkill if there ever was one!

He would deal with that issue later. No way would he want Sally working on his body if she was gagging as she did so. And, frankly, Jake didn't know how much longer he would be around. He was like the long-haul trucker traveling at night; he could see only as far as his headlights. Unlike the trucker, though, Jake didn't have a GPS map in place. His final destination might be California, or Alaska, but a vehicle breakdown might cause him to end up in the Rockies, so to speak.

That comparison is so lame, Jake thought.

In the meantime, he sought to take Sally's mind off whatever was bothering her by engaging in love play. Yes, love play in a car. It wasn't the first time they'd done it, but it had been a long, long time ago. Back when they were easier with each other.

"Hey, Sal, remember that time when we were driving back from Fort Bragg? Matt was asleep in the infant seat in the back, and I was so tired you were afraid I would nod off at the wheel. I had just come off a three-week deployment to Nigeria."

"I don't remember," she said, even as her face flushed to a pretty shade of pink.

"You came up with a car game for us to play to keep me alert."

"*That* was not my idea," she said indignantly.

"Ah, so you do remember."

She narrowed her eyes at him. "What brought this on?"

He yawned, wide and loud, and said, "I'm suddenly feeling really tired. Hope I don't fall asleep at the wheel."

"Do you want me to drive?"

"Nah. I'll get by." He sighed.

"I could sing." She immediately went into an improvised version of "The Wheels on the Car Go Round and Round." then asked, "Would that work?" Even with her excellent voice, that children's song— which was about a bus, not a car—got old fast, as he well knew from days when his boys were younger and more than a half hour in the car was an ordeal for them. Sally and the kids would sing it over and over till they reached their destination and his ears were ringing.

"Not even close. I have something else in mind."

"You have a wicked mind."

"Thank you."

She smiled, and from this angle, gave him a perfect view of her slightly crooked incisor on the left side. Somehow that imperfection gave her an impish look. A sexy imp.

"You first," he said.

"Okay, I spy something blue. Two guesses. One minute." She glanced at her watch and began counting down the seconds.

Jake glanced up through the moonroof, pretending to look at the sky. Then he looked out the driver's window at the ocean. But then he announced, "My eyes—well, my one eye."

"You rat. You are too good at this," she accused him. "What's my penalty?"

"Take off your panties."

She pretended to be shocked, before asking, "How do you know I'm wearing panties?"

What? "Are you kidding me? With the wind earlier, you could have been mooning all those people on the ferry."

"My bad!" she said with a little moue of apology, then reached under her dress and pulled out a black lace thong, tossing it onto his lap. "Fooled ya!"

"Brat!" he said. "My turn now. I spy something rose-colored."

"Knowing you . . . my nipples," she said.

"Good guess, if I could see your nipples. But, no, that's the wrong answer."

"My lipstick?"

"Nope. Your tongue. I win again. Woot-woot!"

"I suspect I've been set up here."

"Fair is fair," he said. "Okay, lift your dress so that your bare butt is sitting on the leather seat, and spread your legs."

"That's two things."

"Just spread then."

She did.

"How does that feel?"

"What do you think?"

"Sexy?" he remarked hopefully.

"I spy something black," she said, declining to give him the satisfaction of knowing she was getting turned on.

But he knew. "Something black, huh? The dashboard," he guessed.

"Nope."

"My eyebrows."

"Nope."

"My eye patch?"

"No, no, no!"

"You win that one. What's your poison, sweetheart?"

"Okay, in the almost nine years we've been married, we must have made love hundreds of times."

"Thousands," he corrected.

She gave him a frown of reprimand for interrupting. "Okay, which one of those *thousands* sticks in your mind?"

He didn't even hesitate before saying, "The first time we made love after Matt was born. We'd just moved into our own home, and it felt special."

"I'm surprised. I thought you would say some of the more perverted things you talked me into doing . . ."

"I don't recall anything perverted."

"Like that vibrator thingee you bought in Dubai."

"I forgot about that." He grinned.

"Or I expected you would go for some unusual position."

"Unlike now when I can bend my body in only a few directions."

"I was thinking more like that ridiculous wheelbarrow nonsense."

"Hey, that was fun."

"Fun? You pulled a hamstring."

"Well worth the pain, baby!"

"Or I would have thought your favorite would be a place, like the kitchen sink."

"No, it was good old missionary style. In my own bed in my own house, no longer living in the guest room at my parents', with my wife, who'd recently given me a baby. And did I mention it had been six weeks since we'd had sex?"

She was silent for a moment before saying, quietly, "Yeah, that was good."

Of course, the next time he won a game, he reversed the table on her by saying, "What was your most memorable sex?"

She didn't answer right away. "It was the last time you said 'I love you' during sex and meant it. Not just a throwaway line."

"Huh? I always mean it . . . meant it," he argued. "When was this?"

"Christmas, three and a half or so years ago. We had just had a big argument about the usual subject—your leaving again. And then we made up."

"Makeup sex," he said dismissively, but she'd given him something to think about. *And, by the way,* he thought, *when was the last time you said those three words to me and meant them, cupcake?* He didn't say that, though, not wanting to provoke her into saying something he might not like, or starting a conversation he wasn't ready for.

"Whoa! This game is getting way too serious," she declared with sudden brightness. "How about we switch to 'Truth or Dare'?"

The ride home from then on was like an hourslong exercise in foreplay. Arousing to the point of pain, tantalizing to the point of almost, but never quite, release. In other words, prolonged sexual bliss.

It was so much fun that Jake could have cried.

It was gaming, but so much more.

It was wicked sex. Not with a stranger, but his wife.

By the time they arrived back at the cottage in Bell Cove, they stumbled out of the car and barely made it into the house before he had her on the kitchen table. Or rather she had him on the kitchen table—shoved him against the edge and on his back, with her crawling up over him. She was the one struggling to get his belt unbuckled and his pants unzipped.

So much for her being repulsed by him!

He was too busy being in shock, and then laughing so hard he choked on his words. Between bursts of laughter, he was trying to say, "Wait—oh, hell—Sally, give me a chance to . . . oh, my God, you almost zipped my cock."

But then she lifted her dress up and over her head. She wasn't wearing a bra. Looking downward, she grinned and cooed, "Oh, good, a big ol' Blue Steeler."

He let out a hoot of laughter at that risqué observation. And grew a bit bigger and bit more blue.

Gritting his teeth, he got his blue-veined self in hand, literally, and was guiding himself up and into her hot, hot, thank-You-God wetness. His eyes rolled back into his head (both of them, he was pretty sure) at the sheer extreme pleasure of her inner muscles grasping him, hard. Leaning up, he took one nipple into his mouth and she was the one choking out, "Oh . . . that feels . . . so good . . . I can't . . ." Then he switched and gave equal rhythmic attention to the other breast until she was keening a continuous "Aaaaaahhhhh!"

He did a mental "Chalk one up!"

No sooner did her inner spasming end than she began to ride him, but he controlled the pace. Her eyes were so glazed with passion that she probably didn't know what she was doing at this point. He wasn't much better off. The sex didn't last long. It couldn't, not with their sexual drives in overload.

And yet, she ordered, "Don't come yet," and reached behind her buttocks to cup his balls.

Which of course caused him to come to a roaring climax.

And she followed soon after when he used a middle finger between their melded bodies to tickle her clit. He didn't know if it was her second or third orgasm. He'd lost count.

In the end, she lay on top of him, his flaccid dick still inside her, her face nestled in the crook of his neck. When their breaths slowed to a mere panting, she raised her head to look at him. She was crying.

And he was the one most shocked when he kissed her softly and said, "I love you."

She was no fool! . . .

What a day!

When Sally thought about everything that had happened since they'd left the house this morning, her mind boggled. And the day wasn't over yet.

After their voracious bout of sex on the kitchen table, she and Jake voraciously scarfed up leftovers in the fridge, from ham and cheese on swirl bread to rice pudding, and everything in between. Salads, diced fruits, crab dip with crusty bits of a French loaf. And two of Delilah's specialty cinnamon rolls, a peach pecan and a ginger apple. Yum! They'd washed it all down with some of Father Brad's wine.

Sally offered to clean up, and Jake made his way upstairs to take a hot shower. Although she'd told him she would join him shortly in the shower, she was going to delay, to give him time to get his act together. The day was catching up with his body aches. As evidenced by his more pronounced limp and the fact that he took the backward method on the steps this time, that's how bad off he was.

Making quick work of the cleanup, she went into the hall and removed her laptop from its leather bag. Taking it into the kitchen, she set it on the table and logged into her account. First off, she wanted to look at that press release that the DOD had put out the day after that bullshit general had come to inform her that her dead husband was, in fact, alive.

Carefully, she parsed out parts of the media document, realizing now what she hadn't noticed before. It was very general, and could be interpreted in many ways. For example:

"Although Captain Dawson suffered serious injuries to one eye and a leg following a HALO jump into the mountains of Balakistan on May 19, 2016 . . ."

She realized that in this statement, it hadn't said, exactly, that his injuries occurred as a result of the jump. *Could they have occurred later?* she wondered. *Like under torture?*

Then there was this statement:

"He managed to survive for three years by living in a remote cave in the middle of hostile territory, with the aid of some rebel friendlies."

So, did this mean he was hiding in a cave, or that he was being kept in a cave? Like, as a prisoner?

And then, "Survival skills mastered during his military training helped the soldier to endure the brutal conditions."

What brutal conditions?

"During recent high-level negotiations between the US and the newly elected Qadir government, the president first learned of Captain Dawson's amazing survival story and demanded his immediate return. The President thanks Balakistan Minister of Defense Nazim bin Jamil for his efforts in this operation."

There were so many questions here. *Why did the Qadir government suddenly notify the US of Jake's existence? And when? Were there negotiations involved? Politics, or humanity?*

"Captain Dawson has been in Landstuhl Hospital in Germany, recovering from his injuries. Two other soldiers on Captain Dawson's team, Sergeant Frank Bailey and Corporal David Guttierez, died on the mission, according to Captain Dawson."

When did those two die, precisely? And how?

"The pilots who were to be rescued, Lieutenant Anton "Ace" Sampsell and Lieutenant Gerald Frank, were rescued in another section of Afghanistan soon after Captain Dawson went MIA."

MIA? Baloney! I'm not buying it! Not anymore!

"For more information, contact US Department of Defense, Press Information, Major Raymond Durand, at the above address."

Ah, the famous Major Durand! Yes, I have a few questions for you and your bogus press information.

She felt like such a fool. What was that old expression? "Fool me once, shame on you. Fool me twice, shame on me." Well, Sally was done being a fool.

Next up, she Googled Balakistan's new minister of defense, Nazim bin Jamil. What popped up were an alarming two thousand and thirty-seven links going back ten years. When she clicked on an early one, her blood went cold and the hair rose on the back of her neck as she read an article in the *Washington Post* accusing the man of brutality on a level with some of the world's worst villains. He'd been a Qadir tribal leader back then.

"Hey, Sal," she heard Jake call from the top of the stairs. "When you come up, would you bring a glass of ice water and that vial of pills in the downstairs bathroom medicine cabinet?"

"Sure," she called out. "Be right there."

Sally had more sleuthing to do, lots more, before she confronted Jake with what she was beginning to suspect. For now, she had more important things on her mind. Like those three precious words he'd said to her, and what they meant in the scheme of all these other issues. Most glaring had to be, at least to him, that she hadn't said the words back to him.

And she wasn't sure why.

Were they night terrors, or night terrorists? . . .

*T*he day had taken more out of Jake than he'd realized. He'd barely been able to continue standing in the shower with the pain racking his back and leg. Even his damaged eyeball hurt.

He sat on the edge of the bed until Sally came up with the ice water and his pain meds. Impatiently, he popped one pill and downed the entire glass of water.

"Are you okay?" she asked.

"I will be. Go take your shower, or a bubble bath. I should be fine by then."

"Don't feel like you have to prove anything to me, Jacob. Lie down. Sleep if you need to."

"Is that what you think I've been doing? Trying to prove something? Am I that pathetic?"

"Don't be so sensitive."

"Sensitive am I now, too?"

"Really, Jacob, sometimes you can be such an ass. Don't spoil what has been a good day."

He mumbled something about good being in the eye of the beholder and he had only one eye.

"Too bad you weren't around last Christmas, Mister Grumpy, you for sure would have been voted Grinch of the Year." She put her hands on her hips and shook her head at him. "Are we having a fight?"

He grinned, realizing that he *had* been acting like an ass, all because she hadn't mirrored back his "I love you." And because he hurt like hell, physically. He'd overdone it today. "Only if we have makeup sex afterward," he responded.

"Deal!" she said.

"Keep in mind, the kids should be back by noon. That leaves us time to do the deed only another, oh, five or six times."

"Dreamer!" She smiled. "I'm going to take a bubble bath, and, no, you are not invited to join me. Relax. When I get back, I have a surprise for you."

"I'm not sure I like surprises. Give me a clue."

She stuck out her tongue and showed him the ball of gum she'd been chewing. Then, before he could say something else snarky, she turned on her heel and sashayed away, giving a little extra wiggle to her hips.

Jake stood and shrugged out of his clothes, then slipped nude between the sheets. The pill was already beginning to take effect. That on top of the wine he'd drunk with dinner, and the overall exhaustion of a full day of driving and rehab, caused him to sink into almost instant slumber.

Unfortunately, for only the second time since he'd been home, he felt himself on the brink of one of his nightmare attacks, this one of the red-tide rage variety. In other words, a monster. He tried to fight it off, but couldn't.

In his dream, he saw the ice pick in Nazim's hand. The point was getting closer and closer to his eyeball, which was being exposed by the grimy fingers of Nazim's assistant.

"Tell me the names of your contacts in Balakistan. Just one. And then we'll let you go home."

"My name is Jacob Lloyd Dawson. Rank: captain. Identification number . . . what? No, I don't know any traitors. I've told you that a million fucking times. Put the pick away, you sonofabitch!"

And then he screamed.

"Rock-a-bye, Baby" . . .

Sally had finished her bath and was applying scented lotion to her legs and arms. The OBX sun was brutal at drying out skin, even when sunscreen was used religiously. That's when she heard Jake's scream. A piercing, agonizing, drawn-out cry that tore at Sally's heart.

Without bothering to grab a nightshirt or any other clothing, she rushed into the bedroom. Unlike the other time when Jake had been flailing about on the floor, seeming to be fighting off some attacker, now he was drawn up into a fetal position on the bed, moaning continuously. He was totally naked. Even the eye patch was off and lying on the floor.

She got onto the mattress behind him, and tried to spoon her body into his. He was so stiff, it was as if his limbs were frozen, like an obscene statue, into this pose. Even so, she pressed her breasts against his back and tucked her knees behind his knees.

She managed to get one arm under his neck and wrap her other arm around his waist. She crooned against his ear, "Jacob, it's all right. You're home. It's all right. You're safe now. Please, honey, wake up."

Sally felt totally ill-equipped for this situation. She had no idea what a person should do for someone suffering from PTSD, and there was no doubt in her mind that this was what was happening to her husband. She would have to Google this tomorrow, along with all her other sleuthing, or seek expert help.

But could she do that behind Jake's back? Would he resent her for what he would consider interfering?

Did it matter? He needed help, that was for certain.

So, she did the one thing she knew how to do. Sing. And the only song she could think of at the moment was the silly one she used to sing to the boys when they were overtired and grumpy and unable to fall asleep. "You are my sunshine, my only sunshine . . ." The whole time she sang, she rocked back and forth, back and forth against him until he rocked with her.

Eventually, she felt Jake's body relax, and then finally shake a little. At first, she worried that he was shaking with shock. But then she realized that he was shaking with suppressed laughter. "Are you trying to torture me, too?" he said, turning onto his back. An inadvertent acknowledgement that his nightmare had indeed been about torture.

She was on her side, leaning over him. "Are you okay now?"

He nodded, but the expression on his face was grim. It was odd to be seeing him with both eyes open. And, yes, it was a little disconcerting to have the one eye not moving like the other. But when he was staring straight ahead, it almost seemed normal. "If you're worried about the boys ever witnessing this, don't be," Jake said. "I won't allow it to ever happen."

A chill ran over Sally as she realized that the only way he could guarantee that, at this point in his recovery, was to not be here. *Oh, no, no! You plan to bail out, don't you? Maybe disappear, like some of those Special Forces guys do sometimes. Uh-uh! You don't get to make that kind of decision on your own. And if you think I can't stop you, just watch, buster.* She had to visibly breathe in and out to calm herself down, not to start an argument when Jake was still in this state. Later, though. Oh, yeah, later! "Jacob, I'm not worried about the boys. You'd be surprised at how understanding kids can be. I'm just worried about you."

"Don't be. I'm going to take care of it."

The silent message was "his way."

But then he said, "What's that smell?" He sniffed the air.

"Oh, it's lilac. My body lotion. Don't you like it?"

"It's okay," he said, "but I'm more in the mood for cinnamon. What happened to the gum?"

"I think I swallowed it when I heard you scream."

"Did you say *swallow*? Hmm. Maybe I could scream at a certain opportune moment, and you could . . ."

"Swallow?" she finished for him. "You are so bad."

"Just kidding." He laughed and tugged her closer. "Stick out your tongue."

When she did, he licked her tongue.

"Jacob!"

"Still tastes like cinnamon," he announced jubilantly. "And guess what? I brought a pack up with me, too." He reached over to the bedside table, pulled out a drawer, and showed her the package of spicy gum. He popped two sticks in his mouth and began to chew in an exaggerated fashion.

"Well, then, cowboy, it looks like we're still on for a cinnamon rodeo."

Chapter 15

*The minds of men, no matter the age,
run in one direction . . .*

Jake and Sally stood on the back porch just before noon the next morning, waiting for the kids to return. His father had called once the boat docked to alert them that they were headed home.

Jake was feeling satisfied with himself in an admittedly macho way. What guy wouldn't after the kind of weekend he'd enjoyed with his wife? Except for the nightmare, everything had been perfect.

And Sally . . . He had only to look at the sex flush that covered her from face to chest to know that Mick Jagger song didn't apply to either one of them. She wore a black tank top and white yoga pants, and he would bet she was flushed in some other places, too. If he had gotten his rocks off, his wife's bells had been rung, a time or twenty. Which gave him even more immense satisfaction.

Just then, with perfect synchronicity, the town

bells began to ring twelve times, and his father's truck pulled into the driveway.

"Stop smirking," Sally said, as if she could read his mind.

He just winked at her—with his one eye, the other was covered with the eye patch today—and walked down the steps with the aid of the handrail.

No sooner did the truck stop than the three gremlins and mangy dog hopped out and came rushing at him, almost knocking both him and Sally over.

"Daddy, Daddy, we caught fifty fith."

"Even a baby shark."

"PopPop says there prob'ly are no more fish left in the ocean."

"I caught the most fish."

"But mine was the biggest."

"PopPop made us clean all the fish."

"I puked on thome of the guts."

"Old Mike said a bad word. Three times! Do you wanna know what it was?"

"Kin we play video games for extra hours t'day 'cause we missed them for two days?"

"Donky Kong firtht."

"No, Space Wars."

"I hafta pee."

"Me, too."

"Me, too."

They all ran into the house, pushing each other aside as they tried to go through the door together and Goofus ran off, presumably to his own backyard.

Jake looked at his father, who was beginning to haul their gear out of the truck. He'd aged about twenty years this weekend, or maybe he just looked tired. Whoever said children were for the young knew what they were talking about, Jake decided. Kids were energy draining, to say the least.

Jake put the gate down in back of the truck and hauled the cooler forward. It really was heavy with their catches. He peered inside and noted trout, bass, stripers, and blues, even a few crabs. "Wow! Who's gonna eat all this stuff?"

"Hell if I know! Give it to the neighbors if you don't want it."

"Don't be so grumpy, Joe," Sally said, coming up to give his father a kiss on his whiskered cheek. "We'll use them all, and we appreciate your taking the boys out for a trip they'll remember all their lives."

Exactly what Jake would have said, if he'd thought before speaking. "Where's Old Mike?"

"We dropped him off at the house. Says he's gonna take a nap for a week."

Jake suspected that his father would soon be doing the same. He reached out and shook his father's hand, then pulled him into a hug. Against his ear, he whispered, "Thanks, Dad."

His father seemed to have trouble swallowing for a moment, then said, "Anytime, son."

They could already hear the sound of the video game blasting from the living room.

"Turn that down!" Jake yelled.

Immediately, the volume was lowered. The kids were probably worried that he would come in and turn it off. Not yet. But soon. By the looks of them, they could all use a shower and fresh clothes.

After they unloaded the truck, including a mountain of smelly kids' clothing that went directly to the laundry, Sally told his father, who was standing with them in the kitchen by now, "We have a lot of leftover food here that the neighbors and friends dropped off. Can we give you a care package to take home?" She opened the fridge to show him how the shelves were still overflowing.

"Sure. A couple ham and roast beef sandwiches would be good, and I wouldn't turn away some of that Norse potato salad of Vana's."

The jaws of Jake and Sally both dropped.

"What? Don't knock it till you tried it. Those lutefisk taste just like anchovies. Yum."

"Yeah, and snake tastes just like chicken," Jake scoffed.

They gave him the whole bowl.

Just before his father left, Jake said to him, "I know you're tired and probably pushed to your limits of patience with the kids, but, well, was the trip successful? Was it all you wanted it to be?"

His devious father looked at Sally, giving her a

full body survey, then looked at him with equal attention. Then, he grinned. "Yep."

Is a half-baked idea better than no idea? . . .

They decided to go to the Rock Around the Clock Diner for dinner that evening, at Sally's suggestion. She and Jake were tired of the leftovers, and Sally didn't feel like cooking, especially since she intended to go into the bakery this evening to prep tomorrow's breads and rolls. Plus, it was a treat for the kids, who loved the Elvis atmosphere, though they didn't have a clue who "the King" was, except for that hound dog song, which they thought was hilarious.

It wasn't until six p.m. that they were able to leave the house. It took that long to get the boys showered and changed, they were so wound up from their trip.

Just before they left, while Jake was on the phone with someone, maybe Major Durand, the three of them cornered her out on the back porch. "We have an idea," Matt said, and the other two yahoos nodded in agreement.

They were up to something, she could tell.

Matt, their spokesman, said, "We want to enter the Lolly talent contest, with you."

She frowned. "Doing what?"

"Singing."

"What?" Unless something had changed dramatically in the past few days, none of them could carry a tune in a bucket, as the old saying went.

"We want to surprise Dad," Matt elaborated.

"What do singing and a surprise for your father have in common?"

"Well, the Lolly celebration is supposed to be about lots of stuff. Treasures and patriotism and heroes and hometown talent," Matt told her, like a little old man who'd rehearsed his spiel. "We think it would be cool if we sang that song about eagle wings and heroes, just to show Dad that we're glad he came home."

It took Sally a moment to decipher what they meant. *Oh, my God!* They meant that old Bette Midler song about a woman asking a guy if he knew he was her hero, that he was the wind beneath her wings. And the boys wanted to surprise their father with *that* song! *Oh, my God!* Jake would die of embarrassment, or from emotion overload. He objected to the yellow ribbons still exhibited around town. She could only imagine his reaction to being serenaded by his family.

"Um, can we think about this before we decide for sure?"

The boys weren't too happy about her lack of enthusiasm.

"Maybe we could even ask Uncle Kevin if he would play the guitar with us?" Mark suggested.

Oh, no, no, no! Talk about awkward! "If we decide to do this, and I'm not saying we are, I don't think asking Kevin to join us would be a good idea. It should be a family thing."

"We been practicin'," Luke told her.

"You have, sweetie? When?"

"Out on the boat," Mark said.

Sally narrowed her eyes with suspicion. "Does PopPop know about this idea?"

"Yep," all three answered.

Sally was going to have a thing or two to say to Joe about encouraging his grandkids with this notion. It would serve him right if they decided to go ahead with the wacky idea, and forced him to join them on stage.

"We got the idea when that song came on the oldies station on the boat radio," Matt explained.

"At first, PopPop said we were scarin' the fish away with our caterwaulin'," Mark noted.

"But then he and Old Mike thaid we were really good," Luke interjected. "Wanna hear?"

"Not right now," she said quickly. "Remember, it's supposed to be a surprise."

The three of them pretended to zip their lips as Jake came out, looked at all four of them, who'd gone suddenly silent, and asked, "What's up?"

"Nothing," they all said, including Sally.

As they walked to the truck, Sally noticed how cute they all looked in almost identical khaki cargo shorts and black T-shirts, father and sons. It had been an unintentional matchy-matchy action, and not worth changing when they realized what they'd done. Jake, who was wearing the eye patch this evening, rather than dark sunglasses, and smelling enticingly like cinnamon, looped an arm over Sally's shoulder.

The boys were already in the back seat arguing and squealing over who should sit where and an occasional "Mom, he's touching me" yelled out. The whole time, they kept darting glances at their father, then at her, and whispering. Secret agents, they would never be.

Jake squeezed her shoulder. "Are you guys ganging up on me?"

"You have no idea," Sally said.

And the (red) tide turneth . . .

Jake had been in Clyde Jones's rock 'n' roll–themed diner many times growing up in Bell Cove, but not of course in recent years. Clyde's niece, Delilah, Sally's friend, had done a great job restoring the place to its former glory.

In fact, the boys insisted that he take a picture with his cell phone of them posing in front of the twenty-foot neon Elvis out front, which hadn't been there in the old days, but was a great addition. Two of them had crawled halfway up Elvis's leg. Matt was stretched on tiptoes, pretending to be patting the King's butt. And Sally was as bad as the kids, hugging Elvis's boot. She looked like a kid today, too, with her hair all spiked up, wearing a pink-and-white halter dress that barely covered her thighs, which was amazing considering how un-kid-like she'd been all weekend, especially with her interpretation of cinnamon sex. *Whoa!*

Just as he was about to round up his rowdy bunch, he heard the loud screeching noise of car brakes being pushed to the metal. Glancing sharply to the right, his Special Forces training on high alert for danger, about to leap into action, he saw a bunch of teenagers in a beat-up convertible, laughing their asses off as they barely missed the curb on the street out front. Without a care for any damage they might have done, the idiot driver did a quick self-correction and zoomed off. He'd either been talking or texting or whatever teens did today to distract them from driving with alertness. There could have been kids near that curb.

He sounded like an old fogey thinking that way, but he realized that the knee-jerk, sharp swivel of his head to the right had been due to his concern for his family. *What did I think would happen? That a vehicle would jump the curb and come barreling over the parking lot, taking down my wife, three kids, and a twenty-foot Elvis? Hey, stranger things have happened. Good thing I didn't have a weapon with me. I might have shot up a terrorist teenager.*

But here was an even stranger thing. When his head had wrenched to the right, so had his eyeballs. Both of them. It felt like something had pulled in the socket. And it hurt now. Not painfully. Just an odd ache. This had never happened before. He needed to examine the situation in front of a mirror once he got home. He'd probably popped a blood vessel, or something.

In any case, time to get this show on the road. "Let's go, kiddos. If we don't hurry, they'll be sold out of grilled peanut butter and banana sandwiches."

"Oh, no!"

"I want bacon on mine."

"Well, I'm not eatin' fried pickles. Yuck!"

"Pickles give you farts. Binky said so."

"I'm gonna eat five banana puddings with whipped cream, and I don't care if I barf, either."

"I like that Elvis song about Hawaii. That's where they do the hula dance."

"Kin we get a hula hoop?"

"Wonder if Maggie will be here?" Matt asked, his face going suddenly red as he noticed his father watching him.

"Who's Maggie?" Jake asked Sally.

"Maggie, short for Magdalene, is Delilah's daughter."

"Magdalene and Delilah, huh? Biblical names. She's as bad as us with Matthew, Mark, and Luke."

"And there's the grandmother, too, named Salome. Wait till you get a look at her. Oh, my! No, I won't tell you what I mean. I can't wait to see your reaction. Let's just say if you think Vana Gustafson is hot, wait till you meet the Glam Gram. That's what they call her." She rolled her eyes. "And as for Maggie, she's only five, Luke's age, but all girly girl. All the boys love her."

Still laughing and talking over each other and elbowing each other, the boys would have rushed up the steps and into the diner, screeching like hyenas, if he hadn't grabbed the hands of two of them and Sally corralled the other. They were laughing as they walked inside.

Right away, they were greeted by a blonde bombshell. That was the only way to describe the tall woman with big bed-mussed blonde hair and a hot-cha-cha figure encased in tight white jeans, a red tank top, *and an apron*. Yes, Jake had developed a thing about aprons.

"Sally! You came! At last!" The woman hugged Sally, gave each of the boys a kiss on top of their heads, then turned to him. "And you must be Jake." She gave him a hug, too.

"Jake, this is my friend, Delilah Good. As you can guess, Lilah, this is my husband, Jacob."

"You can call me Jake," he said quickly. Sally was the only one he wanted calling him Jacob.

"Welcome, welcome," she said to them all.

"Hey, the place looks great. Just like it did in the old days, but better," he said. And it did. Everything was shiny new, including the mini jukeboxes set on the wall of each booth, where you could hear the low strains of Elvis songs playing whenever the diners had put in their quarters. At the back end of the diner, on a far wall, he saw evidence of Sally's parents and their set-designing skills having been there. There was a mural depicting a collage of Elvis images against the backdrop of Graceland.

"Thanks. You grew up in Bell Cove. Did you know my uncle?"

"Yeah, a little. My mom and dad knew him better. But this was a teenage hangout for a while. Old Clyde was a good guy."

"You can take that booth there at the end. Merrill is out back, checking inventory for me. I'll bring him here to meet you, Jake. We've heard so much about you."

Jake looked at Sally, wondering what she'd told everyone.

She just shrugged. "I might have mentioned that you're an ass on occasion." Then she grinned. "Or that you have a great ass."

He grinned back at her and said, "Likewise."

Once they were seated, Jake noticed a little girl wearing a red dress with a black belt and a mop of blonde curls. She was talking to a waitress over near the counter. "I assume that's Kindergarten Barbie," Jake said.

"Da-ad!" Matt protested, his face red with embarrassment as he pivoted to make sure no one overheard him.

"Hey, boys, I could give you some tips on how to draw in the chicks. First off, no picking your nose. For some odd reason, girls consider that uncool."

Now it was all three boys who said, "Da-ad!"

"Stop teasing them," Sally said, fighting a smile.

They ate and listened to "Hound Dog" three times on their personal jukebox. He and Sally listened to the boys chatter about every little thing that had happened on the weekend with PopPop, including a few things that might discomfort the old fellows.

It wasn't until they got up from their booth and Jake was placing a tip on the table that Delilah was able to bring her husband out to meet Jake. She apologized for the delay, explaining that the sudden influx of customers was due to a van load of bird-watchers from Virginia coming in, unannounced. Not that the diner took reservations. The Outer Banks was noted for its nature preserves, and because of both its marsh and beach environments, there were presumably more than four hundred species of birds flying or nesting about. Jake knew because many of his school trips involved birding. It was something all Outer Banks kids knew about, his boys included.

"Jake, this is my husband, Merrill Good. Merrill, honey, this is Sally's husband, Jake Dawson, that we've heard so much about."

Good's handshake was firm and he looked him straight in the eye as he said, "I've been looking forward to meeting you. I understand we have a lot in common."

Jake assumed that he meant the military.

Sally and Delilah stepped aside and were talking softly about something involving Lollypalooza weekend. The boys subtly moved over crablike to where Maggie was now sitting on one of the counter stools helping the waitress fill ketchup squirt bottles. Well, subtle as a clump of three clumsy boys could be.

"Have you decided whether you'll stay in the military or stay here in Bell Cove?"

No beating around the bush with this guy!

"Nope. Not a clue."

"You're welcome to join my salvaging crew, and we're about to start another venture into the mountains, looking for precious gems. We can always use a guy with a military background."

"Are you shitting me? I don't have the physical capability or the coordination to do anything like that." And, frankly, Jake was offended that he would bring it up.

"Bullshit!" Good said amiably. "You and I both know that men can overcome any kind of obstacles if they really want to. I know a guy who lost both legs, and he runs a fleet of trucks."

"Don't you mean Lieutenant Dan, and a fleet of shrimp boats?"

Good grinned. "No, I'm pretty sure Alan Petrie never met Forrest Gump."

"I'll think about it," Jake said. "Thanks for the offer."

"By the way, I've had my own experience with Nazim. Met him during a live op in Kabul one time. He was one mean sonofabitch." Good gave Jake a knowing look, taking in his eye patch and the scars on his wounded leg. "If you ever want to talk, I'm here on the island. Anytime."

Jake nodded.

Just then, several men and one woman walked into the diner, and Jake's three boys exploded in excitement, "Uncle Kevin, Uncle Kevin!" They rushed the one guy, hugging his legs, and he actually picked Luke up in his arms, and the little traitor kissed him on the cheek.

It was Kevin Fortunato, of course, the guy he'd seen Sally talking to in the bakery last week.

Good looked at him with concern, and Jake assured him, "Don't worry. I'm okay with this."

He noticed Sally glancing his way with worry, too.

Am I really such an ass?

Yep.

Does she think I'm going to knock the guy's lights out?

Yep.

"Really?" Good arched his brows. "I'm not sure I would be. Don't get me wrong. K-4 is a good guy, and he and Sally are just friends, but still . . ."

"Really." And Jake did the only thing he could in the circumstances. He walked over to introduce himself. To his surprise, there was no hint of the red tide on viewing his "competition." He stretched out his hand and said, "Hey, you must be Kevin Fortunato, the guy who catches more fish than God, according to my kids."

Fortunato put Luke down and gave Jake's hand a firm shake, just like Good had. "Welcome home, man. You have a great bunch of kids."

"I know," Jake said, looking at his boys, who were at his side now, gazing at him with ill-founded pride. "Thanks for being so good to them while I was gone." The hidden message being "And now I'm back."

But no, that's not what was on his mind. What he didn't say, but thought, was *And I hope you'll be as kind, and fatherly, to them if—when I leave again.*

As for Sally, who'd come up and looped her arm in his, that was another story.

On the other hand, bozo, leave my wife the fuck alone. Crap! Even I recognize "Dog in the Manger." When did I turn into such a selfish bastard? Oh, that's right. I always was.

"Did you say something, honey?" Sally asked him.

"Nothing important," he replied, then leaned down and asked, "How's my breath?" Maybe it was time for another cinnamon fix, although he was pretty sure the boys chewed the rest of the gum, which they'd unfortunately left on the kitchen counter.

"You smell like peanut butter."

He thought a moment. "Works for me."

Chapter 16

*She was shaken, all right,
or was that "all shook up"? . . .*

The next few days went off smoothly with no major glitches.

She and Jake slept together and made love every night, sometimes several times a night. His nightmares hadn't recurred, and he hadn't said or done anything more to indicate he was thinking about leaving. Although there had been that moment back at the diner on Sunday when he'd noticed the kids' affection for Kevin. The expression on his face had been pure hurt, wounded pride of the fatherly sort.

But that moment had passed, and plans were tentatively proceeding on her bakery addition, with Jake's help. Her accountant was presently studying the figures that Jake had compiled, after which she—rather, they—would decide whether to make an offer for the adjacent property. She kept insisting that this was not something she could do on her own.

And since the kids would start back to school on Monday, the week before Labor Day, there had been all the chaos of school prep, which amused Jake to no end, never having been around for this annual ritual before. Like school supplies and new backpacks that had to have just the right superhero or kid theme imprinted on them. Plus, the agony— agonizing to the kids, anyhow—of a shopping expedition to purchase new underwear, socks, and athletic shoes. Mark got lots of hand-me-down clothes from Matt, Luke got a lesser amount from Mark since by then some of them were worn out, but all the boys always got some new T-shirts, shorts, and pants.

This year, Sally had passed the job on to Jake, who'd remarked, "Easy peasy!"

Hah! How quickly he learned!

By the time he was done, he swore, "Never again! We're ordering everything from the internet next year."

"Bite your tongue," Sally had replied. "We support local in this house. Remember, I'm a local business. How would I feel if people ordered their cookies and cakes online?"

Duly chastened, Jake had muttered something about him having to be somewhere else at this time next year.

She and the kids had already practiced that hero song several times this week, after school, when Jake was off to rehab, and they weren't half-bad, but she hadn't given them a definite go-ahead yet. It could be either a huge success or a monumental bomb. She wasn't sure she was ready for that kind of risk.

And she had decided on another monster cookie to offer for the holiday. They were heart-shaped chocolate chip cookies, covered with white icing, piped along the edges in blue, with the simple message "My Hero" in red across its center. A zillion calories, which would launch a sugar high that lasted for days. She would, of course, call the cookies, which were the size of teacup saucers, Heroes.

Jake would probably hate them. Not the cookies themselves. He loved chocolate chip cookies, especially those with chopped walnuts, but the idea itself? No way! She had no intention of asking his permission. This was business, she told herself.

Despite all the seeming peace, Sally felt uneasy. The air seemed electric with something. Was she just looking for trouble, or was this the calm before the storm? And what would that storm entail?

She got a call from Jake just after the lunch rush at the bakery on Saturday. "Help! Save me!" he said.

She was in the middle of icing an elaborate four-tiered wedding cake when she heard those words. Jerking to attention, she almost knocked the whole thing over. "Why? Did something happen to the kids?" she asked with instant anxiety.

"What? No."

"Did something happen to *you*? Oh, my God! Did you fall down those damn steps? Is this one of those 'I've fallen and I can't get up' kind of things? I told you we should rent one of those stair lifts."

"Now you're being insulting. I have an injured leg, but I'm not ninety years old. Jeesh!"

At least he'd said *jeesh,* instead of his usual swear word. She was training him well to watch what he said in front of the kids.

"Well, what is it then? You sound panicked. And, by the way, why are you whispering?"

"Because I'm hiding in the outside shower stall as I make this call."

"Okay. I give up. Why are you hiding in the shower stall? Have the kids finally worn down your last nerve?" She was laughing as she imagined the boys standing outside the door asking their unrelenting questions, always wanting something, even when you escaped to the toilet . . . or a shower.

"No, Sally, I am not hiding from the boys. I'm hiding from your parents."

"My parents? They're there? Two days early!"

They weren't supposed to come until Monday in advance of the Labor Day celebrations that would begin this upcoming weekend—the parade, the talent contest, musical events, including some unique bell choir performances, and so much more.

"Seriously, they're at the house now?"

"Serious as shit. They're here all right."

"Watch your language. Remember, you're supposed to be toning your 'nasty' words in case the boys hear."

He said a nastier word.

"Okay, so they came early." *Deal with it, Jake. I have enough on my plate, literally,* she thought, staring at the half-decorated wedding cake in front of her. "So, what's the problem?"

"They've been hugging me."

Her eyes went wide. Her parents had never been very fond of Jake, mainly because of his military career. Them hugging him was unusual, to say the least. She chuckled to herself.

But he heard her. "It's not funny. They're treating me like Christ risen from the dead."

"Don't be sacrilegious."

"I'm not. They really are treating me like some kind of miracle. And they're being nice. I don't like it."

"Lazarus."

"Huh?"

"Lazarus rising from the dead would be a better example than Jesus rising from the dead."

"Holy hell! You're correcting my Bible knowledge at a time like this?"

"I'll be home as soon as I finish this wedding cake."

"You better stop on the way home for some of that tofu veggie crap they like. They almost had a heart attack when I offered them one of the red meat burgers I was serving the kids for lunch. Wanted to know if I've ever tried those new yummy kale burgers, so much healthier, dontcha know?"

"You're exaggerating."

"Only a little," he admitted. "There is a good side to all this, though."

She could hear the smile in his voice, and waited for the zinger.

"They brought a couple of gifts for me. Some cannabis oil for my leg, and some funny cigarettes for pain."

"Don't you dare smoke weed with the kids around."

He laughed. "I might be tempted. You better hurry home to restrain my impulses."

When she clicked off her phone and set it aside, José remarked, "You're smiling again." Her assistant baker had been teasing her for days about the loopy grin she sported all the time, a sure sign, in his male handbook, that her maracas were being rattled on a regular basis. "Chac-chac!" he added, in case she didn't get the message.

When Sally got home, her parents were sitting on the back porch swing, sipping at lemonades, which Jake, bless his heart, must have made for them. She kissed them both, and marveled at how good they looked.

"I swear, you two don't ever age," Sally said.

Her father preened. Her mother arched her brows sardonically and said, "Lots of hard work on all the drooping parts."

They were a sophisticated couple, more attuned to city living and its attire, especially the Broadway scene with its many opening nights and cast parties. Her father, whose salt-and-pepper hair was designer unruly, looked elegant even in the T-shirt and slacks he wore today. Of course, the T-shirt was aqua silk tucked under a twisted leather belt into pleated white pants, no socks, and white deck shoes. He wore a plain Rolex watch on his wrist and a small diamond stud in one ear, which should go over big with the folks of Bell Cove. It was the kind of outfit you might see at a Long Island afternoon cocktail party where George and Amal might drop by while in the city, or Bette Midler, who was a frequent participant or visitor to the Great White Way and its players' homes, or whoever was the celebrity du jour.

Her mother was casually elegant, as well, in a red short-sleeved, scoop-necked fitted top over multi-colored harem pants and black sandals. Her brown hair, like Sally's, was long and coiled into a loose chignon at her neck. Her only jewelry was the set of ruby drop earrings that her father had gifted her the night they got their first Tony Award for set design. It had been for the musical *Magi*. As far as Sally could recollect, there had been a half-dozen other Tonys since then.

"You look good, too, sweetheart," her mother remarked. "To what can I attribute that beautiful flush of your skin? Some new retinol cream? The healthy climate? Or . . . ?"

Sally felt herself flush some more.

"Whatever it is, you could bottle it and sell it at Saks for a fortune."

"And you smell good, too," her father added. "Eau de vanilla?"

She laughed. "I was making a wedding cake today, and, yes, it was heavy on the vanilla piping."

"We are so proud of you," her mother remarked, and her father nodded.

Sally hoped that was true. For years they'd been

urging her to come back to New York and pick up her music studies. Especially after Jake's "death."

"I need to take these inside," Sally said, indicating the bakery bag she was carrying. "I brought some of my latest monster cookies for you to sample, and a fresh loaf of ciabatta. I also stopped at the deli for some of that roasted pepper hummus you liked so much last time you were here."

"Ooh, good!" her father said. "I'm starving."

Her mother rolled her eyes. "Don't believe it for one minute. He ate two of those horrible cow-meat patties when he thought I wasn't looking."

Her father grinned, unrepentant.

"Where are the kids and Jake?"

"Boys are inside, and Jake is in the garage working out," her mother said. Then, a bit teary-eyed, she whispered, "He looks surprisingly good, though way too thin. I was expecting—I don't know—that he would be changed, I suppose."

"And he was very welcoming to us," her father added.

What he didn't say was that Jake wasn't his usual quietly defensive, almost surly, self when they were around.

Good!

Her parents followed her into the kitchen where she left them to set the table and lay out the light lunch and dessert from the bakery boxes. She told them that the boys would probably join them, even though they'd just finished their own midday meal. They were always hungry.

She went into the living room then to find the three of them kneeling on the floor, hard at work on a hundred-piece puzzle of New York City that was laid out on the coffee table. They barely noticed her entrance.

"Hey, boys, what's up?"

"We did all the corners and are looking for side pieces like you taught us," Mark said, "but we're having trouble. Will you help us?"

"Later. For now, you might want to go wash your hands and eat with Gramp and Gram Fontaine. I brought some stuff from the bakery."

"Cookies?" Mark asked hopefully.

"Yes, and some bread and hummus."

The three were off like a shot to the downstairs bathroom shoving each other aside to get to the sink. She would have a mess to clean up later. Only then did she make her way outside to the garage where the door was open. Inside she found Jake sitting on her yoga mat, his free weights off to the side, along with a half-empty bottle of water. He was leaning back against a wall, his legs outstretched. His eyes were closed, his eye patch sitting on the tool bench along with his weight lifting safety gloves and an open tin of gym chalk.

She had to admit that she was looking for evidence of "funny cigarettes," not that Jake had ever been into illegal substances. He'd always been too health conscious and law-abiding for that. Still . . .

"No, Sally, I haven't been zoning out on weed," he said, without opening his eyes. "Just cooling

down. Mmm. You smell so good. Even from here.
Like a donut. No, it was a cake you were decorating when I called, right? Wanna come down here
and share some sugar with me?" He opened his
eyes, automatically reaching for the eye patch to
cover himself. Then, looking up at her, he motioned with the fingertips of one hand for her to
sit beside him.

"Not a chance! You'd have me flat on my back,
licking me like an ice cream cone."

"Now there's an image!" He grinned.

She remained just inside the door, arms folded
over her chest, refusing to budge.

"C'mon. You know you want to."

"My parents have already remarked on the healthy
flush that covers my skin."

"You gotta love the sex flush, baby."

"And José says I look like I've been having my maracas rattled on a regular basis."

"I *am* fond of your maracas." He continued to wag-
gle his fingertips toward himself, beckoning her
forward.

"You're impossible," she said with a laugh.

He was already shrugging out of his running
shorts, which was all he wore.

She glanced anxiously behind her. "You're crazy.
The boys, or God forbid, my parents, could walk
out here any minute and get an eyeful."

"Now see, that's where you're wrong," he said.
Reaching up behind him on the tool bench, he
grabbed a small black box. With the button pressed

on the remote control, the garage door began to close behind her. "Don't you love technology?"

"I give the kids fifteen minutes and they'll be out here banging on the door," she warned, but she was already walking slowly toward him.

"Fifteen minutes, huh?" Jake thought a moment. "Piece of cake!"

She didn't know if he was referring to the cake she'd been working on, or the efficiency with which he could make love under time constraints. Turns out it was both.

But the embarrassment factor went through the roof when they left the garage and noticed another party had arrived. Also early.

Her parents were still inside, apparently, but sitting on an Adirondack chair, enjoying the hell out of their surprise and discomfort, was Lieutenant Isaac Bernstein, peering at them over the top of dark sunglasses, which he'd moved halfway down his big nose. Izzie wore fatigues, the shirt open at the neck. His booted feet rested on the porch rail.

"Well, well, well!" Izzie remarked. "Dare I say, 'commando'?"

It wasn't a (pity) party, but he'd cry if he wanted to . . .

I have concerns," Jake said.

"No shit!" Izzie replied with his usual succinctness.

They were sitting in The Live Bass, a local tavern, sharing a few beers and catching up on the news.

After Sally had gone with the kids to help her parents settle in at the Heartbreak Motel, Izzie had walked down the street to his uncle's house to shower and change clothes, promising to be back in a half hour to pick him up. Jake had also showered and changed clothes, and they rode to the center of town in Uncle Abe's pristine twenty-year-old Buick, which prompted mutual grins.

"Ah, the memories!" Jake had remarked.

"God bless the bench seat!" Izzie had agreed. "What Detroit idiot thought it was a good idea to get rid of these teenage make-out features?"

"If leather could talk!"

They'd grinned at each other.

Izzie wore a faded red T-shirt, floral Hawaiian surfer shorts, and flip-flops, as far opposite as he could get from a military uniform, compared to Jake's more sedate blue-and-white-striped, button-down shirt over jeans. As they rode along, Izzie had gotten the biggest kick out of all the yellow ribbons still attached to practically every tree, mailbox, and lamppost, some of which were drooping by now. "Are any of these welcome bows for me, or they all for you, Mister Hometown Hero?"

"Kiss my ass," Jake had said.

"Would that be a heroic or nonheroic ass?"

"Always the clown!" Jake had observed. "If you must know, I'm praying for a big windstorm to come along and blow them all away."

"How much longer you gonna have that road-block and guard at the end of the street?"

"Word is, right after Labor Day."

"You worried about the news media knocking on your door then?"

"Not too much. I can handle it, and so can Sally, but the boys are something else. And, believe me, some of these people don't hesitate to get at me through the kids."

"You could hire a private firm."

"Nah. I've got to deal with it eventually." What he hadn't said was that he might not be there that much longer. Then it would be a moot point.

They'd chosen a back table at The Live Bass, rather than the bar, because so many people came up to them thanking them for their service, which was nice and well-intended, but starting to become irritating, as in they couldn't complete a sentence without being interrupted. Besides, a few were starting to ask uncomfortable questions about Jake's three-year absence.

"Do you ever wonder if we're making any difference?" Jake asked Izzie, who was in Delta Force, too, but another unit than Jake's.

"Never! And you don't, either, when you think about it."

"I don't know. It just seems like a vicious circle. We knock out the Taliban, then al-Qaeda emerges. We just about wipe al-Qaeda out, but ISIS gets stronger. Then, before you know it, al-Qaeda pops up again."

"There's evil in the world. You and I know that

firsthand. We can't stand by and do nothing. Someone has to fight. Look what happened with Hitler. Millions of people died because good people did nothing for years and years."

That was a particularly touchy subject for Izzie, whose people had suffered so much during the Holocaust, and still did today in Israel and that part of the world. *I should have kept my mouth shut.*

"So, you mentioned concerns," Izzie said. "Like what?"

"Why is Durand coming here? I sense an agenda."

"There's always an agenda, my friend."

"I see on the news that the new prime minister of Balakistan and Minister of Defense Nazim might be visiting the US for some treaty signing, which probably means they want money. If Durand expects me to come to DC and shake hands with the bastards, he's got another think coming."

"I doubt whether that will even pan out. Too many threats of protests from different human rights and watchdog organizations."

"Well, I'm not going to DC, whatever the reason, and I'm definitely not going to work behind a desk in the Pentagon, or anywhere else where I'm some kind of propaganda tool."

"Check. But what else do you have in mind if you leave the military? You gonna work in that bakery addition that Sally is planning?"

"No. I'm willing to help her get it going, but that's the extent of my involvement."

"Bottom line—do you want to stay in Bell Cove?"

"Want and should are two different things."

Izzie arched his brows at him.

"That's my second big concern. I'm becoming too comfortable here."

"Oh, please! You're too happy. Pity me. Boo-hoo-hoo!"

"I'm not looking for pity, asshole. I'm stating a fact. The longer I stay, the harder it'll be for me to leave. And it's not myself I'm concerned about, either. It's Sally and the kids. I don't want to hurt them."

"Then don't. Seriously, why would you even think that skipping town is any kind of solution?"

"Because I am not the man I used to be. I'm working out like crazy, but I have to be realistic. I will always have a limp, at best. Pain will be my best friend for the rest of my life. What does all that spell for a career, or me supporting a family? Do I go on disability, at my age?"

"There are other options."

"Maybe." He shrugged.

"Jake, where's your usual self-confidence?"

Broken.

"It's not like you to put yourself down this way."

I wasn't broken before.

"What did that motherfucker Nazim do to you?"

Don't ask. Really. Don't ask.

"There must be something other than the torture you've told us about."

Uh-huh.

"Mind games of some kind?"

If you only knew! The things that psychopathic maggot made me do, to think! Suffice it to say, I am no hero.

But he couldn't think about that now or he would go mad, madder than he already was. A change of subject was called for, quickly. "Can I confide in you without your blabbing to Durand or my wife or half of Bell Cove?"

Izzie put a hand to his chest and said, "I'm offended."

Jake lifted the patch over his eye. "What do you see?"

"Uh . . ."

Jake glanced right and then left.

"Holy crap! Your eyeball moved! That's something new, isn't it?"

"Yeah. I'm not sure it means anything significant, but something happened when I glanced sharply to the side one day last week. There was a hard pulling sensation, and ever since then, I've noticed differences."

"Has your vision changed?"

"No. Well, there is a slight change in shading. What used to be pitch black is now gray along the edges. And the border of gray has been increasing a bit every day."

Izzie reached across the table and squeezed Jake's forearm. "This is great news. No, you don't need to warn me about being overly optimistic. Every change has to be promising."

"Anyhow back to my concerns. I was at the diner

the other night with Sally and the boys when that Kevin dude walked in. Man, you wouldn't believe the kids' reaction. You'd have thought God had walked in the door, or some superhero. They love the guy, and he clearly has affection for them, too."

"Your point?"

"If I'm gone, they would forget me soon enough."

"Bullshit!"

"Everyone's always talking about how resilient kids are."

"I repeat, bullshit!" Izzie said. "And what about Sal? Would she be resilient, too?" He put up a halting hand before Jake could answer. "It's obvious you two have been screwing each other's brains out. A regular sex marathon would be my guess."

"If you mention commando again, I might just belt you."

"You could try." Izzie smirked.

"Sex doesn't equate with forever after," Jake told him.

Even Jake realized how lame that sounded, and he laughed along with Izzie.

"So, no red tide of rage when you ran into the boyfriend?" Izzie asked. "That's what I was afraid of."

Jake shook his head. "I was surprised, too. In fact, I haven't had any of those episodes since I got back. A few nightmares, but none of the rages. Which is another reason for me to get out of Dodge. I wouldn't want any of my kids, or Sally, to witness one of those psycho outbreaks. What if they were directed at one of them, and I harmed them, physically? Nope, they're better off without me."

"What are you aiming for here? Sainthood? Saint Jake? I just don't see it."

"Sometimes love means walking away, and, yeah, I know that's the oldest cliché in the book."

"Assuming you're right, where would you go, and what would you do?"

"I don't know. I'm researching it. The Northwest is looking promising."

"And what? You'd become a regular Grizzly Adams?"

"Who?"

"Never mind. Don't do anything rash, Jake. Give yourself a chance to heal more, and get yourself a shrink, for God's sake, or something. Maybe a lobotomy. I hear there are two psychiatrists, twin brothers, living over at the Patterson house. Why don't you try one of them?"

"Izz! They're about eighty years old."

"So? I hear they're veterans, too."

"Of what? The Revolutionary War?"

Just then Jake noticed something over Izzie's shoulder. "Uh-oh! Incoming at one o'clock. You better duck." Jake was the one grinning now at being able to reverse the discomfort tables on his friend.

Approaching with fire in her eyes was Laura Atler, and she was baited for bear—the bear being Lieutenant Izzie Bernstein.

"I think I'll leave you to take care of business here. I can hitch a ride home with Sally."

"Traitor," Izzie muttered, then looked up at Laura who was wearing a gray business suit and carrying a briefcase. "Nice to see you again, Laura. You're looking good."

"Save it," she said and sat down, not waiting for an invitation.

That was Jake's cue to leave.

To show how conflicted Jake was in his thoughts and actions these days, he grabbed a handful of mints from the dish beside the front register on his way out. *Mints are a close second to cinnamon*, he told himself, and popped a half dozen.

Chapter 17

Triple trapped . . .

*H*e was trapped.

"Nice to see you again, Laura," Izzie said. "You're looking good."

And she did. Laura was one of those women who grew into their beauty, and then just went on improving as they grew older. Like the class nerd with dark-framed Coke bottle glasses who showed up at a ten-year class reunion looking sensational, making one wonder how she'd kept all that hotness hidden back in the day or if she was just a late bloomer. Like himself with the big nose he'd grown into, as well. Come to think on it, he'd first fallen in love with Laura in kindergarten when she'd smiled and come to his defense when some of the other kids called him "Nosey Posey" just because his nose took up half his little face back then. Later, the rude nickname became "Schnoz."

In high school, Laura had been a little bit overweight, not enough that Izzie noticed, but she had always been on one half-assed diet after another and she'd worn clothes that she thought made her invisible. Not to him, though. And her skin hadn't always been spotless. Whose was, during those zit years? No wonder she'd been a bit on the shy and timid side, not wanting to call attention to herself.

Now she was slim—petite, actually—clear skinned and hot, wearing what she probably thought was a boring gray suit, but she wore no blouse underneath, which he noticed, horndog that he was. The skirt was narrow and short, leading down to a pair of black "fuck me" high heels, the kind that left the toes and heel exposed, which he also took particular notice of, including the pink polish. Her silvery blonde hair, which used to be a mass of untamable curls, now hung straight about her face and onto her shoulders, probably due to one of those crazy ironing devices women used. And, yeah, she might not be wearing much makeup but that siren-red lipstick gave him ideas.

He still felt a little bit tight in the chest just looking at her.

"Save it," she said, noticing his perusal, and sat down, not waiting for an invitation.

So much for shy and timid!

But, hey, he liked this new Laura.

Since she didn't say anything right away, he searched his brain for something to fill the awkward silence and came up with, "You must be excited that Wendy moved back in town. You two were always best buddies."

She nodded, and still said nothing, just gave him the stink eye.

To fill the continuing silence, he babbled on, "She and Ethan finally got their acts together, right?"

Wendy Patterson and Ethan Rutledge had been an item since practically toddlerhood here in Bell Cove, but they broke up before college when he'd gotten another girl pregnant. Wendy had gone off to be a female Navy SEAL, of all things, and Ethan stayed here to run his family's Christmas tree farm, another huge surprise. But now they'd come full circle.

"I thought you would have been here for the wedding," she commented.

"Couldn't. I was in Kabul at the time."

"You better not be thinking we'll do the same thing."

"Huh?" He sat up straighter in his chair. "Why would you think that I would think that?"

She shrugged. "You're suddenly back in Bell Cove after all these years. You probably heard that I'm practically engaged to Gabe Conti. In case you don't know, he's an architect who moved here to take over his family's Bell Forge factory." She was the one to look embarrassed now, at her nervous babbling.

"Practically? What does 'practically engaged' mean? Is that like 'sort of pregnant'?" he teased.

"You don't have to be sarcastic."

Yeah, I do. Either that or lean over and see if that lip-

stick tastes as good as it looks. "I thought you were engaged to the Great Dane."

"Turns out Dane Hollis was marking every tree in the neighborhood."

"A real dog, huh?"

"Yeah. How did you know about Dane?"

"My parents gave me all the news until they moved last year. And Uncle Abe and Aunt Rachel have made sure I'm up to date on all the Bell Cove gossip since then. But let's be clear—I'm not here to cause trouble in your love life." *Or not much.* "I'm here because of Jake," he said, before biting his tongue.

"Ah," she said and laid a cell phone on the table, which he noted had a record button on it. Being in Special Forces, he was accustomed to noticing crap like that. *Scan your perimeter. Always be alert. Carelessness is your number one enemy.* She sealed the deal when she took a notepad and a pen out of her briefcase, which she laid out before her.

Whaaat? Is that why she wanted to meet with me? Not to return something, like Jake said, or to hook up with me again, but to get a scoop on Jake. Well, shiiiit! She better not think she's recording me.

He slid her phone across the table toward him and looked at her before he clicked off the record button. "No way, Lois Lane."

"How do you know I don't have a recording device planted on me?"

"Do you?"

"No. I don't need a recorder. I have an excellent memory."

This was a ridiculous conversation. It was like there was some big elephant in the room they were dancing around, and Izzie wasn't a very good dancer. "Jake said that you have something to give me."

"I do," she said. Reaching into her pocket, she pulled out a college class ring from the Citadel. She shoved it across the table.

"My ring?" he asked dumbly. "You kept it all these years?"

"Not out of any sentiment. I just didn't feel right about throwing it in the trash."

"In the trash?" He looked at her and couldn't help but notice her chin rise a notch. Also, her hands were trembling a little. *Hmmm.* "Do I sense a little hostility here?"

"Now why would you think that? Do you remember what you said when you gave me that ring?"

"Give me a break. That was ten years ago, Laura."

But, yeah, I remember. I told you that I would come back after basic training, and we would get engaged. Should I tell her why I didn't—couldn't—or is it too late for that?

"The shelf life for being a jackass is like . . . forever."

"Ouch. Would it help if I said I'm sorry?"

"No. And don't be thinking I'm going to jump into the back seat of your uncle's sex mobile with you, for old times' sake."

Izzie blinked with shock. He hadn't in a million years been thinking that. But he was now.

She waved a hand dismissively when he was about to say something more. "None of that matters. Returning your ring and a boring rehash of your dumping me a long time ago is not the reason—"

"Whoa, whoa, whoa. I did not dump you."

She waved a hand dismissively again. If she kept doing it, he might just grab her by the wrist and haul her over the table and . . .

"I need to talk to you about the parade on Saturday."

"Huh?"

"I'm on the parade committee."

He shook his head to clear it. "Did I miss something here? What does a recording device, Jake, and my class ring have to do with a friggin' parade?"

"I never said they were connected. You're the one who made assumptions about why I wanted to talk to you."

He rolled his eyes and sat back in his chair, but not before taking a long drag on his beer. "Okay. Give it to me. What about the parade?"

"I just wanted to make sure you're wearing that hottie uniform like in the picture on the wall of the deli."

"You think I'm a hottie?"

"Not you. The uniform."

"Wait. Are you under the delusion that I'll be participating in a parade?"

"No delusion. You're in, buddy. Riding in a convertible with Major Durand."

Oh, crap! "How do you know Major Durand?"

"I don't know the man. Jeesh! Don't get bent out of shape. Mayor Ferguson is the one who contacted him after your aunt mentioned that she was going to have a high uppity-up Army guy as a weekend guest. And she wasn't talking about you."

"I never said I was a high uppity-up."

The look she gave him said that he probably thought it. "So, it's settled? You'll be in the parade."

He assumed that Durand had approved this already. "I guess so," he said. "About that other thing. The nondumping. What say we have dinner together tonight and straighten out some misconceptions?"

She stood and was gathering her stuff, preparing to leave. "Not a chance! I'd probably find myself on the back seat of the Buick with my legs through the sunroof."

He grinned. That didn't sound like a practically engaged woman to him.

"Tsk-tsk! What happened to the shy, modest girl I used to know?"

"She grew up."

"Too bad," he said, but he liked this new version of the old Laura. Maybe too much.

If Izzie thought he'd dodged a bullet with Laura, he was wrong. No sooner did Laura leave and he was standing, about to leave himself, when Sally approached.

"Are you looking for Jake?"

"No, I sent him home with the kids. He'll pick me up later at the bakery. It's you I'm looking for."

"Uh-oh!" He tilted his head in question and sank back down into his chair. He nodded to the waiter for another beer and asked Sally, "What'll you have?"

She sat across from him. "A Bloody Mary sounds good."

While they waited for their beverages, Sally pulled an iPad out of her purse, set it on the table, and logged in to some news website. Turning it so that they could both see the screen, he saw that there was a Reuters news story from ten years ago with the headline "Nazim and Qadir Rebels Torture Villagers."

The hairs rose on the back of Izzie's neck. "What exactly do you want me to see?"

"This article, plus dozens of others that I've been Googling, all point to a totally different Nazim and Qadir government than what our administration is currently portraying. And this Nazim is the one who turned Jake over?" She gave Izzie a pointed look. "Something is rotten in the state of Denmark, my friend. So . . . ?"

"So . . . ?" he repeated back to her.

"Exactly what happened to Jake during those three years he was MIA, lounging in a cave, waiting to be rescued?" she asked in a scoffing tone.

Fuck, fuck, fuck! Jake is in such trouble! Durand is going to be furious. If Sally could figure this out, or be

suspicious, the news media must be digging even deeper.
The shit is going to hit the fan, one way or another.

"Have you asked Jake about this?"

"In the beginning, I did. But not lately. He's clearly hiding stuff. And he's hurting, Izz. Real bad. And I don't just mean physically. I want to help, but I don't know how." She had tears in her eyes.

"I hope you haven't been discussing your concerns with anyone else."

"I haven't." She paused. "Why?"

"It could be dangerous."

"For whom?"

"Everyone. Starting with Jake."

"Dangerous in what way?"

"Nazim wouldn't want him talking. Our government wouldn't want him talking. I can think of a dozen different people and agencies that wouldn't want him talking."

"Oh, my God!"

"You need to discuss this with Jake. In the meantime, I'll speak to Durand."

The waiter brought Izzie's beer and Sally's drink. They each drank for a few moments.

"You think I'm meddling, don't you?" she asked.

He shook his head. "No, I think you love the guy."

A tear slid down her cheek. "He's planning to leave. I know him. I see the signs."

And if he finds out you or the kids might be in danger because of his presence here, he'll be off like a shot. "Sal, don't say or do anything until after the holiday. Let me see what I can do."

"And in the meantime, I just twiddle my thumbs?" she asked.

"Just continue to screw his brains out, like you have been."

On that happy note—at least Sally was laughing as she left—Izzie planned to scoot out of the bar and make a quick call to Durand, who wasn't supposed to arrive until Friday. But he was trapped again. For the third time!

This time it was Jake's father, Joe Dawson, and Old Mike, both of whom looked as if they'd just stepped off their fishing boat, complete with suspendered hip boots and canvas bucket hats. Izzie didn't even bother to stand, just waved for them to sit down and put up two fingers for the waiter to bring two more beers.

"How can I help you gentlemen?" he asked with a long sigh.

"We need help keepin' Jake in Bell Cove," Joe said right off.

Why me?

Because I'm his best friend.

But maybe staying in Bell Cove isn't the best thing for him.

"We already got him and Sally havin' sex like rabbits," Old Mike added.

Izzie wasn't about to ask what he meant by that.

"But that might not be enough to keep my boy in town," Joe continued.

"We see the signs," Old Mike said with a nod at his partner.

"A baby, that's the answer. We need to find a way to get Sally pregnant again. And this time Jake will stick around to see it born." This from Joe.

Izzie's eyes widened at that outlandish statement. And he didn't like the sound of that "we." *Do they mean me, too?* "What? Are you serious? What can you—we—do about Sally getting pregnant? I don't understand." And wasn't an unplanned pregnancy supposed to be the worst reason for a couple to stay together?

"Well, she takes them birth control pills," Joe told him. "Maybe you—bein' in Special Forces and knowin' all kinds of tricks—could tell us how to doctor 'em up so they're just placebos or whatever you call them dummy pills."

Izzie put his face in his hands. "That is the dumbest idea I ever heard. Unethical at the least. And illegal. Don't . . . you . . . dare!"

"Okay. So, what's your idea then?" Old Mike asked.

Izzie's only thought was, *I've landed in Bedlam. No, I've landed in Bell Cove. Same thing.*

Chapter 18

*And then they hit him with their best shot,
and it was a shot to the heart . . .*

He just needed to get through the Labor Day weekend.

Jake felt pressure building all around him, and he was being pulled in five different directions at one time, which had to stop. If he wanted to avoid a recurrence of the nightmares or, God forbid, one of the red-tide rages, he needed to step back, and, yes, he had to admit it, just breathe, like Dr. Sheila had advised. Furthermore, once the hassle of all the Bell Cove hoopla was over, Jake had some important decisions to make, the least of which involved PTSD counseling.

The rages, he'd come to conclude, were triggered when some huge anger issues popped up, and hadn't happened at all since he'd left the hospital in Germany. Then, the red tide had been sparked by the news that his "rescue" was being announced to his wife and the world, without his consent. He had feared a recurrence when he first met "Uncle"

Kevin, but that hadn't happened. So, no sweat on the rages. So far.

The nightmares, or night terrors, on the other hand, followed a pattern that he was better able to understand now . . . and control. They usually followed a day when he'd overdone things, physically and mentally. In other words, stress. With a determined effort to cut back on overexertion and tense situations, he'd thus far avoided the humiliation of having his kids witness him in the throes of a wild flashback.

Now, he was in uniform for the first time in years, preparing for the friggin' parade. "It's a little big. What do you think?" he asked Sally.

"It's fine." She walked around him in their bedroom, adjusting the jacket in places and patting the myriad colored stripes on front, including the Silver Star bar he'd attached for the first time. "In fact, don't you dare take it off when we get home later."

He turned to look at her in question.

"You are so hot. Seriously, dude, you can still make my bones melt when you're in uniform."

He grinned.

"And you know it!" She slapped his arm in fake reprimand.

"And when I take it off? What happens to your bones then, baby?"

"Up in flames, baby." She gave him a quick kiss and darted away before he could grab for her.

She was looking damn good herself. "Thanks for wearing the dress."

"Pfff. This thing is going to be in shreds pretty soon. I've been wearing it so much." She said it with a smile, though. He could tell that she liked doing things to please him. And that made him want to do twice as many things to please her. If only he could!

It was the peach sundress, of course, the one that reminded him of that time when they'd first met in Central Park. A time when things were so much . . . less complicated.

Just then, the boys barreled in. They never just walked into a room. They stopped dead in their tracks when they saw him in full uniform. "Wow!" Matt exclaimed, immediately echoed by his brothers.

"'Wow!' back at you, guys," Jake said. They were wearing their scout uniforms with all their impressive badges, including Luke's recently earned one for knots, which you would have thought was a Medal of Honor. "I still think all of you should ride in the convertible with me."

The boys' faces lit up.

Sally shook her head. "No. The boys should march with their scout troops."

"And you?"

She shook her head some more. "I want to be on the sidewalk taking pictures of you all. Besides, I told my mother and father I would meet them in front of the bakery. Your dad and Old Mike will be with me, too. Your own personal cheering section."

Yippee!

Luke tugged on Sally's hand, and she leaned

down to hear him whisper something in her ear. It had something to do with singing, which the little, still front-toothless guy pronounced as "thinging." When she straightened, she told Jake, "Don't forget. We're going to the talent show over at the Conti mansion after the parade."

Jake groaned. They'd already attended the first of the shows last night, and it had been hokey beyond belief. Well, not all of it. There had been some surprisingly good solo songs, a performance by the St. Andrew's Bell Choir that brought tears to the eyes, not his, but some other people's, an acrobatic performance by a troupe of Nags Head teenagers, an amazing salsa by the Swinging Seniors dancers from the Patterson house in colorful, Spanish, very un-senior-like costumes, and a puppeteer who depicted the early history of Bell Cove, but there had also been the ten-year-old violinist who screeched his way through "The Star-Spangled Banner," the ninety-year-old clog dancer who lost his false teeth on the makeshift stage, and the comedian who was quite funny but borderline X-rated.

The town council, who'd first put out the call for talent for the Lollypalooza had been shocked at the number of entries they received, especially when the prizes were only fifty dollars in a number of categories. Thus, they'd had to put a limit of fifty contestants and break the performances into two parts, Friday and Saturday.

He gave Sally a "Do I have to?" look, and she nodded, emphatically.

The kids gave a visible sigh of relief, which he thought was kind of odd. But then, kids liked hokey crap. Besides, they were still unsure of their newly returned father. Jake supposed it was the least he could do for them.

"Okay. Just so there are no more violins."

"Jacob!" she chastised, not wanting him to influence the kids in mocking the talent. But then she added, "There is a yodeler, though. Flossie McCormick from the Bayside Retirement Community."

"And Binky Jones is going to show his dog, Sparkie, doing dog tricks," Matt said.

All three boys gave Jake their doleful looks then. As in a silent "If only we had a dog!" It was a decision Jake felt unable to make when he was pretty sure he wouldn't be around to help train and care for the animal, and Sally was too busy at the bakery.

To forestall further questions on that subject, Jake commented, "Isn't Binky the master farter?"

"Yeah, but his mother says Sparkie can only do the high jumps and walking on his hind legs. No showing his dog's farting tricks, or he'll be grounded till Christmas," Mark told him.

"And that's too bad 'cause the farting tricks are really cool. Binky feeds Sparkie chili dogs to get him gassy," Matt explained.

TMI!

Sally put her face in her hands.

"No more talk about farts," Jake warned the boys.

Before they left the room, he asked Sally, "Should I wear the eye patch or sunglasses?"

"Either is okay," she said, pretending to give him an extra study. "The patch makes you look wicked good and will have the women salivating. You better wear the dark glasses, but put the patch in your pocket in case you're feeling in the need of an ego boost."

He pinched her butt on the way out of the room. "Wicked good, huh?"

"I didn't know it was okay for a boy to touch a girl's hiney," Matt remarked as they walked slowly down the stairs, all of them pacing themselves to Jake's slower gait.

"It's not!" he and Sally both burst out at the same time.

That's all they needed . . . a sexual harassment suit against an eight-year-old for pinching Kindergarten Barbie's butt, and Matt explaining that it's what his daddy does; so, it must be okay.

Man! The kids saw, and heard, everything. He had to be more careful.

This being a father was harder than Jake had ever imagined. Still, as they all piled into the car, he was smiling.

But not for long.

Of course, once they were all loaded in Sally's car and buckled in, one of the kids decided he had to pee, which resulted in Sally ordering all of the boys back inside to take care of business. "I swear those boys are going to frazzle my nerves today," she said.

He just grinned at her. Sexy Momma, that's how

she looked to him at the moment. Soon they were on their way again, with Sally warning Luke that his fly was open.

Along the way, Jake could swear there were twice as many yellow ribbons as before, and miles of bunting, and enough flags to put a flag-making company out of business. The place was beginning to look like either a veterans' convention, or a cemetery. Then, when they finally got to the center of town after parking behind the bakery, they saw nothing but bedlam. Traffic was a bottleneck of yelling and honking horns as dozens of vehicles vied for limited spaces in the off-street parking lots and were directed back to the ferry lot where hired buses would shuttle them back and forth to the town square. In addition, there were at least ten news vans taking up slots that some locals felt they were entitled to. A bunch of unhappy campers, to say the least. Sheriff Henderson and his temporary deputies had their work cut out for them today.

The media hadn't given up on Jake, and no doubt they would be approaching him again today. But he had his polite refusal speech down pat. He wasn't worried . . . at the moment, anyhow.

"Oh, no!" Sally said, noticing the line leading out of the bakery. She hadn't gone in this morning, and must be feeling that she'd left her staff ill-prepared for the tourist rush.

"Go ahead in and take care of business," Jake advised. "I'll take the kids to the scouts' assembly place over on Cove Street."

"Thank you," she said with a sigh of relief and had to reach up only slightly to kiss his cheek. With high heels on today, she was still several inches shorter than him, but at a more level playing field. And, yes, he meant "playing." He had plans for those high heels, as well as the dress, later. If he was going to be wooing her with his uniform, she was going to . . .

"Daaaad! C'mon. I hear a band tuning up." Matt was tugging on his hand.

Jake had his cane with him today, but he hoped to use it only if things got too bad. He had to limp, though, and his slower gait had the boys practically dancing in place with impatience. Along the way to the meeting spot for the scouts, Jake ran into Izzie who was also in full dress uniform. He accompanied them because the place where they were scheduled to be, midway through the parade, was along this route, too.

"Hey, kiddos, you look hotter than asphalt," Izzie remarked.

"Huh?" the boys said, and then they giggled, not knowing what asphalt meant, but homing in on the "ass" part of the word.

"He means that you look really good in your scout uniforms," Jake interpreted.

The three of them preened and said a communal "Thank you."

Izzie arched his brows at Jake to show how impressed he was at their politeness. "Way to go, Father of the Year."

"I can't take credit for that. Sally's the etiquette police in our house."

As they walked along, he and Izzie got more attention than they wanted, or needed . . . well, their uniforms did. Many people stopped them to say, "Thank you for your service." A few old vets saluted them. And females gave them a second and third look.

Once Jake handed the boys over to the scout leader and promised to pick them up at the end of the parade, he and Izzie headed over to the street where new convertibles were parked awaiting the parade marshal's signal to begin the festivities. In exchange for free advertising, local car dealers had donated convertibles in red, white, and blue colors. There were at least ten of them, two of which would carry Jake and Izzie. Others were designated for state and local politicians and a few notable folks of the Outer Banks, like a former Miss America, and last year's winner in the Blue Marlin Tournament.

Right off the bat, he and Izzie recognized Phillip Franklin, the World War II POW and longtime senator before his retirement a decade ago, who would be riding in the car with Jake. He was wearing his old uniform which was neatly pressed and as spiffy as it once had been.

Hurrying up to introduce them was Mayor Doreen Ferguson, who operated a shoe store on the square since her husband's death. Leonard Ferguson's shoe store, named simply Shoes, had been a fixture on the town square for as long as Jake could remember.

"Had to get a new pair of dress shoes today," Izzie told him in an undertone. "Couldn't find 'Shoes' until I realized its name was changed to 'Happy Feet Emporium.'"

"What's an emporium?" Jake whispered back.

"Hell if I know, but these black leathers cost me a hundred bucks, and they pinch."

Doreen, a senior by anyone's definition, was dressed today as a cross between Betsy Ross and Anne Bonny with her clearly dyed, reddish-brown hair all poufed up like a big bush, no doubt thanks to the special Jake had seen advertised this week in the window of her daughter Francine's hair salon, Styles and Smiles. Francine was married to Sheriff Henderson. The family connections in Bell Cove boggled the mind.

"Senator Franklin, this is Captain Jacob Dawson and Lieutenant Isaac Bernstein, whom we told you about," the mayor chirped happily. Doreen was in her element with these kinds of affairs, always had been. Either that, or she was high on hair spray. "Boys, this is Senator Franklin."

Boys?

"You can call me Colonel or just Phil," he said after giving them a smart salute, accompanied by a click of his heels, which almost caused him to tip over.

Jake grabbed for him and almost fell over himself when his cane fell to the ground.

The colonel jabbed Jake in the arm and laughed. "Us fellows with war wounds gotta stick together."

"What about me?" Izzie asked. "I got wounds, too. Inner wounds."

The colonel looked at Izzie like he had a few screws loose or was suffering what they had called "shell shock" in the Great War.

Just then Major Durand came up, greeted Jake and Izzie, and carried on a brief conversation with the old guy about some mutual acquaintance who still served on the Armed Services Committee. Jake was impressed by the amount of color on Durand's uniform. Some of those bars had been given for valor in battle.

So. Apparently the asshole wasn't a desk jockey all his career, Jake mused. He still didn't like the guy.

In fact, when Durand walked up to him and insisted, "We need to talk," Jake actually groaned aloud and said, "Don't spoil my day."

"Your day or days are going to be more than spoiled if you don't learn to take advice, young man."

Blah, blah, blah. "I'll talk to you tomorrow. When are you leaving?" *Hopefully, tonight.*

"You're still in the service, Captain Dawson. And I'm still your superior officer."

Jake nodded his acceptance of that fact.

"This afternoon at the Conti mansion, after the show." With a curt salute, the major dismissed him, for the moment.

A short distance away, someone with a bullhorn

walked by announcing, "Fifteen minutes till show-time, everyone. Rev your engines."

Jake saw Izzie do a double take. Then he did the same when he realized it was Laura Atler, wearing a red, white, and blue halter dress that ended midthigh, leading down a length of bare legs to red high heels. Her pale blonde hair was piled on top of her head where there was a red, white, and blue bow. Her lipstick was a bright, really bright red.

When had timid, slightly overweight Laura turned into a centerfold? It was amazing that Jake hadn't noticed the transformation when they'd met last week. Yeah, he'd seen that she looked different, but not in this way. Wow!

Jake waved at her, which prompted Izzie to hiss, "Stop!" Which of course prompted Jake to glance at Izzie to see why he objected to a mere wave to an old acquaintance.

Before he could make some "What the hell?" type comment, Laura noticed them and stopped. She was staring directly at Izzie, who was staring at her like she was a cherry snow cone on a warm Outer Banks summer day.

She blushed, gave a little wave, and continued on her way, yelling into the bullhorn.

"She's on the parade committee," Izzie said dumbly, and then he blushed, too.

Taking one look at Izzie's red face, Jake said, "Do I sense a romance brewing, or rather reheating?"

"Hell, no!"

"Uncle Abe would lend you his make-out mobile."

"What are you? Like fifteen years old?"

"Maybe you could ask her to go steady like you did in ninth grade."

"Bite me."

Jake just grinned.

"She's practically engaged to someone else."

"*Practically* being the key word to a player like you."

"I'm not a player. I've never been a player."

Jake shrugged, as if that was debatable.

Mayor Ferguson blew a whistle, the signal for action. Apparently, she was second-in-command and only merited a whistle while the high honcho got the bullhorn.

Izzie and Durand got into the back seat of a convertible with a driver wearing a pirate outfit, complete with eye patch. Jake was glad he hadn't gotten that particular ride. Instead, he and the colonel sat in the back seat of another convertible driven by a college kid dressed in red, white, and blue—*What else?*—as Uncle Sam complete with top hat and gray beard.

It was hard to tell exactly what the theme of this parade was. Patriotism. Pirates. Treasure hunting. Local pride. Or something else. When Jake had first talked to the mayor about this parade, she'd suggested "Hometown Heroes" as a theme. But, when he'd said he would be damned if he would be the highlight of a parade, she changed it to "Hometown Spirit," which was much more inclusive. In other words, a potluck of whatevers.

From their seats in the open vehicle on the side street, while they waited their turn, they were able to watch the first half of the parade go by on the main drag leading into town, starting with a local high school marching band. Then there were antique cars, truck-drawn boats worth a fortune for sale from some marinas, motorcycle clubs, baton twirlers, color guards, more bands, including a colonial drum and fife one, and a small Army unit from Fort Bragg that must have come at Durand's request. Scottish bagpipers added yet another type of music.

There was a pet parade section that marched along, or were tugged along, featuring everything from the usual dogs and cats, along with a goose on a leash, a llama, ferrets in a cage on a red wagon, a potbellied pig, a pygmy goat, several snakes, and a monkey. These were followed later by some of the wild ponies from Ocracoke and Corolla.

Intermixed with all these were local floats put together by a garden club and several bell choirs, not to mention some local stores, like Abe Bernstein's deli, making the most of his Reuben's Masterpiece. The float featured a huge canvas depicting the artist Rubens painting his own self-portrait, shown eating one of Abe's corned beef sandwiches. An impressive Bell Forge float held early bell-making equipment being fired by laborers in early 1900s–type clothing. Then, historic Southern quilts were displayed by Blankety-Blank, a town square quilt store, which included a huge frame being worked by a woman in period costume sitting on a stool. The Rutledge Tree Farm float showcased a funny display of their famous Rutledge trees, which were horribly misshapen examples, not unlike Charlie Brown trees, that had become an Outer Banks sensation *because* they were so bad.

The Bell Cove Treasure and Salvaging Company float starred Merrill Good, "Uncle" Kevin, and several others, including two women, who must all be part of the team. They were gathered around a fake sailing ship of the 1800s, supposedly the one they'd uncovered recently, tossing candy gold coins to the crowds. They were dressed, not in pirate attire like Mayor Ferguson wanted them to, but jeans and T-shirts with the logo "Bell Cove Treasure Hunters."

From other sectors of the Outer Banks, there were floats depicting the historic Wright Brothers flight from Kill Devil Hills, sponsored by Wright Brothers National Memorial, and a drama enactment of Virginia Dare and the Lost Colony of Roanoke.

There were also some OBX fire trucks, representatives of the *Wicked Tuna* TV show, and more bands.

"What a great town to live in!" the colonel remarked beside him.

"You think so?" Jake asked. "They can be irritating as hell."

The colonel shrugged.

"Where do you live?"

"With my nephew in Richmond. I always thought it would be cool to grow up in a small town, though."

Jake's attention was drawn to the scout troops who were marching by then in haphazard rows that would drive a drill sergeant nuts. They must have been advised to keep their faces forward, but his boys darted glances and little smiles his way.

Jake stood up in the seat and waved, yelling, "Hooah!" at them, despite the scoutmasters' glares his way. One of them, a female, gave him a little smile, though.

"Are those your sons?" the colonel asked.

"Yep. Three of them."

"You're a lucky man."

Jake knew he was, but he looked at the old guy in question. "Do you have a family? I mean, other than your nephew."

"Nope. Was married once, but we never had any babies before we got divorced. Heard she remarried a few years later and had three daughters. Coulda been mine." Those last words were said on a kind of choked whisper.

Jake didn't know what to say to that.

But no words were necessary as the old guy continued, "I was a wreck after I came back from that German war camp. And they didn't have any of the services you young fellas have today for handling those kinds of problems."

Jake still didn't know what to say.

"You make sure you take advantage of all the help they give you," the colonel advised him, squeezing his arm for emphasis. "Don't lose those things most precious to you through fool pride. Y'hear?"

Jake nodded, and wished he'd been in the car with the pirate, after all.

But now, there was a signal for the convertibles to begin entering the parade. Not all at once, just a few at a time, to be interspersed with other parade events.

Jake found the whole experience uncomfortable. He didn't like calling attention to himself in this way. But it wasn't awful. Mostly, he just smiled and tossed individually wrapped hard candies to spectators who lined the streets, especially the kids. Everywhere along the route, they saw handheld flags being waved.

Until they turned a corner where a dozen protestors, presumably from that hateful Westboro Baptist Church, carried placards that said "Thank God for Dead Soldiers" and "Thank God for 9/11" and the usual anti-gay ones.

"Oh, shit! Them wackos again!" the colonel said.

Jake blinked behind his sunglasses, and saw red behind his closed eyelids, even the bad eye. Apparently the red tide of rage was not dead. It was rising and rising and rising. He was about to launch himself out of the slowly moving vehicle to knock a few heads together, or worse, bad leg or no bad leg.

The colonel put his hand on Jake's arm and cautioned, "Don't do anything stupid. That's what the idiots want. Besides, the sheriff is about to put their sorry asses in jail. Don't do anything to land yourself there, too, son."

Jake did the "just breathe" exercises for a few moments, even as their car passed the protestors. He heard a flurry of activity behind them as the law did in fact arrive, and he relaxed somewhat, knowing he was not going to go psycho with rage.

Not this time anyhow. But it was a wake-up call to Jake, knowing that the rage condition had been only dormant, not dead. What would be the trigger next time? And who might he attack when in a rage?

"Pick your battles, my boy," the colonel advised, like he was reading his mind. "As a soldier you already know that. Those kind of protestors are like flies on a manure pile. In the end they're just full of shit. If you give yourself time to think, you'll realize they aren't worth the effort."

"Yeah, but in the moment I don't think, that's the problem," Jake admitted.

The colonel shrugged. "I can't promise it will ever go away, completely, that you'll ever forget, completely. But it should get better. Don't let the bastards win by giving in to it. I did, and I lost everything."

Jake was saved from having to comment on that because they were approaching the bakery where Sally, her parents, his father, and Old Mike stood in front of a six-deep crowd. Cheers and waves greeted him, and Sally threw him a kiss which he threw back. Most disconcerting was that all five of them appeared to have tears in their eyes. He lowered his sunglasses to midnose to peer over at them.

Yep! Tears. That is just great. He raised his shades again, and they moved on.

When they got to the end of the route, he shook hands with the colonel and they exchanged phone numbers and email addresses. Soon the colonel was overrun with autograph seekers and old veterans wanting to exchange war stories. Jake caught up to Izzie and they went together to find the boys. When they found them, they all hopped onto a jitney bus, one of a number that the town council had hired for the occasion. It took them directly to the Conti mansion, where the talent show would be held. The rest of his family would be meeting them there.

In the meantime, they walked up the steps to the impressive mansion built by the Conti brothers more than a hundred years ago when they founded Bell Forge. The white-shingled mansion, named Chimes, sat on a man-made bluff overlooking the Atlantic Ocean on the one side, and a view of Bell Sound in the distance on the other side.

The main ballroom had been set up with a make-shift stage and at least a hundred folding chairs for the audience. While they waited for Sally and the others to show up, they walked through the side rooms, which had once been a massive glass-walled garden solarium. An author sat at a table in one room signing copies of a book he had written about shipwrecks, including the *Falcon*, which was the one recently discovered by the town's new salvaging/ treasure-hunting company. The town council had set up a table with brochures for tourists, highlighting all the events to be held in Bell Cove throughout the year, as well as the Outer Banks in general. In another room, they saw the big honkin', totally garish trophies that would be awarded to the winners of the first ever Lollypalooza talent contest in various categories. The local bookstore, The Book Den, was selling books in another space, ones dealing with Bell Cove or Outer Banks history, and also related to shipwrecks, treasure hunting, heroes, and pirates. Quite a mix! Jake bought the kids a book called *Talk Like a Pirate*, and for a long time afterward they heard lots of "Aaarr's!" and "Ahoy, mateys!" and "Shiver me timbers!" and their favorite, "Thar she blows!"

When it came time for the talent show, Jake found himself in the center of the fifth row with Sally and the boys, her parents, Joe, and Old Mike on one side and Izzie, his parents, Abe, and Rachel Bernstein on the other. Jake had tried to plant himself on the aisle chair but Sally had insisted he move over, probably because she suspected he might try to slip out midshow. Which might have been a possibility, though he wouldn't admit to that.

Finally, the show was about to get underway. He took off his sunglasses and put on the eye patch so that he could see better. Then, he linked his left hand with her right one, laying their doubled fist on his thigh. He winked at her with a promise of better things to come, later.

The senior citizen yodeler that Sally had mentioned started off the show, and she was as bad as Jake could have imagined. Then Binky Jones stumbled through his dog Sparkie's tricks, but you had to give the kid credit for having the nerve to get up on stage. He couldn't imagine his kids ever doing that, or himself at that age, for that matter. After that, a pianist played a classic piece that was probably really good, but Jake felt himself dozing off. It had been a long day.

Sally nudged him awake, and he got to see a ventriloquist do a pretty funny routine with his dummy named Bad Luck Chuck. Then a lady from Nags Head carrying an umbrella and an outfit that looked a little Mary Poppins–esque did a tap dance to "Singin' in the Rain." After that, it was Irish folk dancing by a local group. He was whispering to Izzie, "Not one of them is giving Michael Flatley any competition," when he noticed Sally and the boys were getting up.

"What? Are we leaving?" he asked hopefully.

"Shhh," she said. A barbershop quartet had just started singing. "Stay put. We'll be back."

He assumed the boys needed to visit the head. Jake could swear they had bladders the size of peas.

"Any clue how we can escape from this nuthouse?" he asked Izzie.

"Chill, my friend. I'm trying to impress Laura with how well-behaved I can be."

Jake glanced over to the side where Laura was indeed checking Izzie out. "She looks like a cross between Betsy Ross and a *Playboy* centerfold in that outfit," Jake observed.

"I've always had a thing for Betsy Ross."

"Be careful. You may find yourself landlocked in Bell Cove again."

"Like you?"

No, he hadn't meant like himself.

While he'd been looking the other way, at Izzie, Major Durand slid into the seat that Sally had occupied. Jake was about to tell him the seat was taken when Durand leaned closer and said, "We have to talk."

"Here? Now?"

"No, not now. But right after this frickin' show. You're not sneaking out of here without our discussion."

Was I so obvious? "What's so important that it can't wait?"

"Your wife is suspicious about what happened to you in Balakistan, and if she, a civilian, is savvy enough to dig up dirt on Nazim, the newshounds are surely three steps ahead of her. Plus, some Qadir dissident claims to have firsthand knowledge of your imprisonment and is going to announce it to the world if the US/Balakistan deal is approved."

There was only one thing Jake heard or cared about in Durand's spiel.

"Sally? What does Sally have to do with all this?"

"She told Bernstein about internet research she's been doing about Nazim, and—"

"Hey," Izzie leaned forward around Jake and addressed Durand, "I told you that in confidence."

"Urgency takes precedence over privacy," Durand contended.

"You knew . . . You talked to Sally about this? And didn't tell me?" Jake asked Izzie, incredulous that his friend would betray him in this way.

"She swore me to secrecy."

"Bullshit!" Jake said.

"Shhhhhh!" at least a half-dozen people hissed around them, and another half dozen shot glowers their way.

They all sat back and shut up, but Jake's mind was simmering with a mixture of emotions. Hurt, anger, disappointment, fear. What to do, what to do? He needed to get out of here and think, but he was trapped, unless he wanted to make a scene.

But then Mayor Ferguson stepped out on the stage and announced, "We have a new, last-minute addition to our program. Please welcome Sally Dawson, and her sons, Matthew, Mark, and Luke."

Whaaat? Jake jerked, his attention riveted to the stage now.

"This song will be a tribute to Captain Jacob Dawson, our own hometown hero, and all the hometown heroes out there, those who are fortunate enough to come home, and those who have not been." The mayor bowed back, and Sally came forward.

Sensing his dismay, Durand and Izzie clamped hands on Jacob's forearms to prevent him from vaulting from his chair and out of the ballroom.

When the audience went silent, with no musical accompaniment, Sally belted out the first line of the song that asked some guy if he knew he was her hero. People were surprised when they first heard Sally's voice, which was so powerful, coming from such a small body, clear toned and sweet. Like Norah Jones. But then, before he could digest her verbal message to him, his sons stepped forward in their scout uniforms and repeated the refrain in voices that cracked and were tone-deaf, more like shouting. Utter heartrending love. Then all four of them, with piped-in background music kicking in, repeated the refrain as one and went on to the lyrics about the wind beneath their wings.

Jake was stunned and frozen in place. Durand and Izzie no longer held him. He couldn't move if he'd wanted to.

Surely Sally knew how humiliated he would feel? He'd told her that he hated being in the parade because it called attention to himself. How much worse was this?

How could she?

And she'd been researching a terrorist behind his back?

How could she?

And talking to his best friend about her suspicions, also behind his back?

How could she?

What other secrets was she keeping from him? Maybe her claims of celibacy had been a lie? Maybe she had been having an affair with Kevin after all? Maybe the affair was still going on? She'd never said that she loved him since his return, even when he'd said those three words himself. Wasn't that telling?

What a fool I've been!

"Jake, simmer down," Izzie whispered to him. "It was the boys' idea. They wanted to do this for you."

And that should make me feel better? "You knew?" The circles of betrayal around him just got wider and wider.

Durand, on the other hand, shared Jake's dismay, though for other reasons. "If this debacle lands on TV, your mug is going worldwide. The nightly news will make this their Labor Day color story. Nazim and his cohorts could nail you or your family in a nanosecond then to keep you quiet. I've got to go and do some damage control." On those words, Durand made his way out of the aisle, apologizing here and there for stepping on feet.

"Oh, my God!" Jake was just beginning to digest the ramifications of this goat fuck.

"He's overreacting," Izzie said.

The people around them were shhh-ing again.

And then the song ended, and the crowd was giving them a standing ovation. In the midst of that chaos, Jake saw his cue, and made his way across the aisle. People patted him on the back as he passed, probably thinking he was going up on the stage to join his wife and kids.

When pigs fly!

He stumbled up the aisle to the back of the ballroom and then out into the hall and through the door. Because he'd left his cane behind and because he was seeing a red mist in his eyes, he stumbled here and there, almost falling down the wide front steps. He hailed a caterer's truck which was about to take off and hitched a ride to the town square where he was able to make his way to the car parked behind the bakery. From there, he somehow made his way home before he was able to surrender to the mist.

Jake was hardly aware of his actions then as the mist took over. In his rage, he threw dishes, broke chairs, banged his own head against the wall till he felt blood running down his face. He punched a cushion on a rocking chair in the living room till the feathers went flying. It was only when he saw the crack in the window, right through the stained glass border that had withstood a century of wind and storms, but not his rage, that Jake began to calm down. But only enough to realize that he needed to get out of here before his children came home and saw what kind of hero their father really was.

Tears streaming down his face, he went out to

the garage to get his go-bag, then made his way upstairs, backward, because his pain was so great, and began to pack. Where he would go, he didn't know. It didn't matter.

Some heroes shouldn't come home.

Chapter 19

*She cried him a river . . . until the
damn came, as in dammit! . . .*

Sally had a hard time getting by all the well-
wishers once they'd finished their performance.
Everyone wanted to tell them what a wonderful,
touching job she and the boys had done with their
homage to Jake and other heroes.

Everyone except Jake.

Where was he?

But then Izzie approached, and the worried expression on his face told her all she had feared. "Did
he leave?"

Izzie nodded and drew her aside. Her parents,
understanding the situation, took the boys in hand,
diverting them from their search for their father by
promising ice cream cones from a truck that had
just pulled up outside.

"What happened?"

He shrugged. "He was probably embarrassed."

"That's all?"

"Well, he found out just before your stage act that

you've been researching Nazim's torture record, and talking to me about it . . ." He paused.

"Behind his back," she finished for him.

"He's feeling betrayed, I suppose. That on top of the fact that Durand told him that his life, and maybe yours and the boys, could be in danger if a video of this performance today went live on national TV and Nazim got it into his head to send someone here to . . ." He let his words trail off again, then added, "Durand was being his usual asshole self, overcautious and premature, but you know Jake would take it seriously."

"Anything else?"

Izzie shifted from foot to foot, avoiding her eyes.

"What?" she demanded.

"You have to realize that Jake suffers a double handicap, with both his eye and his leg being damaged. If even one of them could be healed, his overall recovery could be much, much better."

"And . . . ?" Getting info out of Izzie was like watching bread rise. Slooow.

"Something's been happening with his eye," Izzie blurted out.

"Dammit, Izzie! Stop beating around the bush."

"There have been changes lately. Little things that might be promising."

She threw her hands in the air. "And he couldn't share that good news with me?"

"It might not pan out."

She breathed in and out for patience. "Where did he go? Home?"

"I don't know. Probably."

"I'll go talk to him."

"I'll go with you."

"I don't think that's necessary."

"Actually, it might be."

She cocked her head in question. Sometimes a ball of dough needed a good punch to get it to work.

"The red mist might have taken over, which makes him unpredictable."

"The red mist?" *More secrets that I don't know about?*

"Uh-oh! He didn't tell you about the red mist?"

She shook her head.

"It's a kind of rage he goes into where he sees a red mist behind his eyelids."

"What triggers it?"

"Who knows? Stress. Extreme anger. The last one I know about occurred when he learned that you and the public were going to be told about his rescue. I mean, after three months in that hospital with him being in control of when or if the big reveal would happen, suddenly that decision was taken out of his hands."

"Wait a minute. Three months?" Sally asked. "Are you saying that Jacob was rescued three months before I was told?"

"What? Yeah. You didn't know that?"

"Actually, I did know, but it didn't sink in until now. The question is why."

"Do you really think that's important in light of today's events?" Izzie was clearly squirming now.

But she wasn't about to let him off the hook. "I do. It's all part of a pattern, in my opinion."

"How so?"

"I know Jacob. If he'd wanted to tell me that he was alive from the get-go, he would have found a way to do it, the Army or hospital rules or Uncle Sam be damned. So, it had to be his decision to keep me in the dark. The ass! But worse than that, what I'm beginning to suspect, is that Jacob never wanted to come home at all."

The blush that seeped into Izzie's cheeks told her all.

For a moment, her heart felt like it was in a vise. She could barely breathe. "So, he was planning to leave from the moment he came back."

"Maybe," Izzie conceded. "But give him a break, Sally. He's been through hell, worse than anything you and I can imagine. God only knows what's going through that brain of his. Bottom line, he loves you and the boys. That's the most important thing."

Sally tried to assess the situation, to make some sense of it. Jake had found out that she knew he was hiding the story of his three missing years and that she'd been researching the guy who presumably handed him over to the US government and that she'd discussed her suspicions with his best friend. Then, the major had instilled a fear in him that the terrorist might be a threat to him and his family. Top that off with his unwarranted embarrassment, rather than pride, in the musical performance she and his sons had put on for him.

On the other hand, she had some legitimate bones to pick with her husband, as well. Like the secrets of his POW, not MIA, experience, that he kept from her. Like the fact that he'd never wanted to come home at all, and he'd been planning to leave even before he got here. Like he didn't trust her enough to be honest with her. Like he didn't respect her strength.

"Can you tell my parents to take care of the kids?" she asked. When he agreed, reluctantly, she added, "Don't let them think something's wrong. Just say Jacob and I want a few hours alone together."

"You know what they'll think."

"Let them."

Before she left, Izzie gave her a hug and advised, "Be careful, and give Jake a chance."

She wanted to say that she'd already given him plenty of chances in the past weeks, that if he felt betrayed, imagine how betrayed she felt. But, instead, she just nodded.

Luck was with her when she saw the local taxi driver outside and she didn't have to ask someone for a ride. She assumed Jake somehow got to the car parked behind the bakery, leaving her without a vehicle. If he was thinking at all, he would assume there were plenty of family and friends to give her a lift.

Her first clue of how bad things were was the open driver's door on her car parked in the driveway. What kind of state must Jake have been in to leave the vehicle like that? In her mind, she pictured him staggering toward the house.

The kitchen door was open, too.

She gasped and put a hand to her mouth at what she saw. Broken dishes around the room. A chair smashed to pieces. Water running in the sink from a faucet that had been yanked from its flange. Then in the living room, dismembered pillows making the room look as if a snowstorm had hit. And the precious stained glass border on the front window had a crack in it. Most alarming of all, when she went back in the hall, she noticed blood on the wall.

"Ja-cob!" she screamed and raced up the stairs. There were drips of blood on some of the steps.

He wasn't there, she saw immediately.

In the bathroom, she saw evidence of blood on a washcloth. He must have cleaned up whatever wound he had. In the bedroom, his blood-spattered uniform was scattered about on the floor, something he would never do. The Army trained its men to be neat. Defiling his uniform was telling, if all the other evidence of his rage was not.

She didn't need to go to the window overlooking the driveway to see what she hadn't noticed before. His truck was missing. She also didn't need to go into the garage to check if his go-bag was missing.

He was gone.

Just like he'd planned all along.

Maybe sooner than he'd planned.

But he was gone.

Should she follow after him?

But where? What direction?

And would he want her to follow?

Did it matter what he wanted?

Yes. Yes, it did.

It was then that she saw the note on the dresser. It was written on a program from the Boy Scout banquet. He'd scrawled on the back, "I'm sorry." That's all. No salutation. No signature. Just "I'm sorry."

"Oh, Jacob!" she cried, sinking to the edge of the bed as the tears came like a river.

What you must be going through at this moment! The anguish you must be suffering to have done this!

I feel like such a failure. I should have been able to help you.

Don't do anything stupid, Jacob.

Hold on.

And come back.

But he didn't come back.

She wailed aloud and cried some more, falling back on the bed, then curled into a ball of misery. Eventually, she fell into an exhausted sleep. Which didn't last long. It was still light outside when she opened her swollen eyes, realizing there was a noise downstairs.

She jumped up and rushed down the steps, only to find it was Joe, on his knees under the sink, turning off the water valve.

He stood and looked at her. If he'd been going to ask about Jake's whereabouts, he stopped at whatever he saw on her face. Instead, he opened his arms to her and they cried on each other's shoulders.

"I never even asked him to come into the fishing

business with me. I kept waiting for the right moment."

"He knew," she assured him.

"I didn't tell him that I love him," he said. "What kind of father am I, that I couldn't say those words to a son that's been missing for three years?"

"He knew," Sally assured him again, but thought, *I didn't tell him I loved him, either. I showed him, though, didn't I? Oh, God, I hope he knows that, at least.*

Izzie came in then. He might have knocked, but they hadn't heard him. He took one look at the mess, winced at the blood on the wall, then sat down heavily on one of the undamaged kitchen chairs. "Fuck! Fuck, fuck, fuck!"

There were tears in Izzie's eyes, too.

"Do you have any idea where he went?"

He shook his head. "I went to the ferry landing, heading north, to see if I might catch him, but he wasn't in the lot. And with all the tourist influx today, it was impossible to ask anyone if they'd seen him."

"Maybe he didn't leave town at all. Maybe he's over at my house. I should go check," Joe said hopefully.

Sally put up a halting hand. "He took his truck."

"Could he have gone out on your boat?" Izzie asked Joe.

Joe shrugged. "I suppose he could be on the boat, but he didn't have keys."

None of them were inclined to go check, it was that improbable.

"Dammit!" Sally said finally. "I have things I have to do."

"What can I do to help?" Izzie asked.

"Go. Find out whatever you can about where Jacob might be, but be discreet. I'm just going to tell people . . . to tell the kids, oh, my God, the kids!" She choked on a sob and continued, "I'll say that Jacob was called away suddenly on some military duty, and that he'll be back as soon as he can make it."

Joe looked at her, questioning. It wasn't like her to lie.

"Whatever the hell has happened to him is related to military duty, and he will be back, dammit, if I have any say in the matter," she insisted defiantly. "You better tell that Major Durand what's going on, Izzie. But make sure you let him know that if he shows his face here, I might just rearrange his nose with a whack from my favorite rolling pin."

When Izzie left, she asked Joe to help her clean up while she made a few calls. First off, she called José and Mary Lou to see if they could handle the business for the next day or two. "Jacob had to leave suddenly on some hush-hush Army business, and I need to do some things with the kids." The first of her little white lies. They, of course, agreed readily, then added compliments on her singing routine that day. Turns out she and her sons won a trophy, according to Mary Lou. That would please the boys to no end.

After that, she called her parents, who were clearly distressed at both Jake's and her leaving the Conti mansion so suddenly. She assured them that she was all right, using the same excuse she'd given her employees.

"I have a big favor to ask of you, though," she said to them both, as they used their speakerphone. "Would you be willing to take the boys back to Manhattan with you for a week or so? Sort of a mini-vacation."

"Now? Won't they be missing school?" her mother asked.

"Yes, but they're only in elementary school, not college. I can get them an educational leave of absence, and I'm sure their teachers would give me their assignments for that period."

"Sally, what's going on?" her father asked. "You know we're always willing to have the boys, but this is an odd time for them to come. Has something happened?"

"They're going to be upset that their father had to leave so suddenly, and so soon after their being reunited with them. I figure this trip with their grandparents and the city itself will distract them enough so they won't be too sad. By then, Jacob might be home again." *More lies.* "By the way, tell them we won a trophy. That should make them happy. Even Binky Jones didn't win a trophy."

"Who's Binky Jones?" her father asked.

"You don't want to know."

"Are you sure you don't want to come with the boys? It would be a vacation for you, too," her mother said.

"No. Too much going on with the bakery right now. Maybe later." She had to stay here, in case Jake called, or came back, or there was news about him.

Twenty-four hours later, Sally was all alone.

Her sons, with her parents, had left, carting the Switch video game system and games with them. No way were they going without those. Major Durand and Izzie had left the island. Izzie's parents had presumably stayed for a few extra days, but Sally didn't see them. Most of the tourists were gone. Joe and Old Mike went back to work on the fishing boat, at her insistence, since word was out that the bluefish had come in early.

It was almost like the awful period after a funeral, when the real loss begins to set in. If Sally allowed herself, she could easily sink into a deep depression. But Sally was strong. She would not allow herself to believe that Jake was gone for good.

And so she did something she hadn't done for a long, long time. She dropped to her knees, bowed her head, and prayed, "Please, God, help my husband. And bring him home to us."

Better late than never . . .

Jake was no fool.

And he was a soldier.

Fighting the good fight was what he was all about. *Surrender* wasn't in his vocabulary.

And so, he left his pride and everything else of importance behind in the Outer Banks. Maybe it was too late for him. Maybe not. On the chance it was the latter, he drove for hours, never getting out of his truck, not even on the ferries, until he got to the nearest full-scale VA hospital. After parking and locking his vehicle, he went inside. "Where's the mental health unit?" he asked the older woman at the receptionist desk, a volunteer, according to her name tag.

Up one flight, and over to another wing, he was directed. "Do you need an escort?" she asked kindly.

Even though he'd changed into civilian clothes and the cut on his forehead had stopped bleeding, he probably looked a wreck. Plus, he'd limped in. So, her question was understandable. "No, thank you, ma'am," he declined. "I can find my way."

"Use the elevator over there," she advised.

When he got to the second floor and exited the elevator, Jake noticed that corridors to the right and left had closed doors with signs reading "Code Needed to Enter Locked Units." Another sign said "Visitors Must Sign In."

He went up to the desk in the center where a young male nurse sat, working a crossword puzzle. There was no one in the lounge waiting area, although a television was turned on, low volume, a newscast about a local Labor Day festivity. Jake had almost forgotten that today was a holiday.

"I'm Captain Jacob Dawson." He shoved Major Durand's business card across the desk. "This is my liaison, who can answer any questions about my history."

The guy's eyes widened and he sat up straighter at the Pentagon name and address on the card. "Friends in high places, huh?"

"You could say that."

"What can I do for you, Captain?" the guy asked.

"I need to be admitted."

Chapter 20

Lady with a mission . . .

Two weeks later, the boys were back with Sally in Bell Cove, and they resumed their normal school routine. Their father's absence was a looming worry to the kiddos, but they seemed to accept their mother's assurance that he would come back as soon as he could. It helped that she'd told them that their father had loved their song routine and was so proud of them.

Another of the many lies she'd been telling.

She cancelled plans for an addition to her bakery. Somehow, she'd lost her enthusiasm for the project. Without Jake here to watch her back and help with the boys, she needed to set some priorities. And, frankly, she felt no great loss. Bigger wasn't always better. Thus, a surf and kite store would be taking over the adjacent space next month.

She was worried about Joe. He'd taken Jake's departure even harder than she had. The fact that he hadn't said goodbye seemed like a double blow to his father. Sally tried to tell the old man that it was because his son intended to come back.

Was that another lie?

And so, Jake's father plodded on with his daily routines, just as she did. Eat, work, sleep. Day in, day out. But in a holding pattern.

And the weeks went on.

Oh, she knew where he was. Izzie had informed her, the day after Labor Day, that Jake had admitted himself to a VA hospital's mental health unit. An inpatient dealing with intense PTSD.

"Oh, Jacob!" she had cried. "That would have been so hard for him."

"Yeah, but it's a first step . . . a positive step," Izzie had countered. "He never should have come back so soon. He needed more counseling."

Sally had a few thoughts about that, but it did no good to berate Izzie. It wasn't his fault.

"I should go to him," she'd told Izzie, but he told her that Jake was adamant in declaring, "No visitors!" And that included Izzie, Durand, family, friends, everyone. He wanted to handle this himself.

The ass!

"Will you give him a message from me?"

"He won't see me, either, Sal."

"But you could get a message to him. Or Major Durand could. I'm going to email it to you. Then, you are going to print it out, and make sure he gets it, dammit. Do you hear me?"

"They heard you in the Bahamas."

Then, days later, something happened that shook her world. The nightly news was full of reports on another government overthrow in Balakistan, even more violent than the previous one when Jake had been returned to the US. In the melee that occurred, another dissident tribal group executed many of the top leaders of the Qadir cabinet, including the prime minister and the minister of defense, Nazim bin Jamil.

Sally called Izzie right away. "This is good news for Jake, right? Now that he has no reason to fear that he or his family are in danger, he can come home."

"Um . . . well . . ."

"What? Don't tell me. More secrets."

"It's not that, exactly." He sighed and told her, "A member of this new group, in order to justify its case for legitimacy, has released intel on some of the atrocities inflicted by the Qadir followers, some of it on local tribes who failed to support them. We're talking old people, women, kids, and . . ." His words trailed off.

She knew without his saying the words that what he wasn't including in the list of victims was captives, as well, like Jake. She inhaled to brace herself.

"One female member of this new group witnessed some of the prisoner torture firsthand. While she doesn't mention names, it's clear—at least to us in the military—that she's talking about Jake."

"Where is she doing this talking?"

"On the internet. But I'm begging you, Sally.

Don't look. The details are too graphic, and . . ." Izzie seemed to choke up. "And there are some pictures."

Oh, my God! Will this nightmare ever end? "All the more reason why I should go to him."

"No. He is going to feel humiliated by some of this crap. He shouldn't, but you know that he will. Besides, he's not in the mental health unit anymore."

"What? When did that happen? Is he in another part of the hospital?"

"No. He's left North Carolina."

"I knew it, I knew it. I should have gone to him while he was still that close. Where is he now?"

"I don't know."

"You do so, you lying piece of dog . . . barf."

Izzie laughed. "He had an appointment at that orthopedic hospital in New York City, but that was a few days ago. I don't know where he is now."

He knew. He just didn't want to tell her, either at Durand's or Jake's orders.

Aha! In that moment, Sally knew where he was now, too. With the phone to her ear, she went over to the wall calendar. Yep, September 30. The eye clinic in Baltimore. But she wasn't telling Izzie that she knew. Instead, she tweaked him a little, "By the way, what did you do to Laura Atler when you were here? Word is that she's no longer seeing Gabe Conti."

"Me? I didn't do anything. We didn't even do the deed, not totally," he said.

"Oh? Then why did she go to some voodoo woman at the mall to put a curse on you? Have you noticed an itch in an uncomfortable place lately?"

"Whaaat?"

She hung up on him, laughing. Probably hysterically, considering this was not a time for mirth.

Or maybe it was.

She had plans to make.

First off, she called Joe. "Can you come stay with the boys for a few days? I hate to ask you when the king mackerel are hitting heavy."

"What's up, girl?"

When she explained, he said, "Screw king mackerel! About time we did something, instead of sitting on our asses waiting."

Next she called the Outer Banks Airlines to see if she could get on one of the early morning shuttles to Norfolk International. From there, she could book a seat on a plane to Baltimore. It was surprisingly easy.

She called José and then Mary Lou to ask for their help with the bakery. She was not surprised that they readily agreed and asked if there was anything else she needed.

She went upstairs to pack but first went into Matt's room where the video game system was now housed. The boys were halfway through their two-hour weekend daily limit.

Her announcement that she had to go out of town for a day or two met with some whining and protest, even when she mentioned that PopPop would be babysitting for them. Ever since Jake had left, they were much more needy. Maybe they thought she would skip out on them, too. But then they soon conceded, realizing that PopPop was much more lenient than she was. Her trip could work to their benefit, the wily little devils concluded, probably already coming up with a strategy to convince their grandfather that they really needed more game time. No big deal in the scheme of things.

"Don't you guys want to know why I have to go?" she asked them.

They immediately became alert.

"I'm going to bring Daddy home."

Was this a near-death experience, or just God giving him a second chance? . . .

Jake felt himself coming out of the anesthetic at the vision care hospital. As he drifted in and out, he opened his good eye and guessed that he must be in the post-op room, having just gone under the knife an hour or two ago. That's how long the surgeon had said the eye muscle procedure would take.

One of those times when he was more wakeful, he thought he smelled cinnamon. And smiled. *I could get used to this happy juice.*

But wait. *I must have died,* he thought, *and this is heaven.* For some reason, he wasn't alarmed at that prospect. Just sort of sad that he wouldn't see Sally or his sons again.

"Sweetheart, you are only going to wish you were dead when I'm through with you," he heard Sally say.

He must have spoken aloud, or else he was talking to Sally from "the other side." He chuckled and said, "Do they have cinnamon sex in heaven?"

"Shhh. The nurse will hear you."

It sure did sound like his wife, and the cinnamon scent was enveloping him, taking away that medicinal smell that pervaded hospitals. And who was that holding his hand? Was it a nurse? No, he didn't think a nurse would kiss his hand.

Yep, it must be heaven.

Still later, when the opiates had mostly left his system, he came fully awake and realized that he was back in his regular hospital room. Man, he was sick of hospitals. When this was over, he swore he would never voluntarily enter another one again.

That's when he noticed that the cinnamon scent was still with him. Moving his head, he saw Sally sitting in a recliner in the corner, fast asleep.

How long has she been there?

Why is she here?

How did she find me?

I thought I said no visitors. No, that was back at the mental health unit.

Sally is here.

Mmmm.

Instead of being angry, he felt a calm acceptance blanket him and he sighed himself back to sleep.

He hadn't died after all, he supposed. This time his sleep was natural.

"Captain Dawson! Captain Dawson, wake up. That's good. Here. Have a sip of water. Just a small sip. How do you feel?"

"Fuzzy."

"That will wear off," a nurse said.

"I need to use the bathroom."

"Should I bring a urinal?"

"Hell, no! Help me to the head."

After he'd relieved himself and gargled some mouthwash, he let her assist him back to the bed with an arm around his waist. He felt weaker than cat piss.

Once back in bed, he asked, "My wife?"

"She's out in the hall, speaking with your friend."

My friend? Sure enough, he listened and could hear patches of a conversation between Sally and Izzie. The traitor. Izzie must have brought her here. Or was it vice versa? Somehow he couldn't care.

Once he was tucked into the bed and all his vitals taken, the nurse asked, "Is it all right if they come back in?"

He nodded. Might as well get it over with.

"Hey, buddy," Izzie said, coming up on one side of the bed. He was in uniform and must have come directly from the airport. Last he'd heard, his friend had been stationed at Fort Bragg, waiting to go active in Kandahar. In fact, he should be OUTCONUS by now.

"Oh, Jacob!" Sally came over to the other side of the bed.

Great! She pities me. "What the hell are you two doing here?" Jake asked with more hostility than he was feeling.

Sally winced and Izzie shook his head at Jake's stupidity.

"Sorry," Jake said, but then turned on his friend. "Why did you bring Sally here?"

"Hey, I didn't bring her here. She arrived before I did."

"I came on my own when I figured out where you were. On my own. Imagine that. Little ol' me has a brain in my fool head. Fool, for caring enough about you." She had tears in her eyes.

He felt like shit for making her cry, and he reached for her hand, squeezing. "I'm glad you're here," he said, and he meant it. To Izzie, he added, "You, on the other hand, need to leave us alone."

Izzie nodded and winked at him. "Bet you're commando under that pretty gown."

His friend was impossible.

"How do you feel?" Sally asked, moving to sit on the side of his mattress. He was still holding her hand.

"Okay, but I have to tell you, Sal, I'm not very optimistic about the outcome of this surgery." He pointed to his left eye, which was heavily bandaged.

She cocked her head in question. "I talked to your surgeon, and he said there was a thirty percent chance of improvement."

"Yeah. Those odds aren't in my favor, though, especially with my bad luck streak of late . . ." He shrugged.

"What bad luck streak?"

"My evaluation at the orthopedic hospital in New York a few days ago proved to be the bomb I feared it would be. The most I can hope for with this gimpy leg is . . . a gimpy leg."

"I hate when you use that word."

"It is what it is."

"And I hate that expression."

He stifled a grin at her vehemence. "With continued exercise and massage therapy, I might get a little more mobility."

"See, that's a positive."

"If I stop that active regimen or slack off even a little, I could regress to an even worse state."

"So, you don't stop. Besides, you enjoy all that exercise crap."

More stifled grins. "Bottom line. Surgery isn't an option for all the damage that's been done to the muscles and ligaments and tendons. I will always be lame, to some extent."

"Lame, blame, shame! Nazim has a lot to answer for, and hopefully he's answering for it in hell."

Jake had seen the news of Nazim's well-deserved demise while he'd still been back at the hospital in New York. "You got that right."

"How did the counseling go at that mental health unit?" she asked.

"You know about that?"

She nodded.

"Really well. I'm suffering from PTSD, Sal. I might always be, but I'm getting a handle on controlling the symptoms."

"That's good. To me, that's a bigger hurdle for you than the leg or eye injuries."

She was right. If he could get his head on straight, the other problems might be manageable.

"Listen to me, Jake. You are a survivor. And it's time you used that word to describe yourself instead of all those negative ones. And I'll tell you something else. You have a family and a community that care deeply for you. That is no small thing."

"You're going to make me cry, and I'm pretty sure tears aren't a good idea for the stitches in my eye."

"Does it hurt?" she asked, lifting the sheet and crawling under it with him.

"What? Whoa! What are you doing?" he asked.

She cuddled up against him and he lifted his arm so she could rest her head on his shoulder. Her left hand was flattened on his belly, low down. "I missed you," she said.

He kissed the top of her head and said, "I missed you, too."

"Yeah? How much?"

"Isn't that obvious?"

She ignored his remark and rubbed his belly in an absentminded sort of way as she talked softly, giving him the news, inconsequential things that had happened while he'd been gone, including the fact that they'd won a humongous trophy for their song at the Lollypalooza.

"The boys can't wait to show it to you. It's almost as big as Luke. They think it's made of gold."

"Major Durand sent me a video of the performance. I've replayed it over and over on my laptop. It was really nice, Sal."

"You should tell the boys that."

"Are they okay?"

"Uh-huh. I told them you were called away on some mission."

He chuckled. *In my shape? The only mission I'm capable of is a trip to the toilet.*

"I can feel your negative thoughts again."

The whole time they chatted, softly, she continued to stroke his belly and abdomen and chest, then back to his belly. He was beginning to suspect her actions weren't so absentminded, after all, especially when a certain body part began to take notice.

"Are you sure this is a good idea?" No beating around the bush for him. "A doctor or nurse could come in at any moment."

"They would have to get past Izzie first."

It wouldn't be the first time his friend had covered his back . . . or front.

"The question is whether you are capable, so soon after surgery."

He put her hand on his very capable body part and said, "It was eye surgery. Not cock surgery."

"So crude!" He felt her lick the skin on his neck, then nip him with her teeth.

He turned and cupped her face, placing his lips on hers, shaping, coaxing her to open for him. When she did, he slid his tongue inside and tasted cinnamon. He smiled against her lips and murmured, "Ummm!"

"I've been chewing that damn gum for three hours, ever since you went into surgery. Consumed four whole packs. Izzie is suspicious."

He laughed and kissed her again. "Well, no sense putting all that hard work to waste."

She raised her head and grinned at him. "Are you sure you're up for this?"

"What do you think?" he asked, glancing downward at the tent he made in the sheet.

Without further prompting, she removed her blouse and slacks, her bra and panties, and was sliding under the sheet to kneel between his legs. He didn't need to direct her on how to create a cinnamon stick. She'd become adept at certain skills in recent weeks. Actually, long ago. They knew each other's bodies so well.

Soon, way too soon, his blood thickened and lodged down below. He arched his back and moaned.

"Shh!" she cautioned, raising her head to stare up at him. Her lips were moist and parted with her own arousal. "The nurses might hear you on the monitor and think you're in pain."

"I am in pain," he said as she resumed working him. Then, before he exploded, he urged, "C'mere, baby. Up, up, up." He raised her so that she straddled him and then took his erection into her body, one inch at a time. With pure male fantasy, he imagined there were a dozen inches.

"So good," she sighed.

"Tell me about it!"

He helped her raise and lower her hips on him as she leaned forward and he took one breast, then another into his mouth. Licking, teasing with his tongue, sucking.

Soon, she was unable to control the thrusts of her needy body. He held her firmly downward, impaling her with his heat, and she convulsed around him. Only when her spasms ceased did he release himself. He barely held back a roar of satisfaction as he did so.

For what seemed a long time, she just lay atop him, his flaccid member still inside her. He caressed her back and rump. Kissed her face. "I love you, Sally. You know that, don't you?"

She nodded and looked up at him, tears glazing her caramel eyes. "I love you, too. Never stopped. Never will."

Later, when she was dressed and sitting by the bed once again, holding his hand, she asked, "Did you get the note that I told Izzie to give you?"

"I did." He paused, and said, "You told me to come home when I'm ready."

"And . . . ?"

He didn't pause at all now when he said, "I'm ready to come home."

Epilogue

There was nothing spooky about this wedding . . .

Captain Jacob Dawson and Sally Fontaine Dawson renewed their wedding vows on October 19, their ninth anniversary, in Our Lady by the Sea Church in Bell Cove. A reception followed at Chimes, the Conti mansion.

The couple had wanted a private ceremony followed perhaps by a casual lunch at the Rock Around the Clock Diner, hosted by the bride's best friend, Delilah Good, who'd offered to shut her business down for the day. Or else, they suggested, a barbecue in the backyard of their home under a tent if the weather proved warm enough, which it was. But the people of Bell Cove wouldn't hear of that. They'd taken over, as they always did when one of their own took a big step.

It was less than two weeks until Halloween, and since all special events had to have a theme, even weddings, the Bell Cove-ites had decided on "Halloween Heroes." It was either that or "Halloween

Hootenanny," which was thankfully nixed by Ethan Rutledge, a member of the town council, who'd said he'd be damned if he sentenced his friend Jake to "Kumbaya" as a wedding march. That was as bad as that stupid Grinch contest, which was coming up again soon, Ethan, known to be a bit of a grinch, had contended. He'd won out, but they were still stuck with a "Halloween Heroes" wedding.

Thus, everyone attending the wedding was supposed to come as their favorite superhero (or heroine), except for the bridal couple, who'd refused. For some reason, the groom insisted that his bride be dressed in a special peach-colored dress made for the occasion. And she'd insisted on his wearing his dress uniform, something he wouldn't be doing for much longer, having submitted his resignation from the military as of next month. Jake wore no eye patch or sunglasses on this day since he'd managed to regain some vision and movement in his injured eye. He had to wear glasses for close work, like reading, even with a lens implant. And since he didn't use a cane or crutch when walking forward on the altar to meet his wife, he did limp.

No one cared about any of that. He had survived a terrible ordeal and come home. That was all that mattered to any of them.

Lieutenant Isaac Bernstein, aka Captain America, was best man, and Delilah Good was a Wonder Woman matron of honor in an outfit that made her husband blush. There were no other attendants, except for The Three (Mini) Musketeers, who gave their mother away to their father. Many a tear was shed in the congregation at that poignant moment in the ceremony.

Although they claimed it was a bunch of foolishness, Joe and Old Mike came as Batman and Robin. Supposedly, Vana Gustafson was heard to say that she'd always had a thing for Batman. Gus came as Thor, of course. Mayor Ferguson was an unusual Elektra, especially her hair, which looked as if it had been electrified. Merrill Good, with his Navy background, was Aquaman. K-4 was Wolverine. Laura Atler stunned the crowd in a figure-hugging Catwoman costume. Everyone wondered if Catwoman and Captain America might make a love connection with all the kryptonite sizzling in the air around them, or maybe that was just feline hissing. And so it went with everyone participating with laughter and good cheer. A typical Bell Cove event.

At the reception, folks were surprised to see that the table favors weren't the usual coated almonds, which nobody ever ate anyhow, but individually wrapped cinnamon hard candies. "What is that about?" the bride and groom were asked repeatedly, to which they just smiled. The best man kept remarking to the couple about some kind of commando thing, which also garnered secretive smiles.

The bride made her own wedding cake, a six-tiered chocolate cake with a fudge icing, based on a recipe of the groom's mother. There were also monster cookies from the bride's bakery, wedding bell cutouts with the bride and groom's names on them. Some people said they were too pretty to eat, but who could resist?

When the band Nostalgia played the first dance of the evening, Jake managed to hold his own by swaying side to side with Sally in his arms. When the band segued into that Outer Banks favorite "Carolina Crazy," Jake showed that even with his wounded leg he could manage to do an impressive Shag. You couldn't live on the coasts of the Carolinas without learning the basic steps of that regional dance. Sally, a converted Outer Banks gal, moved around him like she'd been born to shag. Even their sons, who joined them on the dance floor, showed that they had moves, like their daddy. Another in the many poignant moments of the day.

Rumor was that Jake had been offered a highfalutin job in the Pentagon, and a promotion, but he'd declined, even when his wife offered to move to the capital with him and the children. Instead, Jake was going to take over his father's commercial fishing business. He would keep his dad and Old Mike on as assistants until he got the swing of things. It had been agreed that if he was physically unable to carry out his duties, or found his heart wasn't in the business, it would be sold. Maybe treasure hunting would be in Jake's future, as a backup plan.

Sally would continue to run her bakery, Sweet Thangs, and had no immediate plans to expand. She had enough on her hands, literally, with three sons and a husband who was very much a handful, and, yes, she knew there was a double entendre when she repeated the sentiment around town.

Later, in their honeymoon suite at the Heartbreak Motel—okay, the Blue Hawaii room, with all its hokey decor—Jake made love to his wife like there was no tomorrow. He had a tendency to do that a lot lately, having almost lost everything himself. But he was getting better at toning down his desperation, thanks to the PTSD survivors' therapy group he led in this very town. Who knew there were so many wounded warriors around? And they weren't just military related, either. Or men only.

Sally gave as good as she got in the lovemaking and constantly told her husband, "I love you," because she knew how much he needed to hear it. Well, she did, too. They made a mutual promise to say the words at least a dozen times a day, starting when they awakened in the morning, and before they fell asleep at night.

Later, when she scooted into the bathroom to relieve herself, she saw a gift that Delilah had left for her in line with the motel room's Hawaiian theme. With a smile, she donned the grass skirt and lei and nothing else, and hula'd her way back into the bedroom.

"What do you think?" she asked Jake, who was still sprawled out on his back on the bed, replete with satisfaction from their last bout of making love. He raised his head, then raised another body part, as he looked her over. "Baby, I am all shook up."

Nine months later, Sally gave birth to another baby,

although she'd sworn there would be no more children. Jake was with her this time, though, and that made all the difference. After seeing what she went through in a long, agonizing, ten-hour labor, he was the one who proclaimed her the hero in their home, and he was the one swearing, "No more!"

They didn't name the baby John, though.

It was Joan.

Author's Note

Dear Readers:

I love a tortured hero with a sense of humor. Don't you?

It was hard writing Jacob Dawson, with his history as a POW and continuing PTSD, while keeping the book in the romantic humor genre. But when you throw three little boys into the mix and the wacky town of Bell Cove, it just had to be funny at times. I hope you smiled in certain places, maybe even laughed out loud.

A fan told me that she was reading one time and burst out with a hoot of laughter. Her husband, who was sitting nearby watching TV, remarked, "You must be reading a Sandra Hill book." To me, that was the greatest compliment.

There were prequels to this book in the Bell Sound series, *The Forever Christmas Tree* and *Life, Love and the Pursuit of Happiness*. And hopefully there will be future books. Surely, K-4, Izzie, Laura, and Gus have stories to tell, and maybe even other treasure-hunting team members, like Bonita Arias or Charlotte LeDeux. And don't forget Navy SEAL Jacob Alvarez Mendozo, JAM, who is lurking in the background.

Please know how much I value your readership, especially those of you who have followed me through twenty years of myriad genres, including historical, contemporary, time travel, and paranormal. Everything from Vikings to Navy SEALs and combinations thereof. Hard to believe, but I am almost to my fiftieth published full-length novel.

I love to hear from you, readers, and I respond to all mail at shill733@aol.com. You can sign up for my mailing list on my website at www.sandrahill.net, or get news on my Facebook page at Sandra Hill Author.

As always, I wish you smiles in your reading.

Sandra Hill

Fall in love with *New York Times* bestselling author

SUSAN ELIZABETH PHILLIPS

THE CHICAGO STARS/BONNER BROTHERS BOOKS

THIS HEART OF MINE
978-0-380-80808-3

A down-on-her-luck children's book illustrator is about to cross paths with the new quarterback of the Chicago Stars.

MATCH ME IF YOU CAN
978-0-06-073456-5

You met star quarterback Kevin Tucker in *This Heart of Mine*. Now get ready to meet his shark of an agent, Heath Champion, and Annabelle Granger, the girl least likely to succeed.

NATURAL BORN CHARMER
978-0-06-073458-9

It wasn't every day that Chicago Stars quarterback Dean Robillard saw a girl in a beaver suit walking down the road. He'd been praying for a little distraction from his own company, so he threw the door open and stepped out onto the shoulder of the Colorado highway.

IMP 0811